INTO THE JUNGLE

To Tyler, Enjoy the adventures.

Ken Panse

Ken Panse 2013

Published by

RSE Publishing

403 N. Harper Street
Laurens, SC 29360, U.S.A.

Copyright © 2013 by Ken Panse

ISBN 978-0-9837103-9-4

Printed in the United States of America
Edited by Amanda L. Capps
Book Design by Michael Seymour
Cover Design and Illustrations by Dan Fowler

Acknowledgments

I would like to thank Mikaela Shupp, Lauren Curtis, Marjorie Stansel, Ramon Nunez, Greg Jones, and Frank Demartini for their contributions to developing this story.

Also, a big *thank you* to my wife, family, and parents who have been a great encouragement and source of inspiration during this process.

Chapter 1

The sweet morning air smelled of honeysuckle, as the sun's rays lit the valley. Emily's eyes were still shut, but her ears were awake—thanks, in no small part—to a wren that bore her state's name: *Carolina*. "The tiny bird with the giant voice," her dad would always say. In the distance, she thought she heard her horse calling for her with neighs and whinnies. Em thought to herself, *if only Maybell would open the door and say, "G'mornin', Sugar, pancakes 'n bacon is served."* She stretched her arms, exhaled a big yawn, rolled over, and looked out her window to see if her horse was poking his head outside the barn window.

Just then, someone knocked on her door and entered. It was their housemaid, a freed slave. The Scroggins did not own slaves. Maybell, chiding her, said, "Rise 'n shine, child, breakfast is a gettin' cold."

Em pulled the sheets over her head and replied, "All right," with a heavy sigh.

A short time later, Em emerged from her room wearing khaki pants and a long sleeved white cotton shirt. A crimson bandana was tied around her neck. Her long blonde hair was pulled back in a ponytail. Maybell's eyes opened wide as she said, "Now you eat that food up and get goin'."

"Where's Mother?" Em inquired as she wrapped the fried eggs and toast in a cloth napkin.

"She's getting the store delivery outside," Maybell answered.

Em could hear the sounds of men unloading the various goods, mostly pantry items. She walked down the hall where she could see the boxes and barrels being lined up and checked off. Each item was accounted for by her mother, who held the itemized list sent along by the shopkeeper. She would check off each item as it was placed on the porch. There were lots of barrels, some filled with grain or rice, and others filled with oats. Sometimes they'd get a sugar barrel, or better yet, some molasses. Maybell could perform miracles with molasses and pancakes.

The family's estate was in the foothills north of Charleston, South Carolina. The year was 1844. Em's mother, Mary, ran the family business, a sprawling horse farm. She had inherited the plantation from her parents who raised melons and cotton on the land. The boll weevil beetle killed off the cotton, so the mission had turned to the breeding of both work horses and Walker horses for competition. They still grew watermelons, cantaloupes, squash, and corn, but the crops were mainly for the family—not the market.

"Good morning, Mother," Em said cheerfully.

"Why, good morning to you, Emily Rose," her mom said. Em's mother used her full name, usually when making a point of it. "I want you to help me train the horses later."

"May I go by Ah-ti-yah's house and see if she wants to help?"

"Don't be gone all day," Mary said.

"Yes, Mother, I won't forget," Em replied as she gave her mother a kiss on the cheek.

Em ran toward the barn to see her horse, Caramel. When Caramel saw Em, he bobbed his head up and down with excitement. Em ran up to him and gave him a big hug around the neck, stroked his mane, and looked into his caramel-colored eyes. She took great pride in knowing that Caramel was all hers. Her parents had agreed to let Em keep him now that she had turned sixteen, as long as she cleaned his stall, fed him, and changed his water bucket each day. Most days, Em would begin her day this way, and sometimes she'd go for a morning ride or "look-about," as she called her wanderings. Today she had a small green apple that she had picked up along the way. It had fallen out of one of the dozen or so fruit trees, planted like a grove, not far from the barn. Caramel greedily munched the sour treat and raked his tongue over her open palm.

"You are too gross sometimes," Em chided Caramel, who shook his head again in a playful manner.

Em walked around the side of the white-washed barn past the red roses. She lifted the latch and went inside. There was a row of a dozen stalls that held the Walker horses. The family had a couple of other barns and buildings for storage. Caramel had the first stall in the row that had an extra window on the barn's side, facing Em's bedroom window.

"C'mere, you!" she called out happily. "Let's get you saddled so we can go see Ah-ti-yah."

Caramel complied by allowing Em to put his bridle over his face and head. Then Em tied him to a stall clasp and got the saddle ready. His tack box was a large trunk in which she kept the horse's bridle, brushes, hoof pick, liniment, leggings, and saddle. She first put a small blanket on his back and then, the saddle, as she reached across his belly for the girth strap. He would always turn to look at her when she'd jerk the strap up snugly to buckle it in place. He stomped his front foot impatiently as if he were thinking, *Let's go already!*

Em untied Caramel, walked him out of the barn, jumped up onto his back, turned him around, and gave him a good nudge with her heels; that was the signal to run! Off they sped down the dirt driveway toward the west meadow. Mary watched Em ride and admired the youthful vigor with which she embraced life. She waved goodbye to her daughter as she rode past their house.

This was Caramel's favorite part of the ride because he loved racing down the dirt and gravel road that led to the pastures of grass, clover, goldenrod, and heather. Em would lean forward in her saddle and squeeze him with her legs, and their rhythm would synchronize. Their hair floated, and their spirits delighted in the feeling of weightlessness. Sometimes on a particularly straight section of the road, Em would raise her arms over her head with delight. Sometimes, she'd have to pull her hat down low and turn her collar up because of the mosquitoes and tiger flies.

Caramel slowed to a trot as they came to a ridge. The pace was then slowed to walking as they made their way downhill across two creeks. Ferns were prolific, and in the dimly lit lowlands, ancient trees grew—some even reaching one hundred feet tall.

She'd often see several bright red birds called cardinals that sang such beautiful songs. She would pretend she was a bird and mimic their whistle call herself. Actually, Em could do several bird calls that she had learned from Ah-ti-yah's father, Ho-ti-mah, who had worked on their farm for years, taming the young foals for a future of competing or working.

Em's horse came to an abrupt stop, halting at the sight of something on the path. It was a large snapping turtle marching across the clearing; its head was the size of a large apple. Caramel snorted in disapproval of the interruption by this dinosaur-like creature. After it passed, Em made a clicking noise with her cheek, signaling Caramel to proceed. They went up the other side of the lowland until they could smell hickory smoke. That meant that Ah-ti-yah's village was just ahead.

Indiantown was an area where the Native Americans had lived as a community among the European settlers for over a hundred years. Em had met Ah-ti-yah years ago during one of her look-abouts. They met upstream when Em stopped to let Caramel have a drink. They became good friends, even sleeping over at one another's house on occasion.

As the pair prepared for the last incline, they were met by some of the Indian maidens coming down to get fresh water. They had deerskin water pouches that could hold a few gallons each. The maidens came down the path in single file. The women spoke among themselves of a particular young man who yesterday did a back flip off the jumping rock into the pool of water below the waterfall.

"Did you see Pah-nee when he smiled just before jumping off?" Tusca-no-la asked.

"Yes, I saw him look right at Ah-ti-yah and swing his arms upward as he leaped over the edge. You know, I once had a suitor who tried to impress me with feats of skill and cunning," Cut-ta continued.

"True, but how many men would attempt to bring fresh honey with the bees still on it?" Tusca-no-la retorted.

They all laughed while spreading out along the bank.

Then, Em came to a stop on the near side of the stream, not disturbing any mud or silt, so the women's flasks would be clean and pure. It was then that Ah-ti-yah saw Em waiting there, and she said, "You're just in time to help carry our water skins back to the village." Em laughingly said, "Hook them onto the saddle horn and we will!" A few minutes later, Caramel had an additional fifty pounds of water strapped across his back. He hardly noticed their presence because he was thinking about the meadow ahead, blooming with wildflowers.

Up the other bank they all went. Ah-ti-yah, Em, and Caramel were last in line, which suited them just fine. Maybe they could return later after they dropped off the water. It would be fun to watch the butterflies flitting about the blossoms. Em especially liked the big orange ones called monarchs.

Just as they had hoped, the meadow was multicolored with yellows, pinks, and purples. It wasn't long before the smell of hickory smoke wafted past

them. The odor reminded Em of mealtimes with her friend. Perhaps she might even be invited to dinner.

As Em and Ah-ti-yah approached the village, they saw a neighbor, Lo-ma-taka, looking over her garden. She grew peas, eggplant, squash, and herbs in a sunny spot in their yard. Ah-ti-yah dismounted; she brought over the water skin and hung it from a hook near the door.

Ah-ti-yah asked her dad if she could take their horse to the meadow for feeding as she usually did. Ho-ti-mah said, "Fine," so off they went.

Ay-ti-yah's horse, Moonlight, was a striking Palomino-like mare that had a few large brown patches randomly laced around her body. Ah-ti-yah rode Moonlight bareback and with a bitless bridle. Most of the time, Ah-ti-yah didn't even hold the reins in her hands, preferring to hold on to Moonlight's mane, steering him with her knees and legs. This was the traditional riding method of her people. Once they reached the edge of the village, the two girls hopped up onto their steeds and raced off for the fields.

The path was wide there because of the wagons that would come and go, so they rode side by side, galloping through the glade in friendly competition. The horses' hooves made rhythmic sounds as they went. They could hear the air blowing out of the horses' nostrils as their feet went one, two, three . . . one, two, three . . . one, two, three.

Along they went until the trees gave way to grass. The girls watched as the sunshine would illuminate patches of fog and dew that lingered into the morning.

The horses came to a gradual stop and put their heads down to feed. Em looked over to Ah-ti-yah and said, "That was so much fun."

"Yeah," Ah-ti-yah replied, "That's a great way to start the day!"

They laughed aloud, and both horses raised their heads and looked over to them while each munched a gob of grass laced with wildflowers. The girls thought it was funny, prompting another laughing session. The meadow's air was heavy with the sweet smell of the nearby privet and honeysuckle vines. A woodpecker tapped on a nearby tree so hard, his assault could be heard for a mile. *Ratta-tat-tat, ratta-tat-tat,* it would go as the bird foraged for hidden grubs under the tree bark. Ah-ti-yah mimicked the woodpecker, pointing her finger off the end of her nose and jerking her neck back and forth, which Em found very amusing.

They slid off their mounts and began wandering down the path looking at the variety of flowers, some of which were barely as tall as the grass and others that were displayed on three to four-foot stalks. There were finches and bluebirds working the field for insects. The birds seemed to gather up several bugs before flitting away to their nests to feed their hatchlings.

When the horses had grazed for a while, they went down to the stream for a drink. The girls, with their horses following them, made their way up the stream's bank, passing time and chatting. Soon, they came to a creek that poured into the stream. They got back up on their horses. Ah-ti-yah stepped onto a stump and swung her leg over from there. Em did the same. The terrain around them had gullies that were steep. There were also many ancient trees, mostly alive, but some were on the ground in various stages of decay, providing nutrients to the forest and bugs.

The sunlight was blotted by the many leaves above, giving the whole place a cooler temperature and dimmer lighting, which was great for the pockets of ferns. Their green leaves slowly unfurled like majestic wings. They would sway as the horses' legs brushed by them, occasionally dislodging a tree frog.

"I have to go to town tomorrow morning to get school supplies," Em said.

"Maybe I can come with you and get some syrup for my parents," Ah-ti-yah replied.

"Really?" Em said. "Let's see if we can go together. My father is expecting me for lunch. He wants to look over my ciphering supplies to make sure they will meet my teacher's approval."

"I'll tell my father that we will be getting back tomorrow evening, before sunset," Ah-ti-yah said.

The girls agreed that they would meet in the morning and ride to Charleston from Em's place near Kingstree.

Doctor Ezra Scroggins, Emily's father, drove his buggy into Charleston each day where he had a medical practice. His office was a modest brick building with large windows for light and ventilation. The original trees of oak, poplar, and sourwood were never cleared off the property. This gave a nice shady effect so the bricks did not get too hot in the summertime. Sometimes, a strong breeze would blow the curtains like sails. It was located on the outer edge of town near the livery, where he would keep the buggy.

Ezra had attended the medical college in nearby Charlotte. While there, he had a chance meeting with his future wife Mary at a sandwich shop. He was a well-liked and respected person. He was a man who enjoyed helping people get well, and he always had a jar of lollipops handy for younger patients.

At the college, he learned to identify things under a microscope, which was a new way to diagnose people's ailments. His instruments came all the way from Bavaria where the best glass lenses were made. Of course, he could also set broken bones or pull teeth, as well as help mothers birth their babies. He even kept a journal of his patients and methods used to help them. As the years had passed, Ezra saved many of these leather-bound books. An avid reader, he also had a library of books, mostly surgical procedures and life sciences.

This morning was like most others, uneventful. He would drive the buggy about an hour each day into town across the gently rolling hills. He'd go past the occasional farm until he got close to town. Then he'd cross the creek and get on the busier road to Charleston. He often enjoyed the ride because he would sometimes see wildlife, like a herd of deer crossing the road, or some turkeys flying, startled by his approach. One morning, he saw a bear on the edge of a meadow. He used the buggy to carry his tools, bandages, and rain slicker—and occasionally, a patient. Arriving at the livery, a stable boy took hold of the horses' reigns and took them to the paddock after unhitching them. His day officially began when he walked over to his office from the livery and greeted his secretary, Grace.

* * * * *

Returning home, Em spent the late afternoon helping her mother exercise the horses. She still had to muck Caramel's stall, which was no big deal, because she had just changed his bedding. She would pour powdered lime over any wet spots to neutralize any odor-causing bacteria.

The afternoon air felt thick as an occasional breeze wafted across the large, sandy courtyard. She sat on her tack box, daydreaming about the ride in the meadow that they had had earlier, swinging her booted feet back and forth like pendulums. At times, it felt as if time could slow down to a crawl, like molasses pouring out a jar.

In another hour or so, the sun would rest behind the tree line again, having travelled its own time worn path. Then, as the air cooled, a fragrant aroma arose that smelled of clover and privet. The bush swallowtails were floating about lazily, circling about as they searched for just the right spot to land for the night. It was important the butterflies chose a spot where they would get the first light of the morning sun, so that their bodies would warm up and flittering about would be easier. As the sun sank into twilight, Em saw the lamps get lit. That meant the iron dinner bell out back of the house rang once, signaling the closing up of the stables and dinnertime too! Usually Maybell would just call for Em a time or two before she shook the cord underneath the bell and yelled, "Supper! Y'all com'n get ya supper!"

Caramel had already lain down for the night in his favorite corner. When he awoke, he could stretch his neck up and see Em's window in the distance. He loved it when she would whistle to him from across the yard.

Dr. Scroggins usually managed to get home before twilight, but he was late on this night. Undoubtedly, he had some sort of call to make. Since the moon was just entering its full phase, the road would be illuminated a silvery hue that was good for riding. He was an excellent horse and buggy man, which is one of the talents that Em's mom possessed. Mary could even ride and race sulkies as well!

Cletus, their top farmhand would wait until Dr. Scroggins returned each day to put away the horse and carriage. Cletus's home was adjacent to the back gate and carriage barn. His wife would set his evening meal out in front of the house on the table where he could rest comfortably and eat, and still see Dr. Scroggins from afar, giving him time to get up and stretch before catching the team's leader by his bridle.

Dr. Scroggins always had a warm greeting for his old reliable friend. Cletus was fifty-ish, although his wife was considerably younger by ten or fifteen years.

As the carriage came to a halt, the two horses, Endeavor and Elixir, snorted loudly, stomping hooves impatiently, as they were eager to get to their stalls to cool off and drink. They nodded their heads up and down, blowing the day's dust from their pulsating nostrils. Cletus had the carriage unhitched in a jiffy. Soon, the horses were stabled, and his only remaining chore would be to brush them down for the night.

Dr. Scroggins washed his hands and face in the basin inside and changed out of his shirt, trousers, and shoes. He entered the dining room rolling up his sleeves and smiling.

"Today I helped deliver a calf," he said to Mary. "I was called out to the Neil's place to look at Kevin's kicked leg, but ended up pulling a calf out of its mama backward. Kevin had to sit there with his leg propped up. He had a real good time cheering me on, saying, 'Go on Doc, give 'er a slow, steady pull,' which I proceeded to do, and, *voila!* Out it came."

"Well, you must be half starved by now after all that work," Mary said, surveying her husband's tall, lean figure. He crossed the room to Mary, gently embraced her, and kissed her softly on the cheek.

"Hello, my love," Dr. Scroggins said to her, which was his custom when he came home from work.

"Hello, darling, shall we get started?" she asked, meaning more like, "Let's dig in." Mary brought in the stew that Maybell had made earlier, and Em brought in the bread that was covered by a napkin.

"Daddy," Em announced, "I want to go to town tomorrow and get some paper and pencils for writing lessons." Her father knew that, while this was true, his daughter would also go about the stores window shopping. He smiled to himself.

Mary also added, "I have a bolt of cloth that is the wrong pattern that you can return to the store for me, dear."

"Perhaps you can stop by the office, and I may be able to get away for a bite to eat with you," Dr. Scroggins said to Emily. Sometimes, her father would buy her an ice cream or a sandwich as they would stroll through the park.

"All right, but I will have Ah-ti with me, too," Em said, getting excited about the next day as she ate her stew and buttered roll. "She has some things to pick up for her family, too," Em continued.

"Well, you girls be careful. I've heard there are several ships in port, and there is quite a bit of commotion in Charleston," Mary said.

The rest of dinner was uneventful, although tasty. When they finished, Em and Mary cleaned up, while Ezra went to the porch to sit and relax. Mary joined him shortly. Em went to her room and flopped on her bed to doodle in one of her scrapbooks.

Em would sometimes draw pictures of horses and some landscapes around

17

her family farm. After a while, her mother came into her room and sat on the edge of the bed next to Em.

"Emily," her mother said, "I have something for you." She opened a cloth sack, taking out two toys—hand-carved wooden horses.

"Oh! Mother!" Emily exclaimed, as she sprang to her feet. "They are so beautiful!" she said, her face beaming.

"Thank you, thank you, thank you!" Em said as she hugged her mom, while Dad looked on from the doorway. They look just like Caramel and Moonlight," Em continued.

"That's right. I had them made that way for you by Chadwick at the mill. They were in the delivery this morning," Mary said.

Em went over and hugged her dad, and he picked her up and gave her a squeeze.

Then, Em ran out the back door to show Caramel his miniature self.

Chapter 2

Carlos bade his homeland of Yucatan, Mexico, farewell, as the ocean-bound ship left the peaceful harbor, setting sail for the East and then north to America. The sun was hovering above the horizon like a hummingbird, its oranges, yellows, and golds shimmered on the backs of the waves. They glided away from his people's homeland in the jungle just beyond the cliffs. He stood next to the ship's rail, transit in hand, hoping his voyage would be on time.

They watched the turquoise waves roll into the lagoon, splashing against the base of an eighty-foot vertical cliff. Immense pressure shot some of the sea water up through small, dormant, volcanic tunnels. It produced a thirty-foot tall flume that the winds would blow across, giving it the appearance of a giant white feather, as the salty spray blew in the wind. The sky was a cloudless azure blue. It seemed to float over the top of the coral inlet, as pelicans soared silently over the surface in a line formation, undulating up and down to hover a meter above the clear water. Although the deeper water was turquoise, the shallow water was so clear, he could plainly see parrotfish and eels along the coral reef.

Carlos had gone to college with Dr. Scroggins. His heritage was Criollo, which is a person who has one Mayan parent and one Spanish parent. He lived next door to Dr. Scroggins during their formative years. They would often study together, share meals, and throw darts, a sport Dr. Scroggins was fond of when they needed a break from their disciplined academic efforts.

Carlos had lost his microscope when a burro lost its footing just above a waterfall. The purpose of his voyage was to obtain new lenses and to seek his friend's advice. He watched the shoreline grow smaller and smaller, until it was lost among the whitecaps of the ocean's waves. The wind was favorable, blowing from the West, filling the ship's sails full and cutting a sizable wake. The trip should last only two weeks. The cargo ship ran this route, among others, trading with a variety of people and locations.

The captain, an old "salty dog," had leathery skin, deeply wrinkled from years on deck in the equatorial sun. His grey blue eyes were clear and usually squinting. He wore typical seamen's garb, a loose, faded cotton shirt and cotton or canvas deck pants. Many of Captain Baylor's sailors went barefoot, but he had leather sandals.

The captain's pilot, Maggot, was an old and trusted friend from many voyages. He steered the ship out of the harbor, through the channels, and through the dangerous reef. If a ship were to hit a reef, in most cases, a hole would be torn in its hull. A pilot's skill, knowledge, and experience would give him rank, so he was sometimes excused from unsavory duties like swabbing the deck and mending sails and nets.

Captain Baylor and Carlos leaned against the rail looking at the skies ahead of them. Captain Baylor said, "These winds be early this year but favorable for us. We be not heavy laden, so we'll make good time with this wind behind us."

"What are you carrying, if you don't mind my asking?" Carlos said.

"Let's just say that gems are less bulky than grain, although we still hold many kegs of rum from the islands before reaching the cliffs of Tulum," Captain Baylor said, while getting his ivory carved pipe out for a smoke. After packing the pipe with cherry weed, the captain asked, "What are ye needing from the Americas?"

Carlos answered, "A very unique tool, not unlike your spyglass, and also the special man who possesses it."

"Aye, knowing how to figure the tool is the secret. Just like with me transit for ciphering latitude and longitude," said the captain. He lit his pipe, drawing a few rapid breaths to ignite the smoke stuff. He let out the smoke, which smelled pleasant as it wafted away in the breeze. The two men stood there at the helm gazing out into the distance, each lost in his own thoughts.

One man reminisced about past voyages, as his grey eyes drank in the shimmering waters. The other looked forward into the cobalt-blue sky and prayed silently for the fate of his village. The limestone cliffs disappeared over the horizon for only the second time in his life. How would the reunion go with his old friend? Would Dr. Scroggins have the answer to the illness afflicting his people? Even the seagulls stopped following the ship as it slipped noisily through the ocean.

The lighthouse in Charleston Harbor was a welcome sight. Carlos was restless aboard the ship for the week or so they were at sea. It would still be another few hours until his feet would hit dry land. He was tired of eating jerked meat for meals; it was too salty. Carlos was also a trained physician and made notes in his journal regarding the ship's food stores and the physical condition of the deckhands, a rather surly bunch. He noticed the captain had some barrels of fresh fruits and potatoes. No one appeared to be suffering from scurvy. He felt that the fresh water barrels were a concern, because the men all drank from a common ladle, dunking it into the large vessel and hanging it on a nearby hook when they were done. Fresh water was always rationed, along with everything else, because the uncouth men lacked the discipline or knowledge to make the supplies last. That was the cook's job.

The captain's guests and paying passengers had a few more privileges than the ship's men, like a clean bunk with fresher air. Meals were served in the captain's quarters on a large wooden table. The table had little rails on it and shallow circular divots chiseled into the top to prevent plates and glasses from sliding during rough seas. The captain, however, preferred to eat from a bowl and drink from his goblet.

Carlos scanned the coastline, noticing steeples and other landmarks. There were already several ships anchored in the harbor.

Before long, Carlos was walking down the gangplank onto firm ground. The captain was continuing farther up the coast to New York for more commerce. Carlos would have to secure passage home by another vessel.

Travelling light, with only a satchel that he had slung over his shoulder, he held onto the rope railing. The ship and plank slowly wobbled a bit as he disembarked from the ship. Already, the crew was offloading barrels and other cargo from a second gangplank located at the rear of the ship near its hold. He waved a farewell to the captain and set off across the boardwalks to inquire about a horse to ride. The harbormaster told him of a livery a few blocks away where he could acquire a steed at an honest rate.

It had been 16 years since he'd seen his good friend. Carlos could only hope that Dr. Scroggins still resided in Charleston. As he strolled up the side of the road, Carlos remembered his university days and wondered how things would be different. He rarely had use for speaking English back home and would undoubtedly be a bit rusty. Still, he greeted passersby with a friendly nod and smile saying, "Good day," as appeared to be the custom.

* * * * *

Dr. Scroggins got ready for his daily trip into town for work. He liked to get up at first light, before the others, and sip a cup of cold coffee that had been brewed the night before. The coffee pot was located in the parlor that overlooked the porch. At dawn and dusk, a whippoorwill often voiced its unique song. Then, when the sun would peek over the horizon, he'd go inside to get dressed. Mary was usually up by then. She'd get the stove lit to boil some water for more coffee, or, sometimes, she'd gather eggs from their chickens and bring them in to boil. Dr. Scroggins usually left before breakfast was made, so he would eat some toasted bread with butter and jelly and opt for an early lunch in town—or eat something Mary or Maybell would pack for him.

He would review any notes he'd made regarding his patients and enter that information on a simple chart with dates and ailments for future reference. He'd get his bag packed and look out the back window to see if Cletus had his buggy and horses readied at the barn. If so, he'd give Mary a kiss goodbye and head off for town. Mary would often wave to him as he passed by the house or blow him a kiss. Yes, the good doctor truly was blessed with a loving family, good health, and ample means.

The horses would plod along, walking off their stiffness, until they got to the back gate where Cletus was waiting for them to pass through, so he could close it and go back to his own house for a bit. He'd head down to the stables to check on the livestock soon enough. When they passed through, Dr. Scroggins would shake the reins a bit and click his cheek, making a sound the team recognized as a command to trot, and they would.

They would go at different speeds, either galloping, trotting, or walking, depending on what the doctor wanted. Dr. Scroggins had no inkling that this morning's normal departure would be his last for a long time as he called out to Mary, "I love you, dear!"

Em awoke at the sound of the buggy as her dad called to her mom. She didn't lie in bed waiting; she was dressed even before there was a knock on her door.

"Mmm," she thought, as she saw the large pot of grits on the stove. Maybell made them from homily, a type of corn that made the grits creamy and rich. Em spooned some into a bowl and added a spoonful of sugar.

Em played with the toy horses as she ate, pretending they were galloping and bucking. Mary came into the room, set the bolt of linen on the table, and said, "Good morning, sweetie. Here's the cloth that needs returning. Be sure Mr. McFadden enters it in his ledger."

"Yes, mother," Em said, even though her mind was far away, daydreaming she was on the toy horse, floating across a sea of wildflowers in a pretty meadow.

"Emily Rose!" Mary said louder to Em. "Are you even listening to me?"

"Yes, Mother," she replied again, not wanting to look up at her mother.

Em finished eating and returned the toys to their sack. She told her mother goodbye and went out the screen door. She strolled down the path with her hands in her pockets, lost in her thoughts, still holding the two toys. A wren was perched on a tree branch overhead. "Why, he's just singing his little heart out," Em thought.

Caramel already had his head out the window when Em reached the shed row. He whinnied a low chuckle-like sound that sounded like a cat purring, but his "pur" was much deeper. She had a carrot with her, so she broke it in half and gave him a piece. She'd keep the other half for later. Near the troughs, Em had to pump the water by hand. When she returned, she hung a bucket on its hook, and Caramel took a long deep drink from it, practically draining the pail.

Em looked at him and said, "Are you sure you aren't a camel? Your name could be Caramel Camel!" she laughed.

Em went out of the stall and returned with a pitchfork and bushel basket, which she filled with manure. She went out again, this time chaining the entrance to his stall, and walked on to the compost pile to dump her basket. Every now and then, she'd see a black snake or a green garden snake on the lookout for mice near the pile of old straw. She passed Cletus along the way, and they exchanged smiles, each going about their own business. Em noticed a large new spider web with a big black and yellow spider on it blowing in the breeze. "Yuck!" she said, feeling a chill go up her back.

In no time, Caramel was saddled and they were halfway to the meadow. Em led him by his reins, and they walked along the edge of the meadow. Caramel was attempting to eat the tasty flowers from both sides of the path at the same time, which was a bit comical. Most of the time, Em didn't even hold his reins because he followed her everywhere, unless he was penned up or tied off.

Em and Caramel had a place where the path had a high side and a low side. Caramel would go down the low side, which was only two feet lower, and stop, and Em would slip onto his back. She knew how to steer with her knees like Ah-ti-yah had shown her, which was less troublesome when ducking through privets and ironwood. There were only two directions Em and Caramel ever took back there, straight onto Ah-ti-yah's village or to the left, which led to the highlands. When Em got on, they proceeded down the trail until they got to the creek. Ah-ti-yah was already there, waiting with Moonlight. She was sitting on a giant boulder, writing in the river with a stick. There were lots of large smooth stones there at the ford, where the sand would silt up after a good rain. Her people would dip out the sand for use around their homes and gardens. The town potter would mix the sand into the red or white clay, giving it a gritty texture for larger flasks, so that they would be less slippery.

The creek curved where the new sand would always accumulate, and that is where Ah-ti-yah was sitting.

"Hello there," Ah-ti-yah said.

"Hey," Em replied.

"Are you ready to go to town?" Ah-ti-yah asked.

"You betcha!" Em replied, and off they went.

＊ ＊ ＊ ＊

Meanwhile, Carlos turned up the slate path, wondering if the directions from a local dock worker would correctly lead him to the house where his friend practiced. He went up the three steps to the front porch that was pretty large and covered by a roof. There was even a round portico on the porch's corner. He knocked on the door and heard voices inside. A man and woman were talking. The door opened, and the woman said, "Can I help you?"

"Yes. My name is Carlos, is this—" he paused.

Just then, Dr. Scroggins exclaimed, "I recognize that voice!" as he rounded the corner to the front door. Grace stepped aside and the two men looked at one another, almost in disbelief. Dr. Scroggins stepped forward welcoming Carlos, and they clasped forearms.

"Whatever are you doing here?" Dr. Scroggins asked in amazement.

"Ah, my friend," Carlos replied, "I have travelled far on behalf of the Mayan people who have been stricken with an illness that we have never seen before. I have come here to ask you for your help. I am in need of the glass lenses that we used at the college, for seeing the small creatures that I suspect are somehow afflicting the people. Young and old alike, even the strong, are succumbing to the sickness," Carlos continued.

"Let us sit and discuss the matter, but first, rest a bit. You must be exhausted from your journey. Please have some coffee or tea," Dr. Scroggins said as they moved toward the parlor. With a nod of her head, Grace scurried to get some refreshments for them.

The two men talked for quite some time about the mysterious problem. Before long, they moved to Dr. Scroggins's examining room to look into the microscope or "looking lens" as he usually referred to the tool. It was on the shelf, contained within a finely crafted hardwood box. The inside of the box was lined with green velvet that was formed to accept the specific shape of the tool and glass slides. They would not shift about once the box was closed and secured by hinged hasps, a type of lock.

They got the looking lens out and set it up on a table, reflecting the sunlight up into the cylinder by tilting the small round mirror at the base. The men looked at some books from Dr. Scroggins's library, scoured the pages, and reviewed the text and plates, which were reproductions of drawings of animals, plants, and miniscule lifeforms called bacteria.

They were totally absorbed in their work when a lad burst through the door exclaiming, "Come quick, Doctor! There's been an accident at the docks."

The men gathered up the scope, fitted it back into the box, and grabbed their coats. Just before walking out the door, Dr. Scroggins remembered to write a note for Emily. He laid the note on top of the scope case and set a small stone on it as a weight.

"Oh, Grace," Dr. Scroggins called out, "please give Emily my regrets when she comes by later for our lunch date and give her this note."

Dr. Scroggins left for the livery to get his buggy with Carlos at his side. In no time, they were riding toward the port with a supply of bandages, not knowing what injuries they might need to treat.

* * * * *

Emiliy and Ah-ti-yah took to the road, which followed the creek downstream until it came to a fork. They crossed it and got onto a path that used to go from Indiantown to the port. Their path paralleled the road, offering more things to encounter along the way, plus it was a bit cooler near the creek. Soon, they came to a place that overlooked the port valley in front of them. They even thought they could see ships out in the water.

"Here we go," Ah-ti-yah said, leading the way.

Em said, "Giddyap!" as she guided her horse over the last upper hill. The two horses and riders made their way down along the trail, which was a bit steep and narrow. The girls leaned back on their steeds as they went down the embankment. Nearby, a squirrel scolded the foursome as they passed below its oak tree.

After a while, the ground leveled out a bit, and they went by some farms and hay fields. They climbed the steep bank onto the road more commonly used where the creek took a hard turn. Here, there were occasionally other riders and wagons going in either direction. The girls chatted about where they were going to shop once they got to town. Ah-ti-yah had to pick up a few items from the grocer too. They proceeded in a timely manner, arriving at the edge of town about 11 a.m.

Emily leaned to her side a bit, checked her saddlebag with her hand, and made sure that the bolt was still secure.

The two girls rode on toward the livery up the street from the doctor's office. When they arrived, Em noticed that her father's buggy was absent. So, instead of dismounting, they rode on to her father's office. They got off their mounts in front of the office and walked the horses to the shady area along the side where Em tied Caramel to a tree. Ah-ti-yah just waited as Em said, "I'm going inside to see what's going on."

Emily went to the door and opened it. Grace was waiting inside and told Em that her father and his friend had departed a while ago for the port because of an accident of some sort. Grace showed Emily the note and told her to be sure that she brought it home for her mother to read.

Em read the note and wondered if her father had mistakenly left the wooden box behind, as he apparently hurried off. Em told Grace that she would go down to the docks to see if her father needed the looking glass. Actually, she wanted an excuse to go see her dad, thinking perhaps they could spend some time together. Em had her eye on a drawing pad that she intended to purchase.

Em went outside, strapped the box over the saddle horn, and said to Ah-ti-yah, "Let's go on over to the grocer and take care of our chores."

Ah-ti-yah replied, "That sounds good to me."

They rode down the streets, looking to see if there was any excitement to be had. Most people were busy taking care of their personal affairs. Some lads ran out across the road in front of them playing tag. Em and Ah-ti-yah saw the women were wearing a new style of bonnet with their puffy dresses. Em thought they looked a bit uncomfortable, since the dresses appeared to have several layers to them.

They stopped outside the grocer's store where Em's family shopped. The girls got down and tied off their mounts to the rail out front. Em got her mother's cloth off Caramel and went inside to see the shopkeeper. He was just finishing with a customer when the girls came in through the screened door. A small bell jiggled overhead, announcing their presence.

"What can I do for you?" the balding man inquired.

"Mother had a delivery out to the house yesterday, and this cloth is not the one she ordered, so I'm here to return it," Emily stated.

"Let's have a look at it, lass," the shopkeeper said, with a Scottish brogue to his voice.

Em set the package down on the counter, and the man unwrapped the cloth. Seeing the cloth was intact he said, "I'll credit her account for you."

"Mother would like a receipt, all the same, please," Em pleasantly replied.

While the shopkeeper began ciphering, Em strolled about the store with Ah-ti-yah, who was also gathering up a few things to take home.

"Oh look!" Ah-ti-yah said. "It's rose perfumed soap."

They both gave it a good sniff, and Em's eyes watered a bit as she tried not to sneeze. Ah-ti-yah began to giggle a bit and made a bulging-eye face at her friend. They both began laughing. Ah-ti-yah got some salt and syrup for her folks.

Ah-ti-yah said, "I like these beads. Aren't they pretty?"

27

Em replied, "They sure are! Are you going to make a fancy necklace for the boys to notice?"

"Well, it won't hurt if they happen to notice, will it?" Ah-ti-yah said coyly.

"Maybe this is what you want," Em said as she raised a corset to herself.

Ah-ti-yah laughed aloud and pursed her lips a bit suggestively.

"Why don't we see if we can find my father?" Em suggested.

"Okay," Ah-ti-yah replied, thinking about how much time they had to fritter away before heading back home.

So the girls continued on toward the port. Em spied her father's buggy outside the port's livery and said, "Let's go over there and ask where my father is."

Ah-ti-yah nodded her head in agreement. So they again got off their steeds and walked them over to a rail to tie them off.

Em remembered the lens box and went back for it. Ah-ti-yah took hold of the reins and made soothing sounds to the horses.

* * * * *

Dr. Scroggins knew he shouldn't make the horses go straight into a gallop, since they had just cooled off from the morning's commute to town. He trotted them for a while, but before long, they were on the main road along with many other wagon teams and people. Dr. Scroggins recognized many people along the way who would throw up a hand and say, "Morning," as he passed by them.

The dirt streets were fairly straight and smooth, but one would have to keep an eye out for slippery puddles and an occasional rut if it had rained recently. His team had years of experience with the good doctor. He would hardly have to flap the reins, but he would make sounds so they knew which way to turn. It was also an easy ride, because the port was a bit lower than the surrounding land, so it was mostly downhill to the water. The team was strong and handsome and had great training.

Soon they were going past the city proper and were walking along at a good clip. The iron horseshoes kept a steady rhythm of *clip clop, clip clop.*

Carlos recognized the park and some of the houses as they went past.

He said to Dr. Scroggins, "There are many fine homes here."

Dr. Scroggins replied, "Yes, the city planners laid out a grid system which works rather well."

They went past the grocer where Dr. Scroggins would get sandwiches and drinks occasionally. There was no time to pull in now. Perhaps they could stop in for a bite on the way back. Briefly, Dr. Scroggins imagined a liverwurst on pumpernickel with a pickle slice. Better yet, two sandwiches, one for himself and one for Carlos.

The turn off was just ahead for the wooden docking area. The lad pointed and said, "Over there!" It was the same ship Carlos had walked past earlier that day. The men had been loading cargo on it for a few days and were probably hot and tired. That's when most accidents occurred, Dr. Scroggins had learned. There was a spot nearby where he could tie his team. A lad there promised to keep an eye on them, while a seaman stood at the boarding plank to receive the doctors.

"Me mates got under the cargo net, when it ripped and some barrels fell on 'em," the seaman said. "Will ye come below and 'ave a look, Doc?" he continued.

"Yes, of course," said the doctors as they all boarded the ship, which was heavy laden.

As they made their way down to the cargo hold, the air became very hot and oppressive, even though a breeze was picking up. The hold was large and almost full to capacity. The sailors, except for a few injured men and the captain, who was with them, were busy tying the nets, boxes, and barrels to the ship's stays.

"I gave them each some rum to numb their pain a bit," the captain said as he stood up. "There's broken bones to set before we set sail this very afternoon. Our time at this dock is almost over, so I will need to vacate the spot for the next ship," he continued.

"How can we treat these men then?" Carlos asked.

"Aye, no worries, I will set anchor out in the harbor, and we'll send ye back to shore on me skiff," the captain said matter of factly.

So they got busy, aiding the first seaman over to one of the mess hall tables.

"Get a roll of cloth to hold his head up and some fresh water," Dr. Scroggins said.

Chapter 3

Mary stood on the porch waving "so-long" to her darling man. Like many a morning, she watched that carriage go up that road. She went back inside to eat and finish dressing.

Before long, the back door near the pantry opened and Maybell arrived, which meant Cletus wasn't far behind. He'd come up each morning to get a list of the day's chores.

"Hmm," he muttered to himself, as he looked over the writing.

"Blacksmith coming out today," he said aloud to Maybell.

"Oooomm," Maybell replied, "that means I will be feeding at least one extra hungry man. Everyone knows it takes a lot of fixins to keep those big arms of his swinging and pounding."

"Yeah, maybe he can help you pound the dough, too!" Cletus said, as he turned to get out the door quickly after that wisecrack. Maybell was already looking for a towel or something to throw at him. The screen door closed with a bang, as he scooted away rather pleased with himself. Maybell was getting things situated in the kitchen when Mary came. She looked over at Maybell, who had a big grin on her face and was humming softly to herself, undoubtedly lost in her thoughts of what kind of pie or stew she could put together.

"Oh, I see Cletus told you who's coming today," Mary said jokingly. She was aware that Maybell didn't mind staring out the window at the blacksmith. "Have one of the boys get a chicken for a pot pie," Mary continued.

"Mmm! That man can eat a whole pie by himself, Miss Mary. We'll need two chickens, if'n you don't mind," Maybell said.

"That'll be fine. There's a new barrel of flour in the pantry," Mary said, as she sat down at the desk to review the previous day's delivery bills and enter them into the household logbook.

Maybell crossed the kitchen to the pantry shelves and looked over all the new supplies, mostly foodstuffs, when she spied a glass jar with orange marmalade. "Oh, Miss Mary, is it all right to open this jar of marmalade?" she asked.

"Why of course, you silly," Mary joked, "I think there's raspberry jam there too." Maybell cut them both a slice of bread and smeared some of the sweet delight on it, and sat down for a bit to enjoy the treat. Mary took a bite and set it down, saying, "I'll finish mine later," as she went out the back door to inspect the shed row.

She could hear the horses' hooves moving about in the stillness of the morning air. There was a chorus of crickets chirping in the distance and a mist was rapidly evaporating from the fields. Mary crossed the courtyard to the office stall, which also had her personal riding gear and tack. She rode with an English saddle, because that was what she was trained in as a girl.

She walked by the rows of stalls, looking in at the mares and their new colts and fillies. Workers were arriving to get on with the chores of the day. Mary herself was going to exercise a gelding in the round pen that morning. Her farm was actually training a dozen horses for working and pulling, either with a harness or a yoke. Some of the horses would be trained for saddle work, but the Walkers would be specially trained for harness racing.

Mary took the thirty-foot rope off its hook on the wall and sat down to change into her boots. This rope was used for cantering a horse around in a circle sixty feet across. Then, she got up and went over to the Walker horse shed row and greeted Cletus with a warm smile.

"Good mornin' to ya, Miss Mary," Cletus said. "Which one are you gettin'?"

"Let's run Chaz this morning," Mary replied.

Cletus opened the bottom stall door, and Mary went in and put a bridle on Chaz. Cletus handed her the rope which she clipped onto the bridle. Then, she led the gelding out across the dirt courtyard, over to the round pen. Cletus undid the chain and opened the gate, closing it behind them after they entered.

Mary started the session by first walking Chaz around the pen. Then, she let the rope out about fifteen feet and made clicking noises with her cheek, which was the signal for her horses to quicken their pace. Chaz responded by trotting, and Mary walked alongside him at a distance in a circular pattern. She trotted the horse around the pen for about five minutes. Then, she slowed him down to a walk for another few minutes and after a brief stoppage, she repeated the process twice more. By the time they were completing Chaz's third time around the pen, his hide glistened from the sweat on his coat.

Some of the other farmhands were watching as they carried out their own chores.

Mary said, "I think he's had enough! Go ahead and open the gate."

Cletus responded by doing so, and he left the gate open in case there would be another horse coming to work out.

Mary led the horse over to a watering trough. Chaz drank several deep swallows of the refreshing water. Cletus came over and led Chaz away to be brushed down, and then put out to a large fenced-in pasture. Mary headed toward her office as a wagon team approached the back gate. It was Virgil, the blacksmith.

"Good morning, Virgil," Mary shouted.

"It's a fine day for work, Miss Mary," Virgil replied.

"Come on into the office and I'll tell you what I need done today," Mary said.

"I'll be right there, quick as a jiff," Virgil happily replied as he cast a glance toward the main house. Maybell had been at the window keeping an eye out for Virgil to arrive. She was already outside on the back stoop, drying off a large mixing bowl with her apron, pretending that she hadn't noticed Virgil's arrival.

"Hallo, Miss Maybell," Virgil shouted as he removed his hat.

Maybell turned to face the strong dark man, appearing to be surprised.

"Why, Mister Virgil, how nice of you to come by," Maybell said sweetly.

"The pleasure's all mine," Virgil replied, visibly licking his lips.

"Y'all come up and see me for some supper atter while," Maybell offered.

"Yes, ma'am," Virgil said as he tried to imagine what kind of vittles he'd be treated to that day.

Mary smiled as she observed the two exchanging glances, wondering if Virgil could ever get up the gumption to court Maybell. He was the strong silent type of man who let his hammers do most of his talking for him.

* * * * *

Down at the harbor, Emily went across the large dock over to the ship. Em said to the seaman at the boarding plank, "Is there a Dr. Scroggins aboard?"

The seaman replied, eyeing the sky across the bay, "Aye, who is ye and what does ye want?"

Em replied, "I am Dr. Scroggins's daughter and I need to give him a message."

"Let me go below whilst ye waits here and see what the captain says about that," the seaman answered as he went up the plank. Em turned around, walked up the dock a short distance until she could see Ah-ti-yah, and waved to her that their mission appeared to be going well.

There was one plank left on the cargo area, and the men had just gone below to store the second to last plank. Em decided to run across the plank, drop off the box with the original seaman she'd met, run down the gangplank, and be done with the whole waiting plan. Em also knew a storm was fast approaching, and she and Ah-ti-yah needed to get themselves and their steeds to shelter.

No one was paying attention to her as she balanced herself and made her way across the plank. When she got to the ship, she heard the men returning with their feet shuffling along. Panicking, she hopped over the top edge of the hold and squatted down. Em watched them struggle getting the last plank aboard, and when they went below, she stood up to jump down onto the deck. Just as she was about to leap, from the corner of her eye, she saw a big wooden pulley that the crew had been using to load the cargo into the hold. It was swinging toward her head. *Pow!* The block and tackle struck her right above her eyes. All she could see was the sky as she fell into the hold onto a large bundle of grain sacks. Dizzy and out of breath from the fall, Em passed out as the box rolled free from her grasp.

"Aye, mateys, make sail before that squall reaches us," the captain ordered.

The seamen drew back the last plank as others unfurled the mainsail. Since the wind was gusting, the sail instantly caught full and the ship slipped silently away from the dock even as the last mooring rope was thrown aboard.

Ah-ti-yah also saw the storm approaching and moved to take the horses to a safe place. She had no idea that Em was aboard the ship as it put out to sea.

Caramel and Moonlight were unsettled by the squall that was racing across the harbor. The wind was steadily increasing, blowing dust, baskets, and straw, along with anything else that was not heavy or tied down. A tarpaulin flew past them like a kite, causing Caramel to rear up on his hind legs, striking out with his hooves. Ah-ti-yah had a terrible time trying to control the two horses whose ears were laid back and eyes showing near terror. She was able to run alongside them toward a nearby warehouse near the dock. A worker was sliding the large door closed as they approached. He called out for her to hurry. Ah-ti-yah had about forty yards to go when the rain caught them in a downpour. She could barely see between the swirling dust and deluge that was soaking everything in sight. Somehow, the horses led her into the warehouse. The man closed the door, barring it shut. They could hear the angry wind pounding the warehouse, causing the old wooden building to moan under the stress.

Ah-ti-yah found an area toward the rear of the structure away from the scurrying merchants and laborers, who were still dealing with their own problems of drying and stacking various crates and bags. The oil lamps used to light the interior flickered, while the wind whistled and slipped between the old weathered plank walls. She tied the horses to a stout post and went to a window to look for Emily. The windows were coated with dust, so she wiped off the glass well enough to see the ship putting out to sea. Frantically, Ah-ti-yah's eyes looked for her friend through the downpour.

Seeing other buildings across the docking area, Ah-ti-yah said to Caramel, "I think Em's over there holed up in one of those shops." She sat down on a burlap sack to wait out the storm.

Some time later, Ah-ti-yah felt a cold wet nudge on her shoulder. It was Moonlight rousing her from her sleep. The excitement of the sudden storm and the ride from Dr. Scroggins's office had worn her out, and she had fallen asleep to the rhythmic rainfall. Moonlight nudged her again as if to tell her, "Get up."

"Okay, okay, I'm up," Ah-ti-ah said, looking first at the horses before peering around a pile of bushel baskets. She noticed the rain had stopped, but twilight was receding behind some distant ominous thunderclouds over the ocean.

"Quick!" Ah-ti-ah exclaimed, jumping to her feet, "Em must be wondering where we are; let's go find her." She gathered up the horses' reins and led them out the warehouse door, thanking the attendant for letting them rest there. Once outside, Ah-ti-ah mounted Moonlight, held onto Caramel, and trotted across the port to the shops.

She spoke with several shopkeepers, but none of them had seen Em. Darkness was almost upon them, so Ah-ti-yah, decided to report Em missing to the harbor captain.

"Aye, lass," the captain replied to her query, "I heard about you two girls, slinking about the dock earlier from my foreman."

Just then, the foreman entered the cabin to hang the keys on the hook for the night. He had overheard the captain's remark and added, "Last I saw, she was alley-catting up the plank to board the ship."

Ah-ti-yah's eyes got big as she exclaimed, "But, but, that ship put out to sea!"

"Aye, she did set sail to avoid the squall lest she be dashed to pieces against the harbor dock. Perhaps she made for the next cove for protection," he continued.

"They'll be back on the morrow, at first light, to return your friend and the good doctors," the foreman reassured her.

"Aye, they best be, because the ship, *Antelope*, hasn't paid her bill for the goods she's loaded for her voyage."

Ah-ti-yah went over to the stables where Dr. Scroggins had left his carriage and team and had them put her horses up for the night. The boy watered and fed both the team and the two steeds. She had to put her mark on the ledger, accepting responsibility for the bill. Since it was evening already, she chose to sleep at the stables in an empty stall next to her charges. She slept fitfully that night, waking often.

Eventually, Moonlight and Caramel lay down, each sighing heavily as they all relaxed in their own way to sleep. Ah-ti-yah prayed to her god that he would deliver her friends from their trials in the morning.

When morning came, the stable boy came by and tossed Ah-ti-yah an apple saying, "There are more of them in the bushel for the taking."

Ah-ti-yah arose and went outside to see the sunrise. When she came back to the stalls, both Moonlight and Caramel were standing. Ah-ti said to them, "Today we ride for home." She had never been away from her family overnight, without prior notice or agreement.

After making sure that Dr. Scroggins's team was properly rested and watered, Ah-ti meandered out to see if the ship had returned yet.

The stable boy came over to her and said, "There's coffee for the taking at the galley."

Ah-ti smelled the fire burning, and, although she was apprehensive, she found her way over to the galley, where a marm was toasting bread over a stove.

"Are ya hungry, girl?" she asked.

Ah-ti sighed.

"That's all right. C'mon over here 'n git ya some vittles," the jolly woman said.

Ah-ti complied and ate some toast and accepted a cup of coffee. "You are so kind," Ah-ti said. The cook's eyes smiled back at her, accepting the compliment.

Ah-ti then turned her attention toward the harbor, anticipating the return of the *Antelope*.

As she felt the chilling dampness settle on her back, the harbor captain came up beside her and said, "Looks as if the *Antelope* has sailed away."

Ah-ti had a sinking feeling in her stomach and replied, "May the Creator bless us and return our loved ones."

Ah-ti resigned herself to the fact that the squall had possibly swamped the *Antelope*, and that she was responsible for the safe return of her friend's horses and carriage. She felt it was best to leave the carriage at the stable, since she was untrained in steering it. Hesitantly, after ample time had passed, with no sighting of the *Antelope*, Ah-ti took all four horses back to the uplands of Charleston.

As she approached the farm, Cletus opened the gate but had a worried look on his face as she passed through. It was almost noon when Ah-ti arrived, and Mary met her at the shed row.

"What's happened, Ah-ti?" Mary asked as calmly as she could.

Ah-ti replied, "Emily and I rode to town for lunch with Dr. Scroggins, but he'd already gone to a ship to tend to some injured sailors. A gale blew across the harbor after your husband and his doctor friend boarded the merchant ship. Em went on board, and I was lucky to find cover from the storm."

Mary said, "Oh, my gosh! Are you telling me that both my husband and my daughter are out to sea?"

"I'm not sure. I think so," Ah-ti replied, as they embraced.

Ah-ti then said, "Here is the note Dr. Scroggins left for Emily."

* * * * *

Dr. Scroggins and Carlos took off their jackets, rolled up their sleeves, and washed their hands in a bowl of water that the ship's cook, Kelly, had brought them.

"We'll need more water," Carlos informed the man.

"And bring it boiling hot," Dr. Scroggins added.

Away the cook went. There were several injured seamen resting about the mess hall awaiting medical attention. The doctors split up and assessed the nature of the injuries. Two of the sailors had broken limbs; a bone was protruding from one man's arm. Another man had a head injury with a deep gash above his brow.

After a brief meeting, the doctors decided to treat the head wound first, as it appeared to take the least amount of time to suture and stay the blood from flowing. They helped the man over to the mess table, sitting him on a bench that they had dragged against a beam. An oil lantern suspended from a hook above them provided light. The cook returned soon with a tankard of steaming water. Dr. Scroggins opened his medical kit that contained a variety of tools, mainly knives, hooks, pliers, chisels, and tongs. Carlos removed a razor and began shaving the hair from around the man's gash, while Dr. Scroggins took some long horse hair out that was coiled in a tidy ring and put it in a cup, pouring the steaming water over it to soak. The hot water softened the coarse "tail hair" enough to thread it into a curved sewing needle. They cleaned the area well.

"Have you any rum?" Dr. Scroggins inquired of the captain.

"Aye, aye," the captain replied, "Me private stock," he continued, as he looked to Jim-lad, who was his personal servant, and nodded his head for the boy to fetch the rum.

Dr. Carlos poured a bit of the rum over the wound, drying it off with a cloth. Then, Dr. Scroggins sewed the gash shut. Carlos completed the job by applying a salve over the area and bandaging the man's head for protection from dirt and insects.

The ship began to sway a bit more than normal, so the captain begged leave from them to see to ship's business, casting a final glance toward his men and his bottle.

Next, the doctors aided the worse of the two wounded sailors over to the

38

table. They propped his head up on a rolled up blanket.

"What is your name?" Dr. Scroggins inquired.

"Robert," he replied, eyeing the bottle, "but me mates calls me Two Bits. Will ye spare me the pains and numb me a bit with that there rum?"

"Yes, I think that is fair," Dr. Scroggins replied, as he asked the lad to fetch a cup.

Before he could react, Two Bits snatched the bottle from the doctor and guzzled several swallows.

"Ahhh!" he said, wiping his mouth with his good arm. "That'll help some." Dr. Carlos grabbed the bottle.

"You'll need this," Dr. Carlos said, as he pushed a wooden bite bar into Two Bits's mouth.

"Now, bite down on this and lie back so we can take care of this break," Dr. Carlos continued.

Two Bits lay back, sighing heavily, as he braced himself for the pain.

As the doctors were cutting off his shirt, the ship pitched from side to side, almost tossing the seaman from the makeshift examining table. They heard the scurrying of boots and feet above and around them. Then, they heard the captain order, "Make sail!" Again, the ship lurched, this time forward, as the sound of heavy wind rushed below into the galley and mess hall, blowing out lanterns and giving some relief from the oppressive heat as well.

"Young man," Dr. Scroggins said to the lad, "go to the ship's carpenter and tell him that we require some wooden splints." The boy soon returned with the carpenter who brought several pieces of wood with him.

It took the doctors a few hours to get the injured men's bones set in place and properly bound. It was no easy task; the ship was pitching and rolling as the squall overtook it. To add to the problem, sea water would sometimes spill down below deck as the violent waves crashed over the gunwale of the ship.

When the captain learned the doctors had finished mending his crew, he sent his quartermaster below to arrange a place for them to rest after their ordeal.

"The captain sends his regrets that he won't be addressing you in person," the quartermaster stammered, "as he is steering the ship out in the storm."

On behalf of the captain, the man extended an invitation to stay in the captain's personal cabin, as the storm made it impossible to return to port. Carlos and Dr. Scroggins exchanged looks of surprise. They realized they had been racing to stay at the leading edge of the storm for hours and may have gone a hundred miles away from Charleston. Fatigued, they followed the man to the captain's quarters.

Once there, they saw a larger open cabin with windows and simple furniture, including a table, chairs, and a bed. Just then, the ship's cook knocked and entered with Jim-lad, two covered plates, and a pitcher with tin cups. After removing most of their sweaty clothes, the doctors sat down at the table and were preparing to eat when the quartermaster returned with two canvas hammocks. He proceeded to hang them from iron hooks attached to a central post and to the cabin's wall.

"I'll send Jim-lad back soon with some dry clothes. If you require anything else, tell him then," he said, leaving unceremoniously. The boy returned quickly and the men changed, leaving their wet clothes in a pile on the floor.

They uncovered the dinner plates, revealing some sort of stew and bread. The pitcher contained grog, a water and alcohol mix flavored with lime juice to prevent the dreaded sickness of scurvy.

While they were eating, the door to the deck swung open and the captain came inside. He was drenched from head to toe. Casting a sideways glance toward his guests, he crossed the room to his dressing area and rang a brass handbell. Jim-lad entered smartly and helped him out of his overcoat and clothes behind a dressing wall. Getting his tall wet boots off proved to be particularly difficult. The captain had to sit in a chair, put one foot on the lad's rump, and push in order to break the wet suction keeping them stuck to his feet. Jim-lad pitched forward from the force of the boot's release. The doctors found it a bit amusing and chuckled, or perhaps the grog was having a relaxing effect on them. Captain Sanchez heard them and offered his first words to them since entering his cabin.

"Argh," he proclaimed, "Are ye liking the cook's chow?" he asked, as nicely as he could muster.

"Well, yes, thank you," Carlos replied, trying to keep the conversation upbeat.

"Yes, this stew has a flavor that I cannot put my finger on," Dr. Scroggins added.

Captain Sanchez laughed heartily. He was garbed in a stylish, but not too ostentatious outfit, with a loose-fitting cotton shirt that was unbuttoned to his stomach.

"Me helmsman, Lynch, has taken the wheel now that we've gained the deep water on a southerly heading." He squinted slightly, gauging their response to this unwelcome news.

Dr. Scroggins was the first to break the silence inside the cabin. The wind howled outside, still pounding the ship angrily with rain so thick that the ship's bow was not even visible through the windows.

"How soon do you think we will be able to come about to return to port?" he inquired, knowing the answer would most likely be something he didn't want to hear.

"Argh! The tempest drives us furiously, farther away from ye port. It is my experience that it be days before we can do anything other than try and outrun the witch, lest we be swamped and sunk," the captain said, as his gaze looked past the men to a distant memory that seemed to make him uneasy.

With that, Jim-lad returned with the captain's supper and the bottle of rum.

"Aye, Jim me boy, yer a sight for sore eyes," the captain announced, taking the half-full bottle. He pulled the cork out with his teeth, spitting it to the floor, and took a few swigs. Then, he looked at his plate, mopped up some sauce with his bread, and inquired as to the condition of his crewmen.

Hearing there was no hope of returning home immediately, the men continued their meal together, as best they could under the conditions, even sharing in a toast or two as they emptied the bottle.

Full, fatigued, and weary of reports from the quartermaster and first mate, they turned the lamps down to a smolder and went to their hammocks.

Chapter 4

Ah-ti watched Mary as she read the note. Mary's hands trembled, as she tried to focus on the words through her tears. Having read it, Mary said to Ah-ti, "Thank you for telling me what's happened. Please stay for dinner and rest. You can stay in Emily's room tonight if you'd like."

"Oh, Mrs. Scroggins, I appreciate your offer, but really, I must return home to my family. They do not know my whereabouts or whether I am safe or not."

Mary understood her point and offered to have Cletus accompany her back home. Ah-ti just laughed and said as politely as she could, "Why, that old man would just slow me down. The sky has cleared, and I've ridden that trail a hundred times alone. I'll be fine."

With that, Mary walked Ah-ti to the barn where Cletus was giving the horses a drink and wished her well. Ah-ti again leapt onto Moonlight and galloped across the fields, disappearing into the forest.

Mary took the note to the front porch of the house and sat in one of the rockers. She stared into the distance, eventually falling asleep to the buzzing sounds of the nocturnal insects and the calling of a whippoorwill. Her mind played tricks on her, as she dreamt of Ezra coming over the top of the hill and returning to her.

* * * * *

Emily awoke with a start. She'd had an awful nightmare about plunging into a deep black hole. Her head was throbbing, and, when she felt her hair, it was sticky and clumped together.

"This is odd," she thought. She opened her eyes, but it was still black as coal around her. Emily then realized that she did not recognize the sounds around her. Her bed was hard and she was cold. She moved her hands about, searching for her comforter and blanket, but of course, they were not there. She rolled over onto her belly to look out the window for Caramel's stable. Instead of seeing the barn and stable, she fell to the floor with a loud thump!

Still stunned, she got to her feet and reached out into the darkness to feel her way toward a door or exit. The floor was moving back and forth. Emily had difficulty staying on her feet. She could not tell whether she was still caught in some bizarre dream or not. She groped along, feeling odd shapes, canvas, even ropes. She thought she could see a faint yellowish light and stumbled toward it. She tripped over something on the floor, falling into a tool rack of iron hooks and grabbers used to position cargo as it was being lowered. The hooks clattered and clanged together like wind chimes. The dim light suddenly became bright, as a door was flung open, and a menacing figure's silhouette hulked in the doorway yelling loudly, "Who goes there?"

Emily screamed in terror as the nightmare came to life. She could not wake up, or God forbid, she was awake and trapped in some terrible place. Realizing that she truly was awake, Emily sank to her knees pleading aloud, "Please, please don't hurt me."

The man came closer and closer until he grabbed Em by the upper arm and growled, "Stowaways are unwanted aboard this 'ere ship." Jerking her harshly to her feet, he lifted the lantern up and shined it on Em's face. He could see the matted blood in her disheveled hair. He thought her clothes were that of a young man. Em was somewhat of a tomboy and was dressed for horseback riding that day. He dragged Em over to a small paddock used to house swine when they carried them. Thankfully, none were aboard. He tossed her to the floor and locked the gate. As he turned to leave, he said, "Don't give me any trouble lest we keel haul ya on the morn."

Em was dumbfounded. What kind of nightmare had she unwittingly become a part of? She scuttled into a corner, drawing her knees up to her chest, praying that the man would not return anytime soon. For a while, she just sat in the dark, listening to the eerie sounds of the ship creaking and the wind moaning. Those were the last sounds she heard before she lost consciousness again.

When the quartermaster got back to his own bunk, he told his shipmates that the commotion was just a stowaway and that he'd inform the captain at dawn so as to not disturb his sleep and encounter his wrath.

"Aye, aye," they muttered.

When dawn came, the sun was still concealed by the continuing storm. The ocean undulated ferociously, as tall waves crashed against the ship.

Lightning was flashing, and the crack and boom of the thunder seemed to be right above the sailors.

Riggers scrambled about the deck, climbing the swaying ratlines to secure and jury-rig the tattered sails. They reefed the aft sail to the yardarms on the mizzen mast, as it was flapping violently and practically torn loose. The sailors took turns going above into the storm, even aiding the helmsman by steering the wheel for him. This was a big problem for they could not "tie off" the wheel to a stationary course, due to the gigantic swells which they had to both "ride out" and steer the ship around.

Carlos was the first of the three men in the captain's cabin to awake. He lay there in his hammock swaying from side to side. He thought of his homeland, of his family and friends, and their dire need for medical assistance. He also remembered peaceful days prior to the sickness. He dwelled on the pleasant thoughts in order to stay focused. His mission usurped his fears of perishing in the ocean's depths.

Just then, a sailor rapped on the door and barged into their cabin.

"Captain!" the man announced, waking both the captain and Dr. Scroggins from their fitful rest. "We await orders!" he continued, raising his arm to shield his eyes and face from the expected wrath of his cranky captain.

Captain Sanchez sprang to his feet and looked through the porthole. The sea was still angrily stirring about them. With purpose, he quickly donned his boots and coat and made for the deck's door.

"Away with ye," he barked at the seaman.

"Captain, there's more news," the seaman went on.

"Out with it, man," the captain sneered, steeling himself to the stinging rain biting his face.

"There's a stowaway below all bloodied and half crazed," he reported.

The captain barked, "You men go see to this stowaway, and be careful for your own safety in doing so." He turned and slammed the door shut behind him.

The fist mate yelled the captain's orders, rousting the crew from their relatively safe abodes below deck, "All hands on deck!"

Chaos ensued as the men raced to and fro, dressing themselves. No one wanted to be the last hand on deck, lest he risk being flogged for laziness. The doctors, still below deck, made their way to the rear of the ship, passing the galley along the way. The cook, anticipating their request, had a jar full of water, a bowl, and a few rags for them to use. He also offered them a cup of his hot morning brew of tea leaves and honey.

The doctors drank their tea rather hurriedly and proceeded on, unguided to the cargo area. Along the way, they passed the quartermaster's area and saw him at his table, fondling a strange wooden box. They continued past him, but then, Dr. Scroggins halted and spun around, rushing over to the man.

"Where did you get this?" Dr. Scroggins exclaimed.

"I found it in the hold near that stowaway," he answered.

Dr. Scroggins grabbed the box, and lifted it closer to his face. In the dim light, he felt its distinctive casing. Dr. Scroggins turned toward Carlos, and, with a ghastly expression upon his face, he uttered one word: *Emily*. Handing off the box to Carlos, he rushed past them, scrambled across the slippery deck, and made his way down another hatch into the cargo hold. Dr. Scroggins jaunted his way through the rocking and unfamiliar surroundings, searching for the stowaway.

The quartermaster complained aloud, but Carlos flipped the clasp open, revealing the mostly intact microscope inside.

"This, sir, belongs to the good doctor," Carlos flatly stated.

The quartermaster shrank back, recalling his actions from the previous night. He snuffed out his candle and ran up the stairs to get out on deck. Carlos followed Dr. Scroggins to the cargo hold.

Dr. Scroggins made his way aft. He came to a low, heavy wooden door with iron hinges and hasp. Pulling the pin from its hasp, he cautiously pushed the door open. It swung completely open, thumping against its frame. He ducked and entered, his eyes slowly adjusting to the dim bluish light that crept through ventilation hatches. Moving cautiously, he searched for signs of the captive. He, too, bumped into the chains and hooks that clattered.

Through the gate's gaps, Emily spied the approaching figure. Having nowhere to go, she began to tremble. Em cowered, wishing she were a mouse, so she could scamper and hide unnoticed. She betrayed her hiding place as a whimper escaped her lips. At that, her father stopped moving. He waited, motionless, his own heart beating so loudly, he could hear nothing else. Sensing something near him aside from his approaching colleague, Dr.

Scroggins grabbed the gate of the pen and opened it. His eyes adjusted to his surroundings, and he saw a person barely visible, hiding in the straw.

Mustering his resolve, he took a deep breath and said, "Em, is that you?"

Emily, fearing the worst again, barely comprehended the words, but she thought she knew that voice. Afraid to hope, Em replied, "Daddy?"

Dr. Scroggins fell to his knees at her sunken form. He scooped her and bunches of straw up to his chest. Carlos appeared with a lantern, illuminating the reunion.

Dr. Scroggins softly replied, "My child, I am here, and you are safe."

Em threw her shaking arms around her father's neck and said, "I thought I was forever lost."

Dr. Scroggins replied, "Child, as long as I have breath, I will always find and love you. Come now, and let us leave this pig sty."

As they turned with Carlos lighting the way, they left that horrid place, only to again hear the wailing witch of a wind. They went back up on deck crossing over to the galley area, then back below to the mess hall to get Emily cleaned up and to get her something to eat.

"That's quite a knot you have there," Dr. Scroggins said to Emily. "How did you get it?"

Emily recounted the happenings that led her and Ah-ti to the dock, along with how she tried to get the microscope to her father, as the ship was getting ready to leave.

"It's a good thing your friend came along with you," Carlos said.

"Yes, at least mother will know where we are," Em replied.

"Well, yes and no," Dr. Scroggins added. "We don't know exactly how long we will be stuck aboard this vessel."

"What do you mean?" Em said rather surprised.

"Well, the captain informed us that this storm is keeping us from turning around. We are actually in danger from it," Carlos continued with a guarded tone to his voice.

After exchanging stories about how they had come to be on the ship, the three passengers' minds wandered to what was most important to them. They could still hear the sailors above them working in the storm to keep the ship sailing properly. Carlos excused himself, so the doctor could give his daughter a better examination. He wanted to make sure she had no fractured ribs or problems with her back and neck as a result of her fall.

Returning to the quartermaster to retrieve the microscope, Carlos inquired as to what kind of sleeping arrangements could be made for Emily. There would need to be better security for a young woman among all those seamen, some of whom had questionable character from his view.

The quartermaster suggested that Emily and Dr. Scroggins stay in the captain's cabin, while Carlos could stay with the rest of the men. Carlos agreed that would be best, so he obtained another hammock and found a suitable place to hang it. Then, he went back to see how Emily was doing.

Doctor Scroggins had Em cleaned up; he had even washed her hair. The cook was a big help, because he supplied them with a towel, soap, and warm water. Then, the doctors returned to the captain's cabin to rest, along with Emily. Em got into the bed and fell asleep after a short time under the watchful and caring protection of her father.

The doctors settled in at the table and were looking over the microscope, which had sustained minor damages. Its reflecting mirror was cracked, but the glass slides seemed to be intact. They both were relieved that the instrument was still in working order. Before long, the captain returned. Again, he was soaking wet, despite having a full-length slicker to protect him.

"Well, methinks we shan't be overcome by the tempest," he announced as he took off his raincoat.

"That's great news," Doctor Scroggins replied, optimistically.

"Aye," Captain Sanchez continued, "but we shan't be returning to port as we had hoped."

"Why not?" the doctors replied in unison.

"We've come too far, and the gale still be chasing us around the horn," the captain continued.

"The horn of what?" Doctor Scroggins asked.

"Argh, the horn of Florida, of course," he answered.

"Where do you intend to go?" Doctor Scroggins asked in shock.

"All the way to Mexico with this here cargo," he said, "as we are already near halfway there." The captain pointed to the ever shrinking strip of land in the distance.

The doctors looked at each other, stunned. Despite the bad news, Carlos was somewhat relieved; this unfortunate development was advantageous to his cause.

Carlos asked, "Where do you intend to go in Mexico?"

"Thar's a small city of sorts on the southern tip of the isthmus to do trade with, but the sky be concealed by clouds, and all I can do is dead reckon a heading," he replied.

Carlos's heart leapt as he processed the news and realized that the destination was very close to his hometown.

"What is the name of this place?" Carlos asked the captain.

"It be called Tulum," the captain replied.

Again, the doctors' eyes found one another in amazement.

"Good sir," Carlos continued, "that is exactly where I need to go."

"Aye, then it's all set. I agree to bring ye thar in exchange for tending to me crew," Captain Sanchez said.

"And to you, Doctor Scroggins, I be paying a small stipend for services rendered," he said with a wink.

"Business being finished, I need to see about some scallywag bilge rat stowing away on me ship," Captain Sanchez said, crossing the room toward his changing area. Passing by his bed, he noticed a lump in it. Upon closer inspection, he could see that the lump was a young woman sleeping.

"Blow me down!" he exclaimed, stopping in his tracks. "What be the meaning of this?"

Dr. Scroggins replied, "The scallywag to whom you are referring and the young woman sleeping there are one and the same: She's my daughter!"

"Shiver me timbers!" Captain Sanchez bellowed.

With that, Emily awoke and sat up. The captain spun around, turning his back to his bed. Emily scanned the room to make sure that her father was still there. When she saw him, she lay down and went back to sleep. Captain Sanchez saw the bruise on her head and suggested that the good doctor and his daughter remain in his cabin for the voyage. He would move some of his things out later and stay in a supply room off the galley.

"A strange chain of events we've had since docking in Charleston," the captain said, sinking into a chair.

"Yes, I'd have to agree," Dr. Scroggins replied.

"It all seems as if the Creator has made these things happen for a purpose,"

Carlos added, as he quietly pondered how the storm was bringing his friend and medical expertise to his homeland.

"Well, I'm not what you'd call a man of faith," the captain said, "but we should make Cuba by the evening with this tail wind a blowin' as she is."

"Then what?" Dr. Scroggins asked.

"Why, then, it's across to Mexico we'll sail, avoiding the Cuban coast as there is unrest in their city of Havana. We need not provoke any Spanish warships," the captain continued. "Depending on wind and currents, methinks in a week's time, we'll be safely in port on the Yucatan peninsula."

With that, the captain left to make the arrangements for residing elsewhere. The storm continued to a lesser degree for the remainder of the day. The doctors took turns watching over Emily as she rested, and they checked on their patients, who seemed to be recovering well.

Later that day, Emily finally arose and felt well enough for a breath of fresh air. The crew had heard about the drama surrounding the stowaway. They cautiously observed her moving about but were careful to not aggravate an already annoyed captain by openly watching her. Tradition held that women were not usually welcome on sailing vessels, unless the ship was specifically meant to have passengers. Even then, the crew and passengers remained separated from one another for the passengers' safety.

The rain had stopped temporarily, and the crew was busy battening down the hatches and adjusting the rigging. A lookout was even posted in the crow's nest. He was to notify the first mate of any ship or land sightings. The first mate, Vargas, was busy with a sextant, in an attempt to pinpoint their position on the charts. It was imperative to stay out of sight of the Cuban coast. The clouds were moving south, and their ship was heading west. The concealing rain cover was abating.

Emily retired to the captain's quarters, having had her fill of salty air and the rocking motion of the ship. Carlos was kind enough to bring her some chow from the galley when he returned from his rounds. Emily managed to eat the odd food and keep it down despite her queasy stomach. She did her best to continue resting, but boredom was setting in. The captain had a bookshelf with several leather-bound books. Em looked a few of them over. Selecting one, she went to the table, lit the oil lamp, and settled down to read a bit.

It was then that she noticed an orange cat walking back and forth outside the window. Enamored at the welcome sight, Emily opened the cabin door and said, "Pss-ss-ss," calling the cat over. The cat meowed and readily accepted her invitation to enter the room, even rubbing itself against her legs and purring. Sanders, the boatswain, passed by Em and said, "So you've met our rat catcher."

"He's just adorable. What's his name?"

"The captain calls him Cicero, after a great orator, because he always has something to say," the bosun replied.

"That's funny," Em said, showing signs of a rapid recovery.

"Do you think the captain will mind that I let him in here?" Em asked.

"Aye, ye best not let it on his clothes or bed due to the hair," he replied.

"Oh, I won't do that," Em said, shutting the door behind her. Then Em looked for some string or ribbon to play with the cat, like she sometimes did back home.

Forgetting about the book, Emily and Cicero had a playful bout. It was short lived though. Soon the cat lost interest and waited by the door, meowing until she let him out. Carlos watched quietly. He was glad to see her in good spirits and giggling a bit.

Dr. Scroggins returned and found Emily up and about. "I see you're feeling better," he said with a pleased look on his face.

Em responded with a big hug and a deep sigh, burying her head in his strong arms and chest.

"Oh, Daddy, I never meant to be any trouble," she said, wincing a bit from the still tender bruise on her head.

Carlos smiled, but he couldn't help thinking that life back home in Tulum was nothing like that of the happy, healthy family in front of him.

Captain Sanchez shouted out to Vargas, "Meet me at the galley whenst ye figures our position." Then, he went below to his cabin and knocked before entering saying, "May I come in for me belongings?"

Dr. Scroggins replied, "Of course, come, come."

The captain moved about with Jim-lad, loading the boy down with various clothes and personal items. He grabbed an armful of charts, which were tubular rolls of parchment paper with maps on them of various land and ocean features. As he departed through the side door toward the galley, the captain gave his guests a sideways glance, showing them a sneer of sorts, perhaps to remind them of both the inconvenience they were causing and his notable efforts to be a polite host.

"That is one man I would not want to cross," Carlos said.

Dr. Scroggins replied, "A tough lot he has to command, too." He nodded toward the top deck covered with seamen. Emily sat down and was trying to make sense of the situation.

They could hear Vargas barking orders to the men, directing them to adjust the sails.

"Davies, Pierce, Hall, Campbell, bring down the mainsail and release it from the yardarms so ye dogs can put needle and thread to it."

"Roberts, Hughes, Gregor, bring down the mizzen sail to half mast," he continued.

Riggins, the man in charge of the ropes yelled, "To the ropes, men."

Vargas turned his attention to Riggins and said, "Be sure to bring all the sails to half mast so's to lessen our look from any Cuban ship a patrollin'."

"Aye, aye," Riggins responded. With that, he kept the men scurrying around. It looked very confusing to the passengers, but to the seasoned seamen, the work came as second nature. They were an experienced crew, having no lubbers on this trip.

Vargas, satisfied with the progress, spun around and stomped across deck. He was headed below to meet with the captain.

"Argh, Captain, the dogs be carrying out ye orders under Riggins's watchful eye," Vargas said.

"Very well," Sanchez replied as he unrolled a chart onto the table. The men used any available kitchen implements to hold the map in place and keep it from rolling itself back up.

"Methinks we are in this here area," he said, as he set a coffee bean down on the parchment. "Where didst ye sextant indicate we are?"

"Hard to pinpoint, Captain. Me best guess since the clouds still be obscuring the sun is just a bit more this-a-way," he said, gently moving the bean over the map westward.

Sanchez looked up at Vargas's face, not liking the minute difference of opinion. He moved the bean a smidgen to the left and said, "We waits for the stars to show themselves tonight for the readin'. We must stay out far enough to avoid any unwanted attention from the coastline's patrols. Fully laden, as we are, we are too heavy to run and our guns'd be no match for a man-o-war," the captain whispered.

"Jim-lad," Sanchez called out. The boy came smartly. "Go fetch the Indian doctor so we can consult with him a bit."

Off Jim went to retrieve the doctor.

"Dr. Carlos, the captain requests yer presence in the galley," Jim-lad informed.

"Oh, okay, that's fine," Dr. Carlos replied, as he patted his chest to be sure that his records were with him.

Dr. Scroggins and Em stayed behind, observing and listening to the working crew. Once below, Vargas nodded the doctor a welcome, as Sanchez studiously gazed at the charts.

"Are ye familiar with these drawings?" the captain asked.

"Well, if you are asking if I recognize the land area on this side of the map, the answer is yes. This is my third journey across the sea," Carlos said.

"Aye, ye are a learned man, I see," the captain replied. "We are positioned here at this here coffee bean." He continued, with a playful glimmer in his eye, "Will ye tell me of any occurrences we might needs to be aware of, whilst we approaches this here area?" He pointed with a knife to the eastern side of the Mayan peninsula.

Dr. Carlos stood upright and folded his arms. Then, he brought his right hand up to his ear and scratched it a bit. He took a breath, and after what seemed like an eternity to the awaiting officers, he motioned with his finger and said, "There is a strong current that was against our progress once we were out to sea in this area."

"Argh! That be the deep channel that we are entering," the captain confidently replied, as he sought the approval of his first mate.

Their eyes locked on one another. Dr. Carlos then tapped his finger on the map, pointing to the edge of a land mass jutting out next to a small island.

"This is where I need to go," he said.

With that, Vargas warned, "Captain, that is the sea of behemoths!"

Sanchez looked at both the men and replied, "The moon is nigh. Perhaps fortune is upon us, and we'll pass through unnoticed."

Unfazed, Sanchez brought out three glasses and a bottle of rum.

"Will ye join us for a drink?" he inquired of the doctor. Vargas set the glasses in a line and hastily poured the amber liquid into each, reaching for his own quickly before the captain changed his mind.

Raising it up for a toast, he said, "May the sea permit us to pass onward to friendly shores and pretty women." They all raised their glasses and drank. *What is this new predicament that we are approaching?* Carlos wondered.

Having ordered the men to withdraw to half sail, Riggins was focused on seeing that the orders were carried out accordingly when Vargas and the captain came up on deck. "Hop to it, mateys!" he shouted.

Sanchez looked at the sky in all directions. In the distance, they could see the horizon allowing an azure blue splotch of an opening along the leading edge of the storm clouds. With the diminishing evening light, the sky adopted a gorgeous, fiery streak that the sea reflected. The orange hue raced across the ocean as the clouds abated. The sunset's rays eventually reached the port side of the ship, and ignited the wet hull like glowing embers.

The captain shouted, "All sails down!"

He then barked to the helmsman, "Steer hard to starboard."

The seamen raced to loosen the ropes and to gather the canvas sheets to be bundled. They did not ask why, or even grumble, when they heard the tone of their captain's voice. Within minutes, the sails were furled.

Their ship turned at an angle, hiding from the sunlight that might bounce off its surface and catch the eye of someone on the coast.

Sanchez and Vargas read the sextant to glean their position. As the sun sank beyond the horizon, the spyglass showed a twinkling of distant objects at sea coming about.

Emily and her father were alone in the captain's chamber. The ship had ceased its rocking and tossing about as the late afternoon became evening. Emily wondered where the cat had gone and wanted to play with him.

Dr. Scroggins took out his journal and reviewed his notes, which encompassed the treatment of the crew's injuries. He located an ink well and quill and wrote for a while. Emily, seeing that there was not much else to do, decided to read the book she had selected earlier. She sat on the bed, leaning her back against the wall and raised the book to catch the sun's rays through the window. It was titled *The Count of Monte Cristo*.

Soon, they had to light the lanterns in order to continue reading and writing. Right about that time, Dr. Carlos came by, and Cicero ran past his legs as he came in. They made conversation for a while, until they noticed that the business on deck had quieted; the noises were coming from next door or below deck.

"Sounds like the crew is settling down for the night," Dr. Scroggins commented.

"Coming below, perhaps, but settling not," Dr. Carlos quipped. "More like ready to be fed."

"I'm hungry too," Em added.

Soon, the dinner bell rang, and a ruckus began, as the men came to the mess hall awaiting their evening meal.

Cook Kelly doled out a large ladle of "mystery stew," the term the men had come to use for his meals. Also they each got a helping of hardtack, which is a kind of bread baked rock hard, that they broke into pieces and let the broth soften. Of course, there was also a tankard of grog, which helped them to relax a bit. They were hard workers with a difficult and often dangerous job. Suppertime was the part of the day they relished—a time when work was done and they could joke among themselves.

On this night, the captain joined them in the mess hall, and on such rare occasions, he often would double their ration of grog. That always put the men in a cheerful mood. It felt like a reward for a job well done.

"Double rations of grog tonight, me hearties!" the captain ordered.

"Hurray, hurrah!" the crew shouted almost in unison. The first officers had driven them hard. First, there was the loading of the cargo. Then, they had to keep the ship from foundering in the storm. This night would be more festive than most!

Jokes were told, knees were slapped, and jigs were danced. McCarthy, one of the riggers, played the accordion, while Smyth played a flute-like recorder. The captain joined in as well, doing a dance such as performed in the great ballrooms of Europe, dramatically waving his arms about and bowing to his shipmates.

The men broke into song:

"Up jumps a crab with his crooked legs
Saying, 'You play the cribbage, and I'll stick the pegs!'

Singing blow the wind westerly let the wind blow
By a gentle nor' wester how steady she goes.
Up jumps a dolphin with his chucklehead.
He jumps on the deck saying, 'Pull out the lead!'
Up jumps a flounder so flat on the ground
Saying, 'Damn your old chocolate, mind how you sound!'
Up jumps a salmon so bright as the sun.
He jumped down between the decks and fired off a gun.
Up jumps a whale, the biggest of all.
He jumped up aloft and he's pawl after pawl,
Up jumps a herring, the king of the sea.
He jumps up on deck saying, 'Helms a-lee!'
Up jumps a shark with his big row of teeth.
He jumped up between the decks and shook out the reefs."

A much needed time of respite was had by all. Even Two Bits joined in. His arm was in a sling, but he was tapping his foot and smiling.

Dr. Scroggins, Carlos, and Emily had their own party from the security of the captain's quarters, dancing and swirling and laughing as well, while Cicero would wail like an alley cat from time to time.

After what seemed like several hours, the men quieted down one by one—either from exhaustion, drunkenness, or a combination of both. There was many a dream that night of fanciful ladies and strumpets, and there was loud snoring, and sleep talking as well. Dr. Scroggins fell asleep thinking of his loving wife and her warm embrace. Emily also thought of home and her steed, Caramel, and her good friend, Ah-ti-yah.

Chapter 5

The next morning brought fair weather along with a bright sunrise. The moon was setting when the sun came up. It was quite tranquil as Emily sauntered about the deck, having awakened before anyone else. She felt free and relaxed. The breeze was constant and her hair blew back. The salty air smelled refreshing as well. Em particularly enjoyed seeing the sun and moon on opposite sides of the sky at the same time, which was rare back home, due to the hills and trees obstructing the horizon.

She had on her vest since it was a bit cool. She remembered her ride into town with Ah-ti-yah and rummaged in her pockets for the pencils. Her fingers found something lumpy. It was the two toy horses her mother had given her. Em got them out and played with them along the deck rail. In her mind, she was riding Caramel again as she maneuvered the horses along the rail in a galloping motion. She even made whinnying sounds, mimicking her steed. Em's father watched her from a distance. He knew she was no longer a little girl and that moments like that should be cherished forever.

With the exception of the helmsman, who had remained at the wheel through the night, Em was alone on deck. Lynch had set the stop on the wheel during some of the festivities to maintain their course while he had his dinner and partook of the singing, but he returned to his post shortly thereafter. That was a good thing, because when he rang the bell at daybreak, there was a lot of grumbling, even cursing at the arrival of a new day. Many of the men had imbibed and celebrated too much. Their heads were aching, and their guts were unsettled. They went to the bow to take turns at the privy.

When they returned, most of the men ambled past the galley for a bowl of the cold stew. Some were content with an apple. Hoarding could be a problem on ship, so everything had to be doled out accordingly, so that supplies would last and the crew would not be forcibly made to accept half-rations.

After a slightly extended readying period, Vargas shouted, "All hands on deck!"

The seamen came like hornets from a hive, lining up in two rows at midship to hear the plan for the day.

"Lads," Vargas began, "Didst ye have yer fill of merriment last night?"

"Aye, aye!" they responded. They felt a bit at ease but were unsure of this rare good mood from the first mate.

"Argh!" Vargas replied. "Twas a good time! This day, we sail for Mexico. Riggins, have ye men repair the torn mainsail. The rest of you dogs, hoist the sails full and pump the bilge. Now off with ye raggedly hides." His sneering grin indicated that playtime was finished. Vargas relieved Lynch at the wheel so he could get some needed rest below.

Carlos had remained below at the galley, where he was chatting with Kelly and observing his manner of doing things. When he noticed that the plates and utensils were merely wiped off and stacked, he had a conversation with the cook about putting them into a pot of boiling water for ten minutes with some lye to sanitize them. He had a hard time explaining to Kelly the concept of tiny bacteria that made people sick. When Carlos resorted to calling the bacteria "tiny bugs," the cook understood but still doubted Carlos until the captain, who had been listening from his hammock grumbled, "Are ye daft, ye sloppy Irishman? Do as he says."

Then, rounding the corner to eyeball them, Sanchez said to Carlos, "And to think me thought twas just his odd recipes what makes me belly squirm." He gave Carlos a friendly back slap and chose an apple from the basket by sticking it with his knife.

Carlos attempted to tell Sanchez that the knife was also contaminated, but the captain was done listening and went topside to meet the day. Jim-lad was busy tidying up the captain's room before he left to dump the chamber pot.

The crewmen greeted their captain warmly but cautiously as he passed by. Sanchez was known to be a tough, old "salty dog" and did not care for unnecessary speech, especially from the crew. He basically ignored them as he headed toward the cargo area to inspect the battens.

"Guillen!" the captain barked. The quartermaster jumped up from his position aft and came smartly to Sanchez's side.

"Aye, Captain," he replied warily.

"'Tis true that ye accosted the lass, down in this here hold?" Sanchez growled so low that it was almost inaudible.

Taken aback by the inquiry, Guillen's face showed trepidation. He stammered as he tried to reply; thoughts of being flogged rushed through his mind.

"Er, uh, no," he lied. "The stowaway was crazed and out of his mind. All I did was subdue and confine him, er, her, until the morn so as to not disturb ye rest," he whimpered, avoiding the question.

While the answer pleased the captain, he detested the idea of one of his crewman manhandling any woman. With one hand, Sanchez reached out and grabbed the quartermaster by his coat, and spun him around behind the capstan, out of sight of the crew. Pulling him almost nose to nose, Sanchez flung the half eaten apple off his knife into the sea, and pointed it at the man's throat and said, "If ye or any other scurvy rat so much as looks at the lass in mischief, I'll have ye tied to the mast and flogged. And if any of ye rats lay a hand on her, both ye and them be keel drug."

By then, Guillen was trembling on the outside and furious on the inside, but he dared not speak with the knife poking his throat. The captain released the man, and, brushing his shoulder in a kindly gesture, he ordered him to go below and inspect the cargo, ready the bilge pumps to remove any standing water below, and return with a report.

Guillen went aft and selected two men to help with the assignment. As he left, he saw Cicero and yelled at the cat to get out of his way. He attempted to kick it, but Cicero ably escaped the seaman's boot.

"Gustafsson, Moppit," he called out, "Leave yer task there and go with me below."

Sanchez returned to the main mast to evaluate the work assignments and noticed Two Bits sitting idly by.

"What do you think you are doing?" he demanded of the broken man.

"Er, nothing, sir," he replied.

"Get your carcass below and help Kelly with the mess—or is your other arm not fit to work?"

No one even looked up at the captain, whose merry mood had been replaced with a malicious attitude. He stood on the bow for quite some time with his spyglass, enthralled in his own thoughts. Vargas thought the captain was on edge due to the proximity of patrolling warships, and he was correct about that. What the first mate did not know was that they were entering the deep channel, where the demons of the deep lurked.

Dr. Scroggins motioned to Emily to return to the cabin when the men scampered on deck. She knew it was best that she not be in the way, so she reluctantly came back. Then after a short while, when things were quiet below, Carlos knocked on the cabin door.

"May I enter?" he asked.

"Yes, you may," Emily quipped, before her father could respond.

"Ah, I see you are feeling well today," Carlos said, glancing at Dr. Scroggins, who returned an encouraging look.

Carlos and Jim-lad came in with breakfast. They sat down to eat their food and held hands. Jim had never done this before, but he went along with it. Dr. Scroggins led them in a brief prayer, thanking God for delivering them safely through the storm and for the food they had to eat.

While they were eating, Jim-lad asked what it was like to live in Charleston. Dr. Scroggins explained a bit and described their home and horse farm. Emily took out the two wooden horses and handed one to Jim-lad. The two of them played with the horses during the meal like little children.

Jim-lad was obviously enjoying their time together, but it did not last long. He heard the cook calling for him from the galley. So, piling the plates and pot, Jim-lad left to earn his keep on the ship, smiling as he went.

"That was nice of you to let Jim play with your horse," Dr. Scroggins said.

"Well, why not?" Em replied. "After all, he's just a boy."

Again, Carlos's mind went to a place where little boys and girls were not reaching Jim-lad's age, due to the jungle sickness. Carlos felt as if he were trapped inside an hour glass, and the sands of time were running out.

After the meal, the three seafarers busied themselves: Emily focused on her book; the doctors, the microscope. Dr. Scroggins had made slides of the blood he had taken from Two Bits. They were studying it under the magnifying lenses and discussing Carlos's theory about what was behind the jungle illness. Emily found a spot just outside the cabin door where she sat down to read her novel. The story began with a handsome young sailor named Edmond Dantès. Emily was coming of age and was enthralled by the tale of a returning seaman and romance. She read the book at an insatiable rate, mesmerized for hours at a time.

Later that afternoon, in the heat of the day, Em retired to the cabin and was reading the book while lying on the bed. Cicero was keeping her company while the doctors were out and about.

Riggins's men had the mainsail stretched out across the mid deck. They also had procured additional canvas from Guillen to reinforce the stitching. The seamen began singing a song they called *Goodbye, Fare Thee Well* to pass the time:

"We're going away to leave you now.
Goodbye, fare thee well!
Goodbye, fare thee well!
We're going away to leave you now.
Hoorah! Me boys, we're homeward bound.
Ah, give me the girl with the bonny brown hair.
Your hair of brown is the talk of the town.
So fare you we're homeward bound,
Homeward bound to Charleston town.
So fill up your glasses for those who were kind,
And drink to the girls we are leaving behind.
We're homeward bound I hear them say,
We're homeward bound with eleven months pay.
Our anchor we'll weigh, our sails we will set.
The friends we are leaving we'll never forget."

Gazing up from her reading, Emily listened to the crude melody. The lyrics caught her attention. Em's eyes popped open when they got to the part about the town they wished to go home to! It brought a broad smile to her young face. She went outside in plain sight of the crew and sauntered over toward them. By then, word had gotten out; the men had heard about her predicament and had compassion for the young woman who had been swept away at sea. They were also appreciative of the good work the doctors had done for their shipmates and the examinations they were given.

Upon seeing her, the seamen broke into a loud cheer reserved for honored guests or special occasions.

"Hurray!" they shouted. "Huzzah!"

They repeated the shout twice. This cheering brought the doctors above deck too. They met up with Emily and all three stood there enjoying the tribute, or so it seemed. The captain took notice and was glad. Then, the men repeated the song's verses a few more times.

The whole mood of the ship seemed to improve, and morale was high.

Captain Sanchez approached the three and said, "Seems me mates have bestowed an honor upon ye." With a wink of his eye, he added, "Methinks ye be safe to move about the ship freely now, Lassie, but be mindful not to be too distracting." He bowed low with a swoop of his arm.

The men thought the gesture was hilarious. The rest of the day passed as any good day at sea should. The travellers were in harmony with the ocean and with one another. The only exception was a sour Guillen, who was still down below in the hold, splashing about in the stagnant water, tightening ropes and chocks.

By late afternoon, the mainsail was ready to be hoisted. The men climbed the rope ladders and tied it off to the yardarms. When they raised the sail at Vargas's command, the sail caught full, making a noticeable increase in the speed of the ship and the size of her wake.

Fear of being discovered by a patrolling enemy ship had diminished as the day waned, but there was a new danger lurking beneath the hull fifty fathoms deep. The water was remarkably clear. The lookout believed he saw large dark shapes below the waves, but they never surfaced or blew like a whale, so he did not report it to the captain.

Then, way in the distance, the lookout saw faint flashes of light and heard what he thought was a booming sound.

"Captain, I think I see cannon fire off the starboard side."

Sanchez rushed to the gunwale and leveled his scope. It was difficult to make out what the objects were so far away. Pirates could be attacking a merchant vessel such as their own. He could not risk tacking to port because that would bring him closer to Cuba. As the onset of evening approached, the daylight waned. It became clearer that the flashes of light were not cannon fire, but heat lightning, emanating from within the clouds.

This time of year, the region was known for its pop-up thunderstorms, which could be extremely violent. These storms were not of the same caliber as the hurricane they had barely outrun earlier that week, but they were dangerous nonetheless.

Emily asked Sanchez if she could climb up to the crow's nest with the lookout. He told her that would be fine as long as she tied up her hair so it didn't get in the way of her hands or eyes. So, she swirled her long hair like twine and tied it into a knot. Up she went. Em's heart beat faster as she neared the yardarm. She stopped for a minute, because the rope ladder was swaying independently of the motion of the ship. She made the mistake of looking down when she was halfway up and froze tight to the ropes. Her knees felt weak, and a clammy sweat was making her neck and hands slick.

Rojas, the lookout, encouraged Em to keep going. "Don't look down," he said. "Just move one hand at a time."

Emily took a deep breath and kept going. Despite the ever increasing swaying, she somehow kept her mind from panicking and made it into the safety of the crow's nest.

With a broad grin on his face, Rojas said in broken English, "Youa climb like a monkey." Emily clung to the mast with a death grip. As the ship pitched and swayed, they also swayed back and forth, perhaps two feet in one direction, and then just as far in the opposite direction. Emily found the height exhilarating. From her perch, she thought she could make out dark shapes that seemed to be swimming underwater alongside the ship. Em asked the lookout if he knew what they were, but he just shrugged his shoulders. Rojas reminded her that it would soon be dark and told her she'd better go back down.

Emily steeled herself for the descent. She was careful not to look down that time.

When she finally had her feet on the deck, Vargas came over to her and jested, "Tomorrow, your shift begins at dawn."

Emily questioned his humor and hastily retreated to the cabin.

Not long after Emily left the lookout, Rojas noticed something on the water in the distance. He watched it getting closer to the *Antelope* over the next hour. Eventually, it got close enough for him to make out that it was another ship. Rojas called down to alert the crew.

Captain! There's another ship bearing down on us."

Sanchez got out his spyglass and leveled it in the direction that Rojas was pointing.

"Aye, tis true," he said. "But it be not a warship. Perhaps it is another merchant." The captain wanted to subtly assure the crew that they were in no immediate danger. They kept a wary eye on the other ship; the vessel was coming toward them from the direction they were heading.

Vargas ordered Guillen to ready the muskets. Sanchez kept careful watch on the approaching ship. When it was close enough to identify, he announced, "She's flying a British flag, laddies!" He also noticed a white secondary flag on the main mast—a sign that meant they wanted to approach peacefully.

Sanchez told a crewman to reciprocate with their own white flag. When the two ships came close enough for crewmen to plainly see one another, a few of the British sailors let down a rowboat and headed toward the *Antelope*. This was a traditional method to parlay or communicate at sea.

McCarthy tossed a rope ladder over the gunwale for the sailors to secure the rowboat, and two crewmen scrambled up the ladder. The second man had a knapsack strapped to his shoulders.

"Permission to come aboard," a fair-haired seamen requested.

"Permission granted," Sanchez replied.

"Captain Richards sends this sack of papayas over as a gesture of peace."

"A fine gift for any seaman to receive. Vargas, have Kelly change out the contents of this satchel for some green apples," Sanchez ordered. They met for about ten minutes, exchanging information and news. Carlos, Dr. Scroggins, and Emily were watching from near the cabin doorway, when Sanchez surprised them.

"Has ye any letter to be sent home prepared?" Sanchez asked.

"Yes, yes I do," Dr. Scroggins replied, ducking into the cabin. While Dr. Scroggins took his letter to Mary out of his binder, Sanchez was busy writing a note of some kind. He poured hot wax on it to seal it, pushing his ring into the wax and leaving an imprint. The doctor handed the captain his letter, and he went back over to the waiting visitors.

"Here's two letters for ye captain to deliver to Charleston, Carolina, as he sees fit. Notice mine is addressed to the harbor master. Inform ye captain of my intent to return to her harbor and make good on the cargo we sailed out with while escaping a great storm, what would 'ave sunk us."

The two sailors thanked him for the apples, and the first one tucked the letters safely inside his buttoned coat. They scrambled back down the ladder and were off, returning to their own vessel. Upon their arrival to their own ship, they relayed the message to their captain, while Sanchez watched them through his spyglass. The other captain turned to Sanchez and waved that he understood, and the two ships sailed in opposite directions.

*****

Supper was served without the gaiety of the previous night. It seemed even the vessel itself was ready for a rest as she bobbed along the current like a cork in a stream. The captain kept to himself. He had gone to his cabin earlier and gotten one of his books to help pass the time. The men were almost unrecognizable as the rowdy bunch who had spent most of the previous evening singing, dancing, and drinking. Eventually, the everpresent creaking of wood was the only audible sound on board.

When the moon rose, it was quite orange in hue. The tips of the wakes that the ship left reflected the color. Otherwise, the ocean appeared almost black, except for a few flashes of light under the water. The helmsman had an easy time at his post, so he decided to cast a couple of lines off the stern. With any luck, he might catch some fish for the cook to prepare. He baited several hooks with scraps left over from the evening meal. The darting flashes of light eventually took the bait. Lynch hauled in several of the cephalopods. They were a kind of squid averaging three feet in length. Removing the creatures was somewhat dangerous due to their sharp beak-like mouths and the dozens of suction cups that covered their flailing tentacles. He put them in a barrel that was half full of seawater. Soon, the squid almost seemed to be following the ship.

Lynch was rather excited by his success. He was engrossed in his task when there was a tremendous splash behind the boat. Both the lines jerked taught and then, went slack. When he pulled them aboard, he could see that they had been snapped or cut. Not wanting to lose any more tackle, Lynch felt it was best to quit and mind his primary job of steering the ship. Several times during his watch, he heard large splashes. He never did get a plain look at whatever was making the commotion. Of one thing he was sure: It was not whales.

When morning arrived, the ship's inhabitants arose a bit earlier than usual, feeling well rested. Even Guillen appeared to be in a pleasant mood. The crew ate their morning victuals and went topside. Having repaired the mainsail the previous day, they pondered what orders would be given. Some even fancied the idea of a day off. Could there be such a thing? A day off at sea? Certainly not!

Vargas and Riggins were standing by at the helm, awaiting the captain's arrival. When he finally came out, the crew was already standing at the ready. The mustering bell had not even been rung. Sanchez was pleased and a bit surprised, but he gave no hint of that to the seamen.

Instead, he barked to the cabin boy, "Jim-lad, muster the bell!"

Jim-lad's eyes popped open. He was the least of the men, yet he would have the honor of commanding the crew to report for duty. He needed a boost to reach the bell's chord. Moppit raised him up by his waist, and the boy confidently rang the bell. *Ding, ding! Ding, ding!* When he was set back on his feet, he raised his hand in salute and puffed out his lean chest. The men, of course, were already there, so the act was moot. A grin escaped the captain's mouth. He then called forth to his first and second mates to have the other sails removed for more inspection and sewing. Some of the crew groaned at the order. Sanchez spun around to see who the offenders were, but they all remained silent.

It was then that Kelly came above deck and immediately spotted his barrel. He peered inside it and cried out, "Blimey! What manner of beast are in me fish barrel?" With that, he tipped the barrel onto its side and two dozen or so squid poured out onto the deck and began crawling about. A few of them went straight for the rail.

Vargas, shouted, "Dismissed!"

Riggins said, "You men, gather up those squid or ye won't have any supper this night!

The men rallied, chasing the creatures about, slipping in the slime, falling about and rolling as they tried to subdue the catch. Kelly, with a pot in hand, had the worst of it, as he attempted to capture one, but it kept crawling out of his pot onto his arm. He was responsible for the mayhem, so he raced about like a lunatic, trying to do too much and accomplishing little. Sanchez, who had relieved Lynch, was guffawing at the wheel as the comedy ensued. After the chaos subsided, the men were strewn about, catching their breath.

Guillen announced, "Now ye dogs go below for pails and scrub brushes."

With that, the men were no longer amused, because they had two separate work details to accomplish, instead of a light duty day. Such was life at sea. They accepted their fate and did as they were told. Throughout the morning hours, the seamen swabbed a portion of the deck. They conferred with one another on how the cook should prepare the sea creatures for a suitable dinner. Some thought they should be fried; others wanted a stew with vegetables. They all agreed on one thing: There should be lots of grog to wash it all down!

The doctors and Emily witnessed the entire spectacle. Even Carlos got in on the act by using his boot to deter a squid that was trying to take cover inside the captain's cabin. Cicero was also standing by with a raised paw.

It was still early when the focus of the day's chores went back to mending sails. It was not easy for the men to climb the rope ladders, balance on the sail rope, untie the canvas, loosen the ropes, and take the canvas down. Davies even slipped while walking on the foot rope, but he was saved when his knee caught on one of the rungs. The wind was increasing, and clouds were forming.

By mid-afternoon, the clouds were increasing in size and merging into shapeless masses. The humidity in the air negated the effect of the ample breeze. The men were no longer humming and singing to pass the time; they hunkered down to complete their tasks before rain fell. They knew the placid water would soon become rough. The sailors always took their cues from the sky.

The clouds continued to expand, and an eerie gloom fell over the ship. Riggins was busy getting the sails secured. Sanchez ordered the main sail to be lowered and the jib sail to be unfurled. Sanchez's experience, coupled with the abilities of his crew, readied the ship for another tropical onslaught. Even Cicero had retreated to the galley, where Kelly kept an old straw-filled burlap sack in a corner for him to sleep on.

Soon, the clouds obliterated the sun. The lookout was anxious for Riggins to excuse him from his post. Once again, he had seen large, dark shapes that kind of looked like schools of fish around the boat.

He called out to the captain, "Sir, there's large fish about that be not whales nor sharks."

Several men rushed to the gunwale to hear the report. Indeed, they were in the company of some creature—or creatures. They must be fish since they did not breach the surface for air like whales or dolphins.

Emily and the doctors rushed to the deck. Riggins ordered the men to cast lines while others set out the plank. Svensson, an experienced fisherman, cast a net. It fell over part of the bait ball and took several crew members to haul in the catch. Wisely, Svensson retreated from the plank and ran to the stern.

It took three men to heave the net up and into the boat through the open cargo railing. The sardines, which averaged three to four inches in length, were aboard. Other men baited heavy lines, attempting to catch a larger prize. Kelly came up with a barrel that was quickly filled with sardines and capped. He rolled it down to the galley and looked for his whetting stone, so he could clean the fish. This would be a rare delicacy for them all, if he could prepare it with no further distractions. He did remember to toss a fish to Cicero.

Why does that cat always chew off the head first? Kelly wondered.

Gustafsson, McCarthy, and Svensson cast out heavy trolling lines baited with sardines. Svensson showed them how to hook three separate baitfish in succession, to increase the chances of a strike.

McCarthy was very excited to be fishing and said to the others, "I hopes to catch me a tuna, or maybe even a swordfish!"

They all chuckled, realizing that time was short. The men tied off their lines to different cleats and divided their attention between the bait and the hubbub aboard ship.

There was a pensive excitement aboard as the men watched the sea. Gregor made the comment, "I can't wait for supper to eat those squid." The others mumbled various opinions to the same effect. "Most times we 'ave salted pork, but tonight we has fresh squid."

"Hah!" Evans exclaimed, "Ye just desires to chew those disgusting round suckers." With that, he elbowed the nearest seaman in jest.

"Don't ye know they taste like marmalade?" Roberts guffawed.

"Yeah, at least we can see what's in the mystery stew this night," Campbell added.

The waves began to swell and white caps began to break. The ship rose and fell markedly as the captain steered her into the waves. The men were excited by the ship's increasing speed, despite the evident gale that was building all around them.

Thunder sounded and the clouds grew thicker and lower. A whooshing sound could be heard, as lightning emitted from the ominous ceiling. The men looked to their leadership for reassurance. Vargas was defiantly standing on the bow, facing the oncoming sea and raising either his left arm or right as he signaled to Sanchez to steer the way through the swells. Lynch remained port and Guillen starboard. They also shouted observations to Captain Sanchez.

Moppit wrapped a cloth around a cable and gripped it, sliding down to avoid the treacherous climb down from the crow's nest. Just before he made it to the deck, the ship made an awkward jerk aft. Moppit actually tightened his grasp on the line and swung out like a flag. He loosened his grasp and slid the remaining twenty feet to the deck.

All of the crew were wondering what could jerk a 170-foot, 1000-ton vessel such as theirs. Immediately, Svensson shouted, "Fish on!"

As the ship splashed through the ever increasing waves, the swells and troughs dramatically increased. Behind the ship, a behemoth was caught. It dove and breached, trying to spit the bait. One could see that the creature was caught on a predatory fish, like a tuna, which hooked itself to the sardines.

Now it became apparent to the lookout what he'd been seeing for the last day or so. It was an unknown leviathan of the deep. This creature had the jaws of a crocodile and the body of a fish.

The three fishermen looked at one another in disbelief, even wondering if what they witnessed had been an aberration. There were many tales of mermaids, sea serpents, and creatures called mosasaurs that sea lore had not defined. They had also seen crocodiles in the Caribbean and alligators in the colonies—but never an animal such as this.

The monster shook the line terribly side to side, even altering the heading of the ship. Other monsters surfaced around them, as if protecting their caught companion. In the tumult of the spectacle, several of the giants swirled and splashed about their comrade. One of them vaulted over the rest, snapped viciously at the rope and severed it, releasing the other from capture. Little did they know that the predator was furious and bent on retribution. The creatures swam alongside the ship and leapt out of the water, snapping their voracious jaws.

One leapt up onto the cargo loading area. It looked about with its pig-like eyes and searched for a victim. The men retreated and fell onto the cargo tarpaulin as the monster thrashed. Its gaping jaws revealed teeth like daggers, half a foot long.

Murphy and Martinez struck at the giant with pike poles. They were the bravest men on board, next to Guillen, having served on whaling vessels. The behemoth had front flippers like a fish. It used them, along with its fishlike tail, to back off the vessel.

Sanchez, although distracted by the turmoil, had his eye on the clouds above. All the while, he'd been observing the wind. It was assaulting the ocean in a circular pattern. The waves were unpredictable. Vargas ordered the fishermen to abate their activities. He was overcome with the appearance of the oceanic demons and could barely utter orders.

"Away with the poles," he ordered, as the reptile sank back into the depths. Murphy and Martinez stowed their poles and hastened to the side of their awaiting comrades.

Riggins shouted, "Stations!"

Upon delivering the orders, Riggins, and all the seamen, as well as Emily and the doctors, who had been cautiously hovering about their cabin door, felt and heard a blast of wind. Svensson understood that the oncoming gale precipitated the feeding of the baitfish and their predators as well.

Captain Sanchez was not as fearful as some of the crew. He had seen other acts of nature, such as a maelstrom that brought a wave so tall, many ships were overcome and sunk to the depths without warning.

The clouds took on an ominous greenish hue, and the wind began to swirl. The circular motion was slow at first, but it gained momentum steadily. Sanchez knew this phenomenon meant they were on the edge of a storm system.

The wind rushed past the ship, not from side to side, but in an upward direction. The behemoths continued to bite and slash around the sides of the ship, even attempting to break through the wooden hull. Kelly could hear their gnawing teeth as they cut into the wood like saws, leaving behind visible divots and scars.

Still, Sanchez maintained the helm, trying to not white-knuckle the wheel. If ever there were a captain who could handle crisis on multiple fronts, it was

Sanchez. He deftly shouted orders to his men and kept the ship under control. The crew looked bewildered. Fear and shock overcame them, despite the leadership of their strict and reliable captain. Some were watching and helping with the fishing, others cast backward glances toward the ship's rigging, and yet others wondered how they could fend for themselves.

Emily and her father sought shelter below deck, in the galley. Carlos chose to assist the captain. Carlos said to Sanchez, "I will be at your service through wind and wave."

Captain Sanchez admired the Indian's resolve. He looked forward at the developing tempest. He grasped the wheel, keeping the ship steadily pointed into the wind.

"Let the foresail loose," Vargas commanded. The rigging crew complied, letting the wind roll past the upright canvases. Waves broke onto the port side as Captain Sanchez attempted to navigate the increasingly violent sea. Leviathans continued to pursue and assault the vessel.

"They want to eat us," Gustafsson mumbled, as he looked to the second mate for reassurance.

Riggins wiped the rain from his eyes and replied, "The tempest has us in her grasp, whilst the sea condemns us."

Captain Sanchez was at the helm trying to keep the ship afloat. "Aye," he squawked, as they shouted updates to him.

"Hack the aft lines," he commanded, as the fishermen did battle with their quarry.

Even as the fishing went on at the stern, Sanchez was fixed on the storm pattern. His eyes forecast the development of the lowering clouds. He was not at all concerned with squid or sardine catches. He recognized the developing event they could only hope to survive.

All at once, there was calm. The air hovering over the sea rushed toward a central spot. The whitecaps that had been steadily increasing in frequency seemed to disappear. There was an eerie silence, as the weather seemed to give way to calmer times. The sky groaned and the behemoths plunged beneath the waves. They, too, could sense the atmospheric depression surrounding the ship.

The clouds rotated in a clockwise motion. Captain Sanchez looked up and blessed himself with the sign of the cross, scanning the ominous skies.

Vargas shook his fist at the ominous display and yelled, "Waterspout!" A funnel cloud descended to the water's surface. It traversed back and forth across the sea. The vortex randomly sucked up water and beast alike. The churning sound was like that of a hundred stampeding horses.

The tail of the funnel whipped from side to side. Water fell from above in torrents; even fish were falling from the clouds. Sanchez tried to steer the boat away from the encroaching funnel, but the rushing winds drew them closer and closer to it. The mizzen sail tore loose from its mast and flapped violently before flying away into the vortex. Just when it seemed that their doom was imminent, fate shone a reprieve upon them; the funnel suddenly dissipated back up into the storm clouds.

Eventually, the storm moved off in a northerly direction. There was still some daylight left, so Riggins began to assess the damages and have repairs made. Sanchez gave the helm back to Lynch and told him to stay on a course toward the setting sun. Then, he told Vargas to let the men off early that day.

Kelly served up the squid stew, but he also had fried some in grease and flour. After the crew had some time to change out of their wet clothes, they came into the mess hall, each in his own time, to eat and rest. Two Bits helped dole out the victuals with his one good arm.

Dr. Scroggins sought out the captain and asked him to have dinner in his own cabin with Dr. Carlos and Emily. Sanchez accepted, and said that he'd be along shortly. Chuckling at the irony, he said to himself, "Tis has been a day of days!"

After the meal, the waterspout and the mosasaurs dominated most of the crew's conversations, but the men were almost at a loss for words. There was some gaiety, as they had survived the waterspout with no loss of life. It may have helped that the captain had ordered that a keg of rum be opened.

Jim-lad helped Sanchez don a suit of fine fabric. The captain could enjoy the evening a bit more than most, as he knew they should reach land the next day.

As Sanchez stepped out of his makeshift cabin, Svensson noticed him and said, "Captain, will ye 'ave a drink with yer crew this eve?" Sanchez silently entered the room. The men were a bit surprised by his attire, but they were delighted by the presence of both their captain and the keg of rum.

Svensson shouted, "Three cheers for our captain, what brought us safely through the tempest!"

The crew stood and raised their glasses, shouting, "Hurrah, hurrah, hurrah!" Then, they broke into song: "For he's a jolly good fellow, whom nobody can deny!" Sanchez tossed back his drink. The crew expected a speech of some sort, but their captain was overcome with emotion and was unable to speak. He took a deep breath and respectfully waved his hand at them. Lowering his head, he turned and left as the men cheered. Their gruff captain had been humbled by their appreciation.

* * * * *

Emily greeted Sanchez at his cabin door. "Why, Captain," she said in a saucy tone, "you are so handsome."

Sanchez suddenly felt hot about his neck as he removed his hat and entered the cabin. Both Dr. Scroggins and Carlos stood and bowed slightly.

Sanchez responded, "Oh, enough with the formalities, 'ave a seat."

Kelly came in with Jim-lad to serve the food and drinks while Guillen guarded the rum keg. There was a lighthearted feeling in the room, as happy sounds of laughter and instruments penetrated the confines of the ship. The foursome began eating their meal. It was somewhat comical as they poked at the food. The stew was not so hard to handle because the squid was cut into thin slices, but the fried squid was still on the tentacles and a bit awkward to maneuver into the mouth.

Carlos broke the silence and said, "I believe this dinner should begin with a toast." Jim-lad, who was seated in a corner, jumped up and poured four glasses of rum. Dr. Scroggins noticed that there was a glass for each of them, yet he did not object.

Raising his glass, Carlos said, "Here's to a fine, brave captain, whose courage and wit has preserved us this day, again!"

"Aye," "Cheers," "Yes, indeed," and "To the captain," added to the toasts.

Emily's mouth burned, and she gagged a bit upon swallowing the liquor. The men did their best to ignore that. Em had earned the right to an adult drink with all she'd been through in the last several days. It might even help the rubbery squid go down a little easier. After recounting the waterspout episode, Carlos brought up the topic of the sea behemoths.

"My people tell tales of those demon fish," Carlos said.

They waited for Sanchez to respond to the statement.

"Aye, there be legends of terrible monsters of the deep in these here parts," he replied. "But none have seen them so clearly until today, methinks."

"I have seen drawings of whales and of alligators at the university—but never of a creature having the characteristics of both," Dr. Scroggins offered.

Carlos replied, "I have heard of ancient creatures in the jungle, so it makes sense there may still be others in the sea."

Sanchez added, "The waterspout may have had something to do with it, as I've never seen the fish behaving like that."

"Do you know what else I've never seen?" Emily asked.

"Do tell," Sanchez replied, eyeing her empty glass.

"Fish were raining from the sky!" Em said, laughing aloud and slapping the table. They all laughed at her observation and continued their meal after catching their breath.

They could hear the men in the mess hall singing *The Mermaid Song*.

> "When I was a lad in a fishing town
> my old man said to me:
> 'You can spend your life, your jolly life
> Sailing on the sea.
> You can search the world for pretty girls
> 'Til your eyes grow weak and dim,
> But don't go fishing for a mermaid, son,
> If you don't know how to swim.'
> Cause her hair was green as seaweed,
> Her skin was blue and pale,
> I loved that girl with all my heart,
> I only liked the upper part,
> I did not like the tail.
> So I signed aboard of a whaling ship
> And my very first day at sea
> There I spied in the waves,
> Reaching out for me,
> 'Come live with me in the sea,' said she,

77

'Down on the ocean floor,
And I'll show you many a wondrous thing
That you've never seen before.'
So over I jumped and she pulled me down,
Down to her seaweed bed,
A pillow made of tortoise shell
She placed beneath my head.
She fed me shrimp and caviar
Upon a silver dish.
From her head to her waist was just to my taste
But the rest of her was a fish.
Then one day, she swam away.
So I sang to the clams and the whales.
Oh, how I miss her sea-green hair
And the silvery shine of her scales.
Then her sister, she swam by
And set my heart awhirl.
From her head to her waist was an ugly fish
But the rest of her was a girl.
Cause her hair was green as seaweed.
Her skin was blue and pale.
I loved that girl with all my heart.
I did not like the upper part
And that's how I get my . . . "

While some of the men were singing, Dr. Scroggins asked Emily if she'd like to dance with him. They got up and did a traditional waltz, as they had done back home. When the dance was over, Em took the captain by his hand and danced a round with him. Carlos stood by, clapping his hands, along with Dr. Scroggins. Even Jim-lad danced a boyish jig.

Kelly called for Jim-lad, who hesitantly left the festivities to help clean the barrel of fish. They worked through the night until all the fish were cleaned. Guillen put the bung back in the rum keg, bringing groans from some crew members.

Dr. Scroggins and Carlos, sensing the evening was at an end, asked Sanchez how many more days it would be before they made landfall. Sanchez replied, "According to our position, we should arrive at the Mexican peninsula on the 'morrow."

The answer surprised the two doctors, as it seemed rather a short time to cover such a distance.

Sanchez added, as he left the cabin, "The winds have brought us forth quicker than usual." He then disappeared back to the crew's side of the ship.

Chapter 6

When day broke, a dense fog obliterated everything beyond a short distance. The lookout scampered up to the crow's nest and listened to the sequence of the waves. After a while, he detected a pattern of seven. The waves seemed to increase in size and volume.

He heard splashing sounds in the distance and strained his eyes, desperately trying to determine their origin. Just then, the ship passed through the fog bank, and a shoreline of cliffs and turquoise water lay before them.

The lookout, Rojas, shouted, "Land! Ahoy!"

The men mustered onto the deck, not even caring about being properly dressed.

Emily, her father, and her "adoptive uncle," Carlos, also came, and looked upon the cliffs and jungle surrounding them. Carlos recognized the shoreline and spoke to Captain Sanchez. "Steer the ship to the left toward the lighter waters," he said.

Sanchez skillfully avoided the coral reefs just a few feet below the surface. When he was about one hundred yards off shore, he ordered, "Drop anchor."

Guillen, also ordered, "Drop the anchor!"

The anchor splashed down. The waves continued to gently splash the shoreline.

Sanchez ordered them to ring the ship's bell. *Clang-clang, clang-clang, clang-clang!* Within minutes, the tall cliffs were covered by people. There was an uncomfortable silence as the sailors waited to see if they were welcome.

Dr. Carlos called out, "It is I, Carlos. I have returned." When they knew their esteemed friend was on the ship, the Mayan men cheered and began streaming down the cliffs like a waterfall.

The *Antelope* sent a skiff to shore. The small boat ran aground on the beach. The water was so clear. The sand was soft and felt good to the sole of the foot. Dr. Carlos jumped out first and was greeted by several of his native friends. The sunburned sailors relaxed as the locals welcomed and even embraced them with a childlike innocence. The Indians waded into the surf to escort the boat farther up the beach.

Some sailors on the ship were still a bit unconvinced that they had ported in a friendly spot. As the men came down from the cliff, Vasquez, who remained on the ship, watched intently through the spyglass. He tried to count the amassing men and suspected they might be warriors.

Vasquez asked the captain, "Shall we retreat to deeper waters?"

Sanchez answered, "Nigh! Tis our fate and fortune to trade here."

Then, the seamen looked around with anticipation. They hoped their captain would trade with the natives and obtain essential provisions. Captain Sanchez set out for the shore; he intended to make a treaty with the aboriginals, as he had done on previous occasions. The ship's hold contained rice, rum, and tobacco.

The quartermaster inquired in Spanish, "Where is your leader?"

The corresponding official replied, "He is awaiting your arrival."

Sanchez then ordered that a gift be brought forth from his dinghy. That gift, along with the presence of Dr. Carlos, almost assured the sailors security upon the foreign shores.

Captain Sanchez reminded Dr. Carlos, "Ye remembers that ye brought me ship here purposely."

Dr. Carlos replied, "Of course! Thanks to you, we have these goods. I can assure you that my comrades will bring your cargo, and more importantly, Dr. Scroggins, to the top of the cliff and beyond."

"Aye," Sanchez replied, "safe passage for the doctors, and a fair'n reasonable price for me cargo?"

"I tell you, our people will trade with your mates, as long as they are kind and honest." Satisfied, Dr. Carlos and Sanchez parted ways.

The soft white sand and clear water were welcoming. Emily looked up the escarpment and was amazed by the profuse foliage. There was a wide, well built staircase on the cliff that led to the mainland. Atop the cliff was a spectacular stone building that loomed above everything else like a castle.

Emily and Dr. Scroggins were soon shuttled to the shore. Dr. Scroggins held his precious microscope case under his arm. Upon their reaching the top of the cliffs, Dr. Carlos had his friends meet Señor Tejada, who was the town mayor, or an *alcalde*, as they called him. He was a powerful political figure.

"Dr. Carlos," Tejada began, "It is with great favor that we welcome you and your esteemed doctor friend to our town. We hope that you will soon determine what sickness plagues our young ones and makes our elders weak."

Dr. Carlos replied, "We will stay at my village and consider the problem there."

Tejada responded with a smirk, "I can arrange two rooms for the good doctor and his daughter."

"That will not be necessary," Carlos affirmed.

"It's all settled then," Tejada quipped as his attention swayed toward the commotion. Then, he took Scroggins's hand and shook it.

"At least, we are here now," Dr. Carlos said. "My people should welcome your arrival," he added in confidence.

Dr. Scroggins, infatuated by the friendly reception, gladly returned the official's greeting, stating, "I hope to find out what is devastating your village."

Emily had barely heard or cared about the words that were exchanged. She was watching in awe as the horde of Indians methodically hauled the cargo up the steep cliff.

The ship's crew kept the cargo coming to shore aboard the skiffs and dinghies. The blue lagoon where they were docked was conducive to the work. Escobar, Tejada's loyal secretary, kept an accurate count of goods that came off the ship. Sanchez was afforded an hospitable resting place, a shelter made of poles and palm leaves. He also was given a sweet chocolate drink that was usually reserved for dignitaries and festivals. The same was offered to Dr. Scroggins and Emily. The American Southerners were a bit overcome by their new surroundings.

* * * * *

The town of Tulum was abuzz with the activity. It was a tremendous effort to hoist and carry the cargo to the receiving area. Beasts of burden could not be used to haul the goods and cargo up the embankment.

Emily initially wandered about, but soon came back to the area where Captain Sanchez was reclining.

"Aye, lass," he chortled. "Do ye see how the natives convey the goods to their market? They're strong as oxen."

"It's a wonder the cargo is even here after your ship was nearly sunk by storms and the sea creatures," Em replied.

"Aye, lass, 'tis true," Sanchez sniggered, "but we've endured the onslaught of weather and sea and are ripe to be compensated."

With that admission, Emily popped out of her chair and looked at the captain for the first time as a businessman. "Well, I hope you do well after that perilous voyage."

Sanchez replied, "Aye, thankye! I'm counting on a favorable exchange and a wee bit of relaxation for me crew, as well."

The bundles and barrels continued to come up to the staging area. It was past noon when Guillen had the totals ciphered. Although Captain Sanchez had kept an eye on the offloading, he was content to wait for an accounting from his officers.

Several hours passed, and the heat of the day exceeded any temperature the crew had ever encountered. The work pace slowed considerably as the heat approached 100 degrees. Soon, all work stopped, as the intense sun bore down, and the people retreated to their homes to escape the heat. Dr. Carlos and his guests walked up the dirt road toward the part of town where Dr. Carlos had lived as a boy.

After a couple of hours, activity around town slowly began to increase as the local folks finished their siesta. Eventually, the market was full of people selling their wares and foodstuffs. As she ambled from booth to booth, Emily observed the primitive looking village. She saw two girls who appeared to be close to her age. They looked at each other, but the girls did not speak English, and like many of the villagers, they were suspicious of newcomers. There were a few people from the elite Criollo class who watched and wondered how they might benefit from their arrival.

From a distance, Dr. Scroggins observed Emily as she went into the market. She stayed a bit away from the booths, just slowly moving along as she observed the many fruits, clothes, and jewelry items that were displayed. The scene was somewhat surreal to Emily. The shopkeepers were used to passersby who needed a bit of encouragement to stop and have a second look at their products. Em deliberated in front of booths that had oranges and kiwi fruits, or pretty shell necklaces, but she did not pick up any items because she had no money.

Captain Sanchez was busy with Tejada, discussing their exchange of goods. Tejada had barrels of honey, salt, dried fish, and henequen, a kind of twine, as well as cocoa, maize, and some precious stones, all lined up in front of the plaza. The two men, along with their assistants, Guillen and Escobar, were writing proposed cargo lists and assigning values to the products. By the time afternoon siesta was over, they had come to terms. Escobar wrote a contract, penning two copies for them to sign. An exchange of coins would make up any difference in the value of the goods.

"We'll have the goods brought out to me ship, now that an agreements been made," he cooed, winking at Guillen. "When the final tally's been made, we'll have the gold and silver ye be owing me," Sanchez continued more seriously.

Tejada was keen to finalize their agreement because ships did not often come to his shore; he would undoubtedly earn quite a sum of money by selling these imported items to his fellow Mayan Yucatecas.

"Yes, yes, that is fine," Tejada replied. Tejada was daunted by the large sum of money he knew he'd have to pay, as Escobar had invested much of Tejada's money in the goods, leaving very little to operate his other businesses.

With that, Tejada summoned the local men to carry his products down to the awaiting seamen. The tide was gently rolling the boats. There was an easy feeling of calmness and peace, despite the arduous morning of labor that all had endured. It took many trips out to the ship to transport the goods from the alcalde's inventory.

Sanchez's crew was diligent in hauling the goods up the side of the deck by net and rope via the capstans and cargo mast. Guillen's mate, Vargas, supervised the loading of the items on the deck. Riggins supervised as the barrels and bundles were brought below deck and secured.

The ship swayed gently in the tide. Eels could be seen chasing small fish that had been hiding under the boat's keel and shadow. Kelly got excited by the possibility of catching more fresh food for the galley, but Maggot reminded him that they already had enough squid and fish from the prior night's dubious catch, and they needed to remain focused on the task at hand. Although Kelly complied, he baited a hook with a morsel of the aforementioned squid and put a line down the aft side of the boat.

As the sun began to wane and the heat of the day lessened, Tejada announced that there would be a fiesta that night. They would celebrate a true blessing, the bountiful supply of goods from the ship.

At twilight, many torches were lit in a line leading from the beach, up the stairs, onto the flat, open promenade, where the fiesta was to occur. This place was adjacent to the market square and adjacent to the shaded canopy where Captain Sanchez and Dr. Scroggins had been resting.

A formal invitation to the celebration was issued by the blowing of two conch shells. The young local men, who sounded the call, were overlooking the inlet. Sanchez's men scurried to freshen themselves and put in to shore for the festivities. Vargas had the remaining crew draw straws to determine who would have to stay behind. The two losers were to be relieved at the rising of the moon by two participants on shore. It was prudent to keep the ship guarded.

The seamen were excited to have the opportunity to put their feet upon land again and to partake in the celebration. Up the long set of stairs they went, with a spring in their steps. The smell of grilled fish and fruit was in the air, and they hastened to it. The blowing of the conch shells notified the natives that their guests were to receive all the benefits of the Yucatan during the fiesta.

Dr. Scroggins watched from his vantage point, overlooking the ship, as well as the town's settlement, and allowed his mind to relax. From the corner of his eye, he could see Em gliding past the merchants in the square. He all but forgot both his impending work and the perilous voyage. His former life seemed almost like a dream. He was truly happy in that moment, but his heart continually ached for his wife, Mary.

Dr. Carlos left once the festivities began, waving his departure to Dr. Scroggins. Out of sight, Carlos quickened his pace up a dark trail. The path to the village was only eight feet wide, and the jungle pressed in on both sides. About twenty or so minutes later, Dr. Carlos arrived at a village outside of Tulum. As he entered, Carlos put his clenched fist to his mouth and whistled a soft, low, cooing sound akin to a morning dove.

Hearing this sound, the local dogs quit barking. It was a tune known only to these villagers. Dr. Carlos strode up the winding path toward the top of a small hill and blew the tune again. He then sat upon a rocky outcrop and waited. Several minutes went by, but, eventually, torches appeared by the jungle huts that they called chozas in the distance. Carlos could feel his presence was noticed, although no person came to greet him. For an ordinary man, who had risked life and limb for such an unselfish purpose, this kind of reception would be an insult, but Carlos remained still, waiting as the fiesta proceeded below. A dog came to him, licked his hand, and lay beside him.

Dr. Carlos's mind wandered for a while, and when he raised his head, he was surrounded by Indians. They were standing in a semicircle in front of him, holding their torches and spears. Their faces were somber and their demeanor was placid. Carlos scanned the group from one side to the other, looking each man in the eyes, as the fire illuminated their faces and cast contorted shadows. Finally, one of the men stepped forward. Carlos smiled as he gazed upon the face of his childhood friend, Tomas, who said, "Nohoch Aantik (big help), you have returned to your people as the moon shines her face on them."

Carlos replied, grasping the man's forearms with his hands and replied, "Aak Baab (Turtle Swims), it has been too long since I have seen you." With that formality out of the way, the group closed in on Dr. Carlos and touched him about his back and chest in the usual greeting of a long missed friend or relative.

"You must be tired, my friend. Come with me to my choza to eat and rest," Tomas said warmly.

When Carlos arrived at Tomas's hut, Tomas announced, "Ana, Nohoch Aantik is back. Bring him some food and water." Ana complied and left the men to speak privately. After what seemed like hours, Tomas hung an extra hammock for Carlos, and they went to sleep. The dog curled up at the hut's entrance to rest as well.

* * * * *

Back near Charleston, a man on horseback travelled across Mary's front yard. He stopped by her front porch and jumped off his mount. He hesitated for a moment, and before he could knock, Maybell threw open the door.

"Are you lost?" Maybell asked, not recognizing the fellow.

"No, ma'am. This is the Scroggins residence, right?" he replied.

"Yes'm. What business do you have with them?"

"I have a message for Mrs. Scroggins, ma'am," he answered.

"Well, give it here! I'll take it to her directly."

The messenger came up the steps and handed Maybell an envelope.

"It sure's been a hard ride," he stammered, wiping his brow with a rag.

"You just rest yerself a bit whiles I get this note to the misses," she said.

The young man tied off his horse to the porch rail and sank into a rocking chair.

Maybell wasted no time. She hurriedly went out the back door waving the letter and calling her friend's name. "Miss Mary, oh, Miss Mary!"

Mary and Cletus were at the shed row discussing one of the horse's legs. They heard Maybell shouting and saw that she had something in her hand. Mary knew it must be important because Maybell made every effort to avoid the barn and the stables.

"What is it? What's wrong, Maybell?" Mary asked.

"A messenger jest delivered this here letter for you!" she said, almost out of breath.

Mary took the letter and opened the envelope with her horse pick, a small, curved iron tool normally used to dislodge manure, dirt, and straw from the underside of a horse's hoof.

She looked over to Cletus, and back at Maybell and read the letter aloud.

My Darling Mary,

I pray this note somehow finds you. Emily and I are on a ship headed for Mexico. A storm has prohibited our return home. I am headed to Dr. Carlos Caamal's village to aid in the treatment of a terrible sickness. He arrived in Charleston a few days ago, and as we were talking, we were called to treat some injured seamen at the port. Although I was unaware at the time, Emily followed me. The storm arose while we were on board, and the captain sailed to preserve the ship and ensure the safety of his crew. I know you must be frightened and worried, and I am sorry to have disappeared this way. I will send word as soon as I can. Emily is fine, and we both are thinking of you.

All my love,

Ezra

Mary looked up from the letter stunned. Cletus was the first to break the silence.

"I'm glad they are all right," he tentatively replied.

Maybell added, "The messenger is resting on your porch, Miss Mary."

Mary gathered her wits and said, "Cletus, rub some liniment on this gelding's leg and wrap it too. She turned for her house with Maybell right behind. They both went through the back door. Mary proceeded through the house to the front door while Maybell stopped for some cold coffee.

"Hello," Mary greeted the messenger who rose to his feet. "Please tell me…

how did you come by this letter?"

"Ma'am, I was told by the harbor master to get it to you as quick as I could, and I did."

"I was also told you'd be apayin me, as well," he added, forcing a smile.

Maybell came out with a coffee, and Mary invited him to relax in the rocker again.

"I see. Do you know anything else?" she inquired.

"Only that a ship bringing sugarcane and rum came into port this morning, and her captain gave this letter to be sent," he answered.

Seeing that the young man had no further information, Mary thanked him and said, "Go take your horse around to the barn for some water and rest before you go. Cletus will tend to your needs."

Mary took her letter and went for a walk through the apple orchard, thinking about Emily and Ezra, and what it all meant.

She read the letter again, and the pit in her stomach relented as she basked in the news that her family was safe. Just then, she realized that she might have an opportunity to send a letter back to Ezra. She ran back to the house calling for Cletus to detain the messenger. Mary quickly penned a reply.

> *Ezra, my love,*
>
> *I have received your letter and am so relieved you and Emily are all right. I love you both so very much. Please rest assured that everything is fine at home. I will diligently pray for your welfare and anticipate your homecoming. Tell Emily that I miss her dearly, and please, keep her safe.*
>
> *Yours,*
> *Mary*

Mary put her letter in an envelope and addressed it to Dr. Ezra Scroggins and Dr. Carlos Caamal, Mexico.

"Boy!" she called. The young man came over from the stable and replied, "Yes'm?"

"Please take this letter to the harbor master, and tell him to send it out on the next ship headed for Mexico. Here's a dollar for your trouble."

Glancing at the extraordinarily large tip, the messenger replied, "I will do so. Don't you worry, ma'am."

Maybell came out and watched with Mary as he disappeared beyond the front pasture.

"I hope they'll be all right," Maybell said.

"I have no choice but to be confident that things will work out for all of us," Mary replied.

* * * * *

When dawn came on the Yucatan peninsula, the sun's rays broke through some lingering clouds. Animals in the distance wailed and screeched. One sounded like a like witch, screaming from the jungle.

Emily and her father, as well as a couple of dozen Indians, had spent the night under the casa real, a long, open thatched hut. There were many hammocks hung hastily in the night. There were also many grass mats on the ground where people had slept soundly. The seamen, who had leave from their ship, had celebrated deep into the night, dancing, eating, and laughing with the locals. They were strewn about the square in a jumble, lying against the stone walls, in corners, and even under merchants' tables.

Emily awoke first. She was uncomfortable in her net hammock, so she wrestled herself to its edge and got her feet to the ground. She fished around for her shoes, and as she put her feet into them, her toes felt something. The bristly texture caused her to recoil. It was a good thing that she did, because a hairy black tarantula proceeded to quickly crawl out of her shoe.

The eight-legged intruder ran quickly at first, but after it was about a foot away, it slowed to a crawl. The creature seemed to be "feeling its way" as it crept into the nearby foliage. Climbing up into a nearby agave, it settled into the plant's leaves, practically disappearing. Em was now fully awake and ready to find a place to relieve herself.

As she walked toward the jungle, she looked over at her slumbering father and told herself that she would wake him when she returned, as she wanted some privacy. She had no idea about how the others would handle their personal business, but she took matters upon herself while they slept.

As she returned, the sun had progressed from dawn to daylight, and everyone was beginning to wake up. Between the warm rays and the increasing sounds of the awakening jungle, most of the campers were stirring with activity within half an hour. The ship's crew was the last to rise because of their indulgence at the fiesta and the fatigue brought on by hazardous duty.

Emily saw her father shaking off the morning's haze and standing along the edge of the seaward side of the clearing. "Dad, are you well rested?" she asked.

Dr. Scroggins replied, "I feel relaxed as a lad, notwithstanding everything we've been through."

Emily looked up into her father's face and replied, "Daddy, I feel so far from home, and wish that I never tried to get that box that you left on your table to you."

Dr. Scroggins cuddled his daughter's shoulders and said, "Em, I do not know what happens next, but I do know that as long as we stick together as a family, we will be okay."

Riggins, Sanchez's second mate, was first to open his eyes and clear his head. He watched as the father and daughter hugged and spoke softly. Being "a man of the sea," he was not sentimental about relationships, but his heart softened when he thought of the dilemma the good doctor and his daughter faced.

Soon, the locals, who worked for the alcalde, also arose and stoked the campfires from the night before. They knew their positions within the community, so the task was accomplished quietly and orderly.

The morning was quite relaxed. Whispers of smoke rose from the ashes of the previous evening like prayers. Instead of meat, the fire soon had a compilation of maize brewing. The crushed corn simmered down to a paste. Cocoa and eggs were added to it, along with milk to enhance its taste. The women were very pleasant, being sure to serve the guests first. After the visitors partook, the Indians added more hot peppers and had some themselves.

The people slowly set about their business with the intention of completing their trading before the sun's apex brought on the most stifling temperatures of the day. If delays ensued, they'd take a break and resume when the heat and humidity of the tropical forest were more bearable.

When Dr. Scroggins and Emily finished the morning meal, they walked about the place a bit in the pleasant morning air. Escobar caught up with them and told them that Tejada had invited them to his house for lunch. It was Tejada's intent to discover the purpose of Dr. Scroggins's presence in his town. After giving the two Americans directions, Escobar left them to their wanderings and focused his attention on the merchant ship and the trading of goods and cargo.

It was not very long before Em persuaded her father to return to the cliffs where the stone buildings were located. They walked the short distance to the ruins.

Dr. Scroggins commented, "These buildings are massive. I wonder how old they are."

It was apparent that the compound had not been used for a very long time, since most of the stone buildings had plants growing on their sides and tops, as well as trees thriving haphazardly about the open places. Even in its destitute state, the area was obviously designed and laid out well with straight walls and open plazas. There was even an arched entrance to the area made of massive gray stones, over ten feet thick. Upon closer examination, Emily noticed thick arches on three of the four walls enclosing the place.

Her dad called over to her, "Hey Em, come here and look at this."

Emily went over to a rectangular structure that was built on two raised stone platforms. They walked through the entrance. Inside the large room, a dank odor accompanied the gloomy darkness. The place gave Em an uncomfortable feeling, and a shiver went up her spine. Dr. Scroggins was looking at a stone carving that had strange looking pictures on it. The figures appeared to be men, but they looked like animals at the same time.

"What do you think it is?" Em asked her father.

"I really couldn't tell you, Em, but this place seems ancient like Egypt or at least as old as the castles of Europe."

Their voices echoed a bit, disturbing the silence. An animal of some sort stirred in the darkness. They could hear something that sounded like panting and then, hissing. Emily ran for the door with her father close behind. When they exited the place, there were half a dozen men standing at the base of the terrace, patiently waiting. One of them spoke up in a language that the Scroggins did not understand, but his hand gestures clearly indicated that exploration of those buildings was taboo.

The group of men escorted them out of the compound. As Em was about to pass through the arch, she looked back and saw an older man garbed in feathers and bones disappear into the dark interior.

They made their way through the aftermath of the fiesta and to Tejada's residence. The hacienda was grand. The grounds were immense and well manicured with all kinds of plants and trees. Gardeners were pruning, raking, pushing small carts, and watering. There was a post and beam fence that was as long as the eye could see. There were wagons pulled by mules entering and leaving the premises, apparently transporting the last of the ship's cargo. Escobar was overseeing the procedure, counting and writing on his tablet.

When Escobar saw Tejada's guests arriving, he called for a house servant to show the Scroggins into the extravagant abode. It had a wide circular driveway with a stone fountain in the center. The servant showed them to a courtyard with ample shading from an arbor and beautifully designed wooden benches.

"Medico Scroggins," the servant began, "please rest here for a moment while I return with some refreshments and notify Alcalde Tejada of your arrival."

Em and Dr. Scroggins complied, and soon, another servant came out with a portable table, followed by a third servant, who placed a tray of drinks and a pitcher on the table. Emily felt at ease. The place reminded her of her own home back in Carolina. She sat back, enjoying the view, and then, jumped up with excitement.

"Look, Dad," she exclaimed, "those birds are gorgeous!' Emily had noticed some large colorful parrots called macaws on perches. She could see the birds eating fruit from clay dishes. One was even splashing its head in a bowl of water. It seemed that the birds knew that Em was observing them. One of the macaws, which was colored bright yellow on its chest and neck and metallic blue on its tail, back, and head, began to stretch out its wings and bob its head up and down at her. Emily clasped her hands with delight, even jumping up and down with excitement. The bird seemed to feed off her attention and energy. It flapped its wings, making a whooshing sound and began to squawk loudly. The sound was unexpected. It was as loud as ten crows or five roosters, and it hurt her ears a bit.

Em's eyes opened wide, and she turned to her father and asked, "What is it doing?"

Dr. Scroggins began to speak but was interrupted by the sound of Tejada's voice.

"This, my dear, is Paco, one of my wife's indulgences," Tejado said, as he bowed a bit. He then grasped Dr. Scroggins's hand. "Welcome, welcome to my hacienda, my home," he cooed with a strong Spanish accent.

Dr. Scroggins stood and replied, "We are honored by your invitation." He glanced at Emily who gave Tejada an obligatory courtesy.

"A fine young lady," Tejada said, nodding toward Emily. "Come, let us discuss your reasons for being here, so far away from the Americas." He turned and motioned them back to the house and into a magnificent foyer.

"Oh, my!" Emily breathed aloud, as they entered the grand room. It had a smooth stone floor, tiled in an ornate mosaic pattern. The walls were made of tile in the entranceway, but throughout the other areas, stained wooden panels and stucco masonry walls constituted the major building materials. They were shown to a nearby side room which doubled as Tejada's receiving room. Three plush velvet chairs had been placed opposite a massive wooden desk that seemed to gleam from a servant's recent polishing. The furniture looked European in design, probably Spanish, as it was very ornamental.

"Medico Scroggins, it is my understanding that you are a curador, a physician. Why is it that you have come here to such a distant place?" Tejada inquired.

Dr. Scroggins simply replied, "Our ship was blown here by a mighty storm. It was not my intention to arrive here without notice or letter."

Tejada opened a small wooden box, withdrew a cigar, and offered the box to Dr. Scroggins. The good doctor declined.

"Perhaps there is more to your story, as you arrived along with Medico Carlos Caamal, an educated local boy," Tejada said, as he sat back in his comfortable chair, lighting his cigar.

"I am aware that Caamal was educated in America. Is it not odd, or rather, a coincidence that you arrive here together," Tejada continued.

Emily sensed mounting tension that went beyond a "language barrier."

Dr. Scroggins was quite the diplomat and a Southern gentleman. He was about to respond to Tejada when commotion erupted in the foyer. A servant vehemently insisted that a visitor leave the premises. The ruckus continued, and soon, Dr. Carlos Caamal appeared in the doorway of Tejada's office.

Carlos rounded the corner and entered the room, waving off the servant. Tejada was surprised by the intrusion, but he nodded to his servant to allow

Carlos to come into the room. Dr. Scroggins and Emily were also surprised by the peaceful doctor's behavior. His face revealed his disdain for the official.

"Ah, Señor Carlos," Tejada began.

"Medico Carlos, you mean," Carlos rebutted.

"Si, yes, of course. What brings you here to my humble abode?" Tejada asked, as if he did not know.

Carlos was respectful of Emily's presence. He held his tongue, knowing that Tejada, a career politician, could shroud his intentions with flowery words. An outburst at that time would have been inappropriate and ineffective.

Dr. Carlos replied, "I've invited my colleague to help solve a mystery. The doctor and his daughter will stay in my village where we hope to bring relief to the sufferings of our people."

With that, Tejada sighed loudly and said, "Do you really believe that the gods will supply a cure for those people's wickedness?"

Carlos replied, "I did not travel to America to waylay this esteemed curador and friend for the sake of appearances."

Sensing that the rift between himself and Dr. Carlos was prompting Dr. Scroggins to question him, Tejada said, "Manuel!" With that, the servant dutifully and instantly appeared.

"Please show Señorita Emily to her room."

As Manuel approached Emily, she looked quizzically to her father for permission. Dr. Scroggins, although uneasy, allowed her to leave; he sensed the ensuing conversation would not be suitable for a young lady.

Emily left the office, accompanied Manuel, and was shown a large opulent room. The windows went from floor to ceiling on one end, offering a view of the garden, and a pretty pink table with a silver mirror sat next to the four poster bed. There was even a privy through an adjacent doorway.

Em was a bit confused by the body language of her father and Dr. Carlos. They seemed to speak in agreeable tones, but their demeanor told her something was amiss. She felt as if she had suddenly been placed in jeopardy.

Emily went to the window and threw back the silk curtains. She saw a yard, much fuller with foliage and grandeur than the one that was visible from her own bedroom window. Emily was practically smitten with the obvious advantages this hacienda would afford.

* * * * *

After Emily departed, Tejada said, "Let us relax a moment and enjoy the favorable weather." Then, he called for some drinks to be delivered to his office.

Dr. Carlos paced back and forth, while Dr. Scroggins sat in a chair watching the two men. Tejada leaned back in his oversized chair and puffed on his cigar, observing Dr. Carlos's obvious aggravation.

The servant returned, as if on cue, and set another pitcher and glasses on a side table. He poured a beverage for all three and delivered the drinks to them one by one. The process did not take much time, but the men seemed to be holding their breath while they were waiting to speak openly.

"Alcalde Tejada," Dr. Carlos began in a frustrated tone. "Why is it that you do not understand that there is a serious ailment oppressing the local people?"

Tejada replied, "There is always some ailment or reason that these people do not work to our expected levels."

"Always?" Dr. Carlos replied. "It is if as you consider these people to be cattle. Do you not care about them?"

"Of course I care about them; after all, I am responsible for their welfare and product. Sick people do not meet quotas. I think that they are lazy and are looking for ways to avoid being productive."

"Alcalde, sir, I have been educated in the ways of modern learning. It is my suspicion that our people are not just finding ways to skip work. You are aware that the children and elders are dying. That is why I left my home to bring back the techniques used to unveil why a sickness has fallen upon our friends and companions."

Tejada looked back and forth at the two doctors. He puffed his cigar and tried to take in this other perspective.

Tejada placed his cigar in an ashtray, blew out a plume of smoke, and said, "I think that you are trying to undermine all that we have built here, so that you are elevated to the status of our shaman."

Dr. Carlos angrily replied, "You think that I spent my life preparing for this, so that I could be a politico, a politician like you?"

Satisfied with himself, Tejada replied, "Yes. That is what I think."

Dr. Carlos turned to Dr. Scroggins and said, "We must leave this place immediately if we are to have any chance of helping the people."

Scroggins followed his friend, and the two went down the luxuriant hallway looking for Emily. Her door was open, so they spotted the room right away.

"Emily, we must leave this place," Dr. Carlos said.

"But why?" Em opposed.

"It is not our purpose to remain here, but to render service to help the ailing villagers," Dr. Scroggins explained.

Emily was practically numb from the recent developments. She wanted to stay and relax in this place, which seemed fitting to her upbringing, but when her father told her to leave with him, she obeyed with no further questions.

Emily cast a parting glance at the beautiful bedroom view, and they left the hacienda, amid the objections of Alcalde Tejada and his servants.

Chapter 7

Captain Sanchez was content with the exchange of goods and cargo, but he was still concerned with his hasty departure from the Carolina dock. He knew that his vessel could be interpreted as a rogue. He would be thought of as a pirate or scoundrel, unless he could return to the port, flying a flag of truce and anchor in the harbor.

Tejada's men paddled back from the ship, having brought out the last of the cocoa and other cargo. The jewels that Sanchez held were an addendum to the cargo list.

The exchange of gold and silver coins completed, Sanchez gave the order to raise anchor, despite the objections of his crew. It seemed that the crew of the *Antelope* wanted more time in this enchanted tropical land.

Instead, the captain declared, "We be seafarers anointed to the perils of the ocean and the gods therein."

Sanchez took the bag of coins to his cabin. He, along with Vargas and Guillen, counted the sum, weighing it upon the scales prior to setting out to sea.

* * * * *

Dr. Carlos, Dr. Scroggins, and Em left the hacienda in a hurry. Tejada sent a team of mules and a wagon after them, more to save face, than for their convenience, but Carlos declined the ride much to the chagrin of Tejada and Emily. It took an hour for the trio to reach the outlying area. The trip was hot and tiring. Dr. Scroggins and Emily passed by many new sights, one of which was some howling monkeys. The primates were very vocal and kind of scary. As the sun waned behind the foliage, they made a sound that was akin to a troubled forest spirit.

It was late afternoon when they arrived at the village. The sounds of the forest leaves and humming insects created a sense of isolation. Carlos seemed to take on a new and different persona. He spoke less, and Emily saw him paying attention to the sounds emanating from the forest. Dr. Scroggins realized that he was totally out of his element, and relied on Carlos's experience and guidance in the jungle.

They came upon the settlement toward the end of siesta. As they crossed the unofficial threshold, where two short stacks of stones sat on either side of the trail, Carlos turned and put his finger to his lips, signaling that they should be quiet. They walked up the dirt path, which was only a few feet wide, curving past trees and bushes of sawgrass and maguey, until they came to an area that was like a clearing. There, Em saw several huts in a haphazard formation constructed of poles, with thick thatch or palms for a roof. Em suddenly felt vulnerable and alone as she passed through this primitive looking village. As they crossed the place, a sound came forth like a dove's cry. Dr. Carlos halted. They were fully exposed to the inhabitants, some of whom peered out at them from the safety and obscurity of their chozas.

A central fire pit was smoldering. The threesome stopped there and waited. Even the dogs were silent. Only the fowl weren't still. Soon, a call came from the far end of the settlement. It was the call of the dove. Carlos cupped his hands together and blew the dove call again. People began to appear from their huts. They did not come forth directly but lingered cautiously before exposing themselves to the open sky and visitors.

The fire cast more smoke than flame. The smoke burned Em's eyes, as it rotated about in lazy swirls. Before long, there were over fifty people standing or coming forth to the circle. None of them showed any enthusiasm or happiness. Their faces were drawn and sullen. This was a stark difference from Em's experience of the previous evening. Medico Carlos seemed to be the focus of the villagers' attention.

"People of the forest," he began in his native tongue, "I return to you with a curador, a healer. In time, we hope to subdue the sickness that takes our babies and elderly. The plague that brings our village grief and torment can be abated with your help."

"You have brought a gringo among us," a villager objected.

"This is true. I have brought a foreigner here among us to make medicine," Dr. Carlos said.

"Nohoch Aantik," another villager, spoke. "Why do you ask us to accept this medico when we already have a curador?"

Carlos answered, "I have faith that this foreigner can help us. Please accept his help and do as he asks."

With that, the people dispersed and left the trio alone in the clearing. The people had a right to question the wisdom of Carlos's suggestion. For years, whenever outsiders arrived, sickness or military occupation ensued. The indigenous people would invariably comply with the outsiders' promises, and they would live to regret their decision.

Dr. Scroggins could feel their anxiety. He knew the Indians were suspicious, but he also felt that there was more to the situation than he knew. Dr. Carlos showed took him to the choza that he was to occupy. It was on the outskirts of the village. The yard around it was a bit grown up with weeds but the structure was solid.

He said, "This place is your new home. I am confident that my people will accept you in due time, just as your people accepted me at the college." Although Dr. Scroggins was a man of science, he was to be subjected to the traditions of the local shaman.

The relative coolness of the afternoon was a welcome relief, a sign that the shade of the evening would surely come. Carlos illuminated the area with a torch, and scads of tiny creatures scurried away. He set the torch down in a hollowed stone to light the interior and invited his guests to follow him inside. Dr. Scroggins stopped and looked back at Em. "Looks like we'll be here tonight," he said with a forced smile. Emily took hold of his arm and ventured into the dark place behind her father.

Dr. Carlos stayed for a short while, telling Dr. Scroggins his plan for the next morning. As he left, he said, "The day has been long. You are safe here in my village and in this place. Relax, sleep well, and tomorrow, I will have clothes sent for you and Emily."

Ambient sounds from the rain forest soothed them into a deep sleep. Emily and Ezra were finally relaxed—not on the open sea, not amid a fiesta—but inside four walls of their own.

Chapter 8

An hour after sunrise, an old woman whom Carlos had hired, appeared outside the hut in the cooking area. She entered the hut, scooped some smoldering coals onto a flat piece of bark, and took them outside to light another fire. She had a few sticks of wood that she placed methodically over the coals, and soon, a new fire was burning.

The old woman then began the process of making breakfast. She did not speak or disturb the hut's inhabitants in any way. When the corn drink was ready, she brought it inside and set the two cups upon a flat stone. Then, she rustled Em and her father by shaking their hammocks and speaking to them in her native tongue. They did not understand her words, but they understood her request to get up and partake of the meal.

The daylight was easy on their eyes, since the dense foliage inhibited most of the direct sun beams. Dr. Scroggins was first to get his cup, which was a squat ceramic flask. The concoction tasted good. It had a chocolate flavor and a hint of coffee as well. The liquid had an effect on his body that seemed to give him energy. Emily was a bit slower to get out of her hammock. She preferred to watch her father and the old woman. Eventually, she struggled her way free of the hammock's netting and picked up her cup of maize.

Emily had slept well, and the smell of the campfire beckoned her to start the morning. She likened the drink to the coffee Maybell made; it was hard to believe it was made from corn. Thinking of Maybell, Em wished she could talk with the old woman, but it was apparent she was there to work and would likely avoid chitchat even if there were no language barrier.

Em realized that breakfast with her father was among the many new things she was experiencing. Back home, Dr. Scroggins always left before she got out of bed. As she drank the maize-like coffee, she looked over at her father and smiled at him.

Soon, the old woman served their meal. Dr. Scroggins and Emily thanked her and made several gestures to show their appreciation for the food, but the woman barely looked at them.

After breakfast, Em and her dad ventured into the courtyard. The good doctor was dutifully thinking of his patients. After all, was he not invited for this purpose? His confidence was unshaken despite the questionable reception that they had received.

Emily was fascinated by the jungle around her. She focused all the sounds coming from it. This place was very different from her pastures, and the animals making those sounds definitely were not Carolina wrens.

Their mindsets that morning would determine the next phase of their lives.

* * * * *

After breakfast, Dr. Scroggins headed into town while Em stayed at the choza. He felt it was important for the people to understand that his presence there was wholly for the benefit of the village. He had to find a way to relate to the people. Typically, the most difficult part of his work was getting the patient and his family to relax, so he could get the information he needed and provide proper care. In this place, he would be relegated to observing his patients' conditions and symptoms. He was concerned that the language barrier and lack of medicines could pose an uphill battle.

Dr. Scroggins decided to walk to the market to observe the local population, but he was an unwelcome visitor. Although he was polite, he also was shunned when he went to their huts. Things improved when he introduced himself as Medico Ezra, and Dr. Carlos went along with him to translate. In an effort to obtain a complete picture, he would ask questions that didn't directly relate to their health. Where did they work? Were they hunters, farmers, or fisherman? He learned that many people worked with henequen plants, as the fibers from them are used to make ropes. He also asked about the places they frequented and inquired about others who might be experiencing similar health problems. Dr. Scroggins proceeded methodically through the village, performing routine exams and gathering information. He was certain of two things: Many of the villagers had succumbed to an illness, and the ones who remained were terrified that the epidemic would devastate their families as well.

All this time, the local shaman kept a watchful eye on this outsider from a distance. The shaman was the people's traditional healer, and from his view,

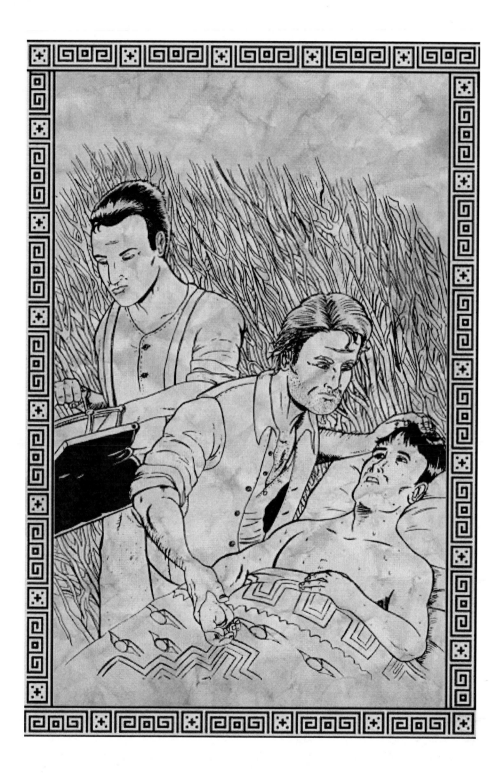

the stranger had no place in his homeland.

Emily spent a considerable amount of time that day in the courtyard, chasing small lizards with a stick, watching the chickens move about, and wondering what else she could do to pass the time. Inevitably, her mind kept going back to her predicament, but she was distracted for a while by all the bugs and scurrying things that were always scuttling away from her to hide or conceal themselves.

She decided to test the methods the insects used to get away from her. Emily would lie-in-wait for them, remaining motionless like a statue at times. When she moved her arms or legs to gain a forward position on some unwitting prey, it would invariably scurry off at an accelerated speed, escaping an anticipated capture. Sometimes the creature would quickly escape, within mere seconds, but some would stay in place, adopting a "wait and see" strategy until she was close enough to touch them. Then, they would take off with lightning speed. Her observances dramatically adjusted her preconceived ideas about wild things.

In Carolina, she would consider these insect games silly, but in this remote place, away from civilization, her perspective was different. She even caught a small lizard with her bare hands and raised it to eye level for a closer look before releasing it at the edge of the jungle where she had found it.

Emily realized that her presence was generally unwanted. The insects seemed to like her more than the girls who were her age. At first, she assumed their hesitancy was due to the fact that she could not speak their language. Later, she assumed the local people simply kept to themselves and accepted her role as an alien.

Em had decided to rethink her way of doing things. Back home, during her studies, she had read a saying, "When in Rome, do as the Romans do." She quickly decided to embrace everything new that surrounded her. She considered all the things she might learn and experience and gave no thought to the ways her new environment—and the people in it—might harm her.

Dr. Scroggins was exhausted when returned. He trudged into their encampment like a runner on his last leg of a marathon. The heat and humidity had depleted him, and the incline stripped away any vestige of strength the good doctor retained. His hands hung limply by his sides. The dogs ran up to him and sniffed his hands and allowed him to continue to the village. They had determined that this person was not an adversary to the village and, from that point on, they didn't bother to bark when he returned.

Emily ran out of their hut when she spotted her father. She did her best to keep him from stumbling sideways. He objected to her attempts to prop him up, but she escorted him into the hut and helped him to a hammock.

Emily immediately got the water gourd and held it to her father's lips. Gasping and panting, he struggled to get it down. Emily stayed by his side wiping his forehead with a wet cloth and fanning him with an elephant ear leaf she had plucked in the courtyard.

The old woman had returned and was making some kind of supper. As the sun waned, she brought tamales into the hut and said some words that Emily did not understand. It was presumed that she was retiring for the night, having completed her obligations to Ezra's family. Emily lit a small fire inside the hut and settled down to make sure her father ate and drank before she relaxed and ate the food herself.

They both slept soundly that night. The village had no fiesta. There was no storm, and there was no visitor or animal to interrupt their slumber.

The following morning, the old woman arrived and executed her duties. She began, as always, to gather a few coals from the previous night's fire to bolster the next day's flame. Having done this, she went outside to her cooking area and began the process of turning raw ingredients into a palatable meal. She had done this countless times—perhaps even 10,000 times during her lifetime. She ground, chopped, boiled, and wrapped, to accomplish the task at hand.

Within a half hour, the old woman had made three plates. She presented sliced plantains, frijoles, and a bean and tomato soup. Dr. Scroggins awoke and was hungry for the sweet-smelling meal. The three of them sat outside on two wooden benches made of a tree log. Ezra spoke to the old woman,

"What is your name?" he asked.

The woman ignored him. It was not her duty to interact with the foreigners but to feed them and supply them with their daily needs. She just sat there, on the adjacent log, eating her breakfast. After a few minutes had passed, Dr. Scroggins spoke some words that Emily did not understand. The equivalent of his words could be translated into Spanish as "What is your name?" The old woman replied, "Mi nombre es Juana."

"So, Juana, thank you for the food." Dr. Scroggins said.

She raised her head and met his eyes for the first time since they had met and smiled just a little bit.

With that, Dr. Scroggins laughed aloud. When he finished his frijoles, he laughed again, and looking over toward Juana he said, "You are one. You are number one with me, and I will speak your name as I hear it. So you are One-a, Juana."

After breakfast, Dr. Scroggins left the hut to make visits. Later in the day, he planned to meet Dr. Carlos and find a place to set up an office in town. He found that being friendly, relaxed, and available was the best medicine that he could offer the people at the time.

The outskirts of town, where most of the village's inhabitants lived, was unstructured and spread out over a vast expanse. It could take a few hours to get from one side to the other or even from the farthermost hut to the market area.

Dr. Carlos assisted him for a few days. The doctors examined many locals. The sick people usually had a high fever combined with sweating, loss of appetite, weakness, and vomiting. They commonly had little hope of recovering. It became apparent that Tejada was not going to help. In fact, he could even become a hindrance.

Chapter 9

Dr. Carlos introduced Dr. Ezra to a proprietor named Perez who managed a maize collection facility. Perez was the kind of man who took orders and performed his job to the best of his ability. He was also intelligent and discerning enough to understand the nuances of "bad business." When Dr. Carlos approached him seeking a clean, secure office, Perez was quick to offer a storeroom beside one of his warehouses, despite any repercussions that he might draw upon himself.

The space was not entirely displeasing. With some effort, they could even get it cleaned up and make it a satisfactory home base. There were also wooden doors with a secure lock. The best part of the agreement was that the two rooms were cheap. Dr. Carlos paid rent for the first two months.

Carlos and Ezra spent the day emptying and organizing the two rooms. Luckily, Perez had one of his boys, Rocio, assist them with moving overstock and other unwanted items.

The dust was thick. The doctors had to step out for fresh air every time they moved a larger box or crate that kicked up a cloud of debris. Fortunately, there were two windows that allowed for cross circulation of air to help waft the dust out of the rooms.

Rocio's assistance was greatly appreciated. He had a way about him and knew how to get seemingly nasty chores done with the least amount of fuss. He also had an uncanny ability to determine the most efficient way to remove old sacks, some of which were dry-rotted. After they had the two rooms completely devoid of objects, Rocio raked and swept them with a surprising quickness. He was also wise enough to wrap his face in cloth to keep the acrid dust from taking his breath.

The men left to let the place to air out for an hour or so. After lunch, they spread a thin layer of powdered lime over the dirt floor. Then, starting in the rear, they dunked a thick straw broom into a vessel of water and swirled it about on the dirt floor, steadily backing up, as they created a thin muddy layer of the mixture. When Ezra came to the door, he told Rocio to place several crates in front of it to keep out anyone who might be curious.

The next morning, Dr. Carlos left to travel to a more prominent city. He intended to solicit some officials and convey the gravity of the situation in his hometown. Before he left, Carlos came by to say goodbye to Ezra and Emily. Juana was preparing the morning meal when he arrived. Carlos greeted her, and she responded in their native tongue.

"Ezra," Dr. Carlos began, "I am going to Valladolid, which is a two-week trek, to solicit the proper people there for assistance."

Ezra, replied, "I will carry on the task at hand. Please send word if you are detained for some unforeseeable reason."

Emily came out of the hut. She had overheard Dr. Carlos's plans and was concerned that her father's only real friend there was leaving them alone in a foreign country. Em asked him when he would return, and he said that he would be back as soon as he could, but it could be as long as "the time when the moon grows dark and then full again in the night sky."

They sat outside on the benches and ate their last meal together. When they had finished eating, Dr. Carlos went over to Emily and embraced her. Looking at her face he said, "Emily, you are a strong young lady, capable of great things. Take care of your father and support his work. It is critical that he succeeds here."

The two doctors then departed—Dr. Carlos with his travel bag, and Dr. Scroggins with his microscope. The two walked back toward the village, discussing their approach to finding a solution to the sickness. Dr. Scroggins recalled fond memories of their walking to the college and talking over the world's problems as younger men.

Soon, the two doctors came to a fork in the road. Dr. Carlos's childhood friend, Tomas, was waiting for him with a donkey that had supplies slung over its back. The friends shook hands, and they parted ways.

Ezra stopped by several families' huts on his way into town. The people were beginning to accept him, because his sincerity was plainly apparent. Some villagers did not like having a foreign doctor attempting to learn information that was previously reserved for the shaman. There was an inherent distrust of any outsider, and the manner in which this man, Medico Ezra, conducted his exams was new to the people. At best, most of them tried hard to tolerate his odd ways of listening to their heartbeats, asking them to take deep breaths and studying their bodies.

Ezra always made notes when he visited the people. He soon had a dictionary of words that he heard over and over again written in his book. He would study these words and attempt to speak them during his visits. The locals usually sneered or laughed aloud when he did so.

Often the children, the village's most precious asset, would stand in front of him and mouth the syllables or dialect slowly. They enjoyed listening to him attempt to speak their language. After all, it is not very often that a child can tell an adult how to act. The few children that were present also enjoyed watching Dr. Ezra draw in his book. Sometimes, he drew letters, and other times, he drew pictures of people or body parts. He often drew strange pictures that were a kind of map, as he struggled to understand the terrain and region.

Regardless, the local people found it increasingly difficult to reject this man, especially after their fellow tribesman, Dr. Carlos, had endorsed him. Another reason they found him to be odd was that he did these exams not expecting payment. It is customary to pay a tribute or to compensate a healer. This man neither followed any of the traditional customs nor seemed interested in their traditional religious observances.

As he went along the way, Dr. Ezra passed several milpas. These were family plots of land that grew a combination of maize, squash, peppers, beans, and tomatoes. Families would plant all of the seeds concurrently. Then, the seeds would sprout and produce fruit in their respective times according to nature.

Before long, Dr. Ezra found his way into town. It was late morning. He walked across the market square toward Perez's establishment. Much of the surrounding area's geography was situated on an incline or depression, but the market area was centrally located around a relatively flat expanse. The market's exterior was surrounded by the permanent structures that contained shops.

Ezra crossed the myriad of businesses near his new office. He traversed the semicircle of the clearing, and went past the establishment of the beekeeper. This building was nicer than most on the outskirts of the square. As he went past, the proprietor stood on the front porch in his white coat, threw a hand up, and waved a welcoming greeting. Dr. Ezra appreciated the gesture and returned the wave, but he kept going until reaching his office. Finally, the rock and stucco walls were free of junk. The main room had a welcoming glow about it. He also noticed the odor of the place. Years of coffee and cocoa bean storage had impregnated the walls, and the smell was pleasant once the dust and mildew were removed.

The lime and clay slurry had set during the night. As he looked in, Dr. Ezra saw large cat-like footprints in the texture. He could plainly see that the cat entered through a back window and left through the front door. The ground was hard, not sticky. He walked through the rooms with a new attitude. Natural sunlight illuminated the place. Dr. Ezra was busy studying the rooms when Rocio suddenly appeared. He said, "Medico Ezra, what work will we do today?"

Dr. Scroggins replied, "Today's task is to situate this place with proper furniture and, hopefully, some medical supplies." Rocio considered his new boss's request and set forth to find what he could.

When Rocio returned a short while later, he found Dr. Ezra sitting on some of the crates that were piled to the side of the entrance. Rocio reported that he had acquired some office type furniture, and that it would be delivered.

A few of the local merchants were concerned about Dr. Scroggins settling near the market area. Since his basement area had never been a point of concern, Perez simply ignored the inquiries about the area being occupied by the new medico.

Having an office to visit was a new idea to the indigenous people. Asking them to come to one collective place was virtually unheard of.

Emily was left to herself again while her father investigated the jungle fever. A normal morning began with Juana's arrival and breakfast. After that, there were a few chores comprised of tidying up, and then, there were a few hours when most of the adults labored at the factories or for their families. Siesta followed, and then the evening meal was usually started.

Em learned the sequence and nature of things. Her father would leave their hut shortly after breakfast and be gone for most of the day until evening. Since Emily felt that she was mostly on her own, she thought of ways to amuse herself.

Emily would walk the path to the market. She'd keep her head high and eyes on the lookout for opportunities to participate in local activities. Even though she paid much attention to this, her advances were often ignored when she attempted to join in. The local girls were still not receptive to her.

Emily looked much different from them with her blonde hair and light colored skin, and when she talked, even the people who knew some English had difficulty understanding her.

It was not long before Emily decided to seek entertainment or acceptance elsewhere. She resigned herself to the fate that the local people really had no use for her. This was a hard lesson, especially since her father was to be their curador.

One morning, while Emily was helping Juana wash the dishes, a butterfly flittered through their yard. She noticed how pretty it was. It was mostly orange with black lines. The butterfly glided about, circling around to their hut. Emily fixed her attention upon this distraction and followed as the butterfly flew away. Deeper into the jungle it went, always seeming to be just beyond reach. Sometimes, it would alight on a flower, and just as Emily approached it, it would flit off, denying her a closer look.

Emily lost track of time as she pursued the creature farther and farther into the jungle. She did not notice that the path she was on soon gave way to a narrow trail. Still, Emily followed the pretty creature along as it made its way toward the flowers.

The butterfly finally landed on a beautiful blossom. This time, she kept her distance so she wouldn't disturb the creature. Emily sat down and watched the butterfly as it nuzzled its proboscis into the aromatic petals, drinking in its nectar. She was enchanted. It had been a while since she had followed a butterfly back home. She observed the creature in detail, even noticing how it used its mouth parts like an uncoiled spring to seek the flower's nutrients.

When the butterfly flew away, Emily realized that she was far from the hut. As a matter of fact, she did not know where she was. The jungle's canopy obscured much of the ambient light. Em felt as if it were twilight, but it was merely afternoon. She watched as the winged jewel flew away. Emily noticed a beautiful bird with vibrant plumage and an equally melodic song. She watched that creature dance and sing for a while and attempted to get closer, so she could see it without obstruction from branches and leaves.

She had steady feet, despite the jungle floor's dipping or rising with rocks and roots. She thought that she would return to the path as soon as the brilliant bird flew away, but while pursuing it, she grabbed hold of a tree trunk covered with little spikes. "Ow!" she exclaimed, as the points entered her flesh. Emily pulled the spine out but felt a sickening, burning sensation. Almost immediately, her mouth became dry and pasty. She had a hard time staying focused on returning home.

Emily realized she was lost and in trouble. She looked around to see if there was anything or anyone to help her. She saw a grayish structure through the trees, not too far away and made her way to it.

The ancient building was the size of a small barn back home. Emily stumbled to the bottom step of the structure and sat down, leaning against its wall. A sunbeam shone through the forest's foliage onto her face. She looked down at the puncture marks on her wrist and thought how nice it might be to rest her eyes and regain her strength. When she fell asleep, she was at the mercy of the jungle.

Palm leaves swayed beside thick agave plants. The jungle's breeze was soft but steady. Emily was dreaming of riding Caramel through the meadows. Her imagination was vibrant. Her mind felt as if her body were being tossed about gently.

Em's dream ended suddenly. She had trouble waking up, but when her eyes finally opened, she was sitting against the stone structures that bordered the perimeter of the village. She got up and slowly walked back into the village.

As Em approached the choza, Juana was preparing the evening meal. She watched Em as she meandered inside. Juana was a bit concerned that Em might have gotten into something that altered her behavior.

It seemed odd to Em that she fell asleep in the jungle but awoke at the edge of town. Emily fell into a hammock and slept for two more hours, having recurring dreams of riding her steed.

"Emily, are you all right? Why haven't you eaten your dinner?" Dr. Scoggins shook his daughter.

"I guess I fell asleep. I was so tired," Em answered. "Is your office ready yet?"

"Yes, we've been working on that for a few days now. I will show it to you tomorrow, if you'd like," he answered.

The next morning, there was a cool fog about the place. They awoke and Juana showed up as expected. After their morning meal of frijoles and fried plantains, Medico Ezra departed as usual and left Emily to entertain herself.

Emily thought that it would be interesting to draw and write about the experiences that she was having. After a while, she walked to look for a place to buy pencils and paper.

As she went into town, Em watched as the women and their children moved toward their milpas to tend their crops. This explained why the local girls were not available for socializing or interaction: They were working.

She stopped for a while at the milpa closest to the town and observed the women and girls tending to various crops, hoeing the furrows or weeding them. One person would hoe, another would drop a seed in the hole, and the younger children would cover it with the soil that had been disturbed. An older child with a pottery jar would then pour water on the spot. The whole thing was rather organized. Everyone had purpose.

Emily continued into town. For a young person, the hike was filled with anticipation of what might happen next. For Emily, the route included both elements of excitement and trepidation. She was still unaccustomed to the traditions and ways of her fellow villagers. She wanted to be friendly, but, when she raised her hand to wave at some of the people, they would quickly turn away or tip their hats low so that their eyes could not be seen. Once again, Emily questioned what she might be doing to elicit negative responses from an obviously good-natured people.

Soon, Emily arrived at the commercial part of town, which bordered the market area. Massive warehouses sat next to lavish offices where exporters conducted their business.

The market itself was a vibrant place. The merchants were organized along the roadside with their various displays of fruits, textiles, and crafts. Emily was bombarded with offers of trinkets, food, and other wares, but she politely declined the offers. As she crossed a clearing, the son of a prominent businessman spotted her. The young man named Hector was enticed by her. He said to his confidant, Rolando, "I would very much like to meet her."

Hector and Rolando watched as Emily approached the building that housed his family's honey business. When she got close, Rolando went down the steps to the road to intercept her.

"Hello, Miss," Rolando said courteously.

"Hello," Em said in return.

"I can see you are bit surprised that I speak your language," Rolando

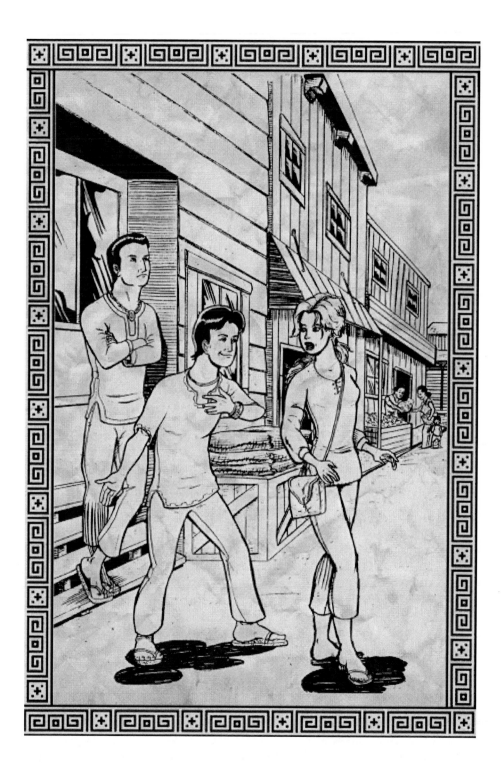

continued.

"Well, yes. That is, I have not met many people here who do, with the exception of Alcalde Tejada."

"Our fathers have sent us to school to learn the ways of business," Rolando said. "Please allow me to introduce you to a good friend of mine." Hector glided down the steps like a bullfighter, looking well groomed and relaxed.

"This is Hector Escalante Chan," Rolando said, as if he were presenting royalty.

Hector smiled and bowed to Emily as if he were inviting her to waltz.

"And, you are?"

"Oh, I'm Emily Scroggins. My father is a doctor here in town."

Hector definitely recognized the name.

"Ah, yes, Medico Scroggins. I have heard of his name before."

"Really?" Em asked. "Can you tell me where his office is?"

"But, of course," Hector replied. "Why don't we escort you there?"

"That would be nice," Emily replied. Hector and Rolando walked on either side of Em, acting as tour guides as they passed various establishments. They arrived at Medico Scroggins's office but stopped short of its entrance.

"I have heard Medico Scroggins is setting up shop over there," Hector said with a disdainful look on his face. Emily saw the change in his attitude. Rolando said, "Miss Emily, there is the gristmill where corn products are sacked for transport. It is dusty and the people are unpleasant. It's not a place for a lady like yourself."

Emily was glad to be making new friends, especially well-mannered boys of proper upbringing, but she was a bit confused about their view of the other villagers. She politely thanked them for showing her the way.

Hector said, "You must stop by soon for refreshments at my father's honey shop."

"That sounds peachy," Em replied, crossing the road to the warehouse. The two boys watched her leave, and Rolando asked Hector, "What is *peachy*?"

They were not the only ones watching Emily.

* * * * *

Emily went inside and found the place to be clean and tidy, just the way her father would want it to be. She had nothing else pressing to do, so she took a couple of crates inside and made herself a place to sit. She reminisced about the time she had spent in her father's Charleston office. She tried to imagine the new one filled with bookcases and desks with lamps and an array of equipment. That was when she spied the paw prints. She looked out the back window and saw that there were patches of jungle nearby. She was noticing the dilapidated shutters when the front door slammed open. *Wham!* The furniture had arrived on a wagon. Rocio was just as alarmed as Emily was when he tromped inside to set up the furniture.

"Who are you?" he asked in Spanish. Emily shook her head indicating she did not understand what he was saying.

"I am Medico Scroggins's daughter," she said. When Rocio heard her surname, he figured she was okay, especially since her features were similar to the doctor's.

The furniture was European in design and old. Rocio made sure the pieces were unloaded with care and brought into the office area without complication. He was an astute assistant and meant to be noticed by his superiors.

Rocio had obtained the furniture from a nearby business that had recently closed. Two wooden desks, four wooden chairs, six cabinets, four large tables, and two end tables were brought in, along with a couple of pictures and some lamps. Rocio directed the men as to where the pieces should be located, and Emily assisted by nodding her approval or pointing to another spot.

As the workers left, Emily attempted to thank them in their native language.

Rocio continued to move the furniture around the space. Emily was excited to see her father's office becoming a place where he would be recognized as an official and reliable doctor. By late morning, Emily and Rocio had everything in place. She was about to excuse herself when she heard familiar footsteps approaching the office.

Dr. Scroggins, otherwise known as Medico Ezra, entered the room holding his precious microscope under his arm. He was pleasantly surprised to see Emily waiting among the newly acquired furniture. As his eyes adjusted to the dim lighting, he was taken aback by the sight of his office.

"Rocio, it seems you've done a remarkable job of furnishing the office, and—Emily, I'm assuming you had something to do with the way the furniture was arranged."

Emily smiled and joked, "If you knew I could do this, would you quit telling me to focus on my homework?"

Medico Ezra conceded the point and hugged his daughter. "I am blessed that such an angel is mine."

Rocio thanked the good doctor and headed to another part of the warehouse. Emily then explained to her father that she had come to town to buy pencils and paper.

"Of course, Em. Get all that you need, and I will settle the debt later. Just sign the receipt with our last name."

Em strode with confidence, as she set out to decipher the town's layout and find a store that had paper, pens, and books. She went up the road and turned onto the first side street which was wide and open. She passed by another warehouse where men were sauntering about. She continued to walk with purpose, and they did not bother her. After a turn or two, Em saw a shop with several pieces of art in the front window. She entered the place wondering what was in store for her.

"We don't need any fruit today." A raspy voice bellowed at her from beyond an interior doorway that was adorned with long strands of beads.

"Oh, I am not here for fruit," Emily replied. "I want to purchase pencils and paper."

"Really?" the voice continued. Emily heard something that sounded like boxes sliding across the floor. A few seconds later, the person brushed the beads to the side and moved from the storage area into the light of the shop. The shopkeeper was an attractive woman with a skeptical look on her face.

In English, she asked, "What kind of paper and pencils are you looking for?"

"Well, I would like a few pencils to draw some pictures and to write some notes. I'm not sure how many, as I've no idea how long we'll be staying here," Emily replied.

The shopkeep looked at Em a bit closer. Realizing that Em may indeed be a fortuitous customer, she adopted a more pleasant tone of voice. "I have two different sets of pencils. I recommend the ones that are carved on the ends for ready writing."

"May I see them?" Em asked innocently. She never thought to inquire about the kind the shopkeeper wasn't recommending.

The shopkeeper showed Em the available stock and was even was a bit enthusiastic, once she realized the young lady was not only a foreign girl, but also a possible repeat customer.

Emily signed for the supplies, as her father had suggested, and left with a tablet of rice paper and twelve pencils. She felt she had found a friend—someone who could speak her language! The shopkeeper frowned as she watched the young miss depart.

Em knew that if she set out for home, she would not be able to get there before darkness fell. Just then, a young man appeared and said, in broken English, "Señorita, my name is Pedro. I will bring you to your father's home tonight."

Emily looked at him and, seeing his clean, strong features, decided to take a chance and question him further.

"How is it that you know where I live?"

"We are in the same village," he replied. "Is Medico Ezra not your father?"

Emily agreed to go with him. Pedro then produced a donkey from nearby and motioned for Em to climb onto it. Pedro walked beside it, guiding the way, and together, they retreated from town, back to the outskirts of the village.

Emily permitted the fellow to take her back to her choza. He seemed genuine and true in nature. She was either going to be greatly deceived or correct in her analysis. Only time would tell. Her ride seemed to take less time than she had predicted.

When they came up to Emily's hut, she got off the donkey and looked to her guide to see his face. Pedro allowed her to see his eyes, which were illuminated by the moonlight. Emily did not attempt to converse with him, since he had been reluctant to do so during the journey. She moved to the donkey's head and stroked his brow saying, "You are a good boy." The donkey seemed to understand that she was grateful.

Pedro watched as she moved away, still not speaking. When Emily came to the entrance of her hut, she turned and twiddled her fingers and said, "Toodle-loo."

* * * * *

Morning began as all other days had. Juana prepared breakfast, Dr. Scroggins prepared for his medical duties, and Em assisted in whatever small way that she could. The air had a crisp freshness about it. In the distance, howler monkeys were wailing their territorial calls. Dr. Scroggins spotted a package wrapped in brown paper and twine and asked Em about the supplies she had bought.

"I bought some paper for drawing and writing, and I got a few kinds of pencils. Oh, and an eraser, too," she replied.

Em got the package and showed him her new things. "I thought I would scout around a bit and do some drawings today," Em said.

"That's fine," Dr. Scroggins replied. "Just be sure you get back here well before nightfall. I've heard a jaguar has been seen in the area."

"Really?" Em quipped. "I saw some kind of paw prints at your new office yesterday."

"Yes, I saw those too. By the size of them, Rocio said it could have been an ocelot. It would be highly unlikely that a large predator would come into the main part of town."

"I'm going to see if I can get close enough to those monkeys to draw a picture," Em said. With that, she gave her father a peck on the cheek and headed down the trail toward the howling sounds. Juana and Dr. Scroggins looked at one another. He said, "I can't keep her here all day." Juana shrugged in agreement.

Ezra and Juana watched Emily walk away, but soon, the jungle swallowed her up. Emily thought her hut on the outskirts of town was one of the most basic in the area, but there were several families living nearby under thatched lean-tos. Em noticed a little girl, kneeling next to a tree. The little girl appeared to be inserting some kind of reed into a hole in the ground. Emily thought this would make an interesting picture, so she began to sketch. The girl laughed joyously as she pulled the reed out. That time, a big, black, hairy spider was grasping it.

Emily gasped in horror as tarantula attempted to flee for cover, but the girl quickly covered the spider with a small woven basket and captured it.

Emily finished the sketch before moving deeper into the forest. There were so many varieties of trees and plants. Distracted by all the foreign sounds and smells, Em found it difficult to focus on any one thing to draw. So, she decided to just go for a hike, and on her way back, she would retrace her steps and narrow the options down to three or four.

Em came upon a mound of densely matted vines. There appeared to be something hidden underneath the tangled leaves, but she could not tell if it was a mound of dirt, or perhaps a rotted tree trunk. She picked up a dead branch and used it to poke through the vines. She hit a solid mass. Her curiosity piqued, and she circled the mound, poking and peering, until she found a space where she could see what was under the vines. Underneath them was a stone. Em assumed it to be ancient. The mysteries of the jungle weighed on her. She began to realize that this area held a secret history that seemed somehow disconnected from the people who resided there now.

Soon she came to a wide ravine, perhaps ten feet deep and thirty feet across. Her heart raced as she chose a side of the chasm and attempted to work around it. The sounds of the monkeys became louder, so she honed in on the treetops . Looking up was risky because she it took her focus off of the ravine. She could hear the tree branches swooshing, as the primates continually moved away from her. At the crest of a hill to her right, she saw a gray, tooth-like object protruding from the ground.

Emily made for the structure. It was farther away than she anticipated, and there was not a direct route to it. Finally, she arrived at its base. It was a mammoth stone with strange symbols carved into it. Em leaned against a tree and pulled her pencils and pad from her pack.

She realized that one of the most difficult parts of a drawing was the initial sketch. More than once, figures would "run off" the page, ruining the drawing. After blocking the various features, she settled in to sketch the details of this intriguing subject.

Em took a lot of time eyeing the stone. Occasionally, she would get distracted by a bird call or an unwanted advance by a buzzing insect. More than an hour passed before she stood up to stretch and take a break. Just then, she thought she saw the jungle foliage shift as if someone or something had hastily retreated.

She crept to the edge of the thicket and pushed aside the leaves. Peering through them, she again thought she saw movement just beyond the dense plants in front of her, so she kept going, hoping that she was not sneaking up on a dangerous animal.

There! That time she did see something moving. It appeared to be a person, although she saw only saw a portion of black hair and tanned skin.

She stooped low, pushing back oversized leaves. Em's heart was racing as she tried to focus her sight from the ground to the forest ahead of her. She knew she was on the right trail because of slight depressions in the soil. She stopped completely and knelt down, gazing in wonder at what appeared to be a dinosaur footprint. She placed her hand into the depression, and it was at least three times the size of her own hand. Practically trembling, Em decided that she had gone far enough. Her foot snapped a twig as she began to turn. Suddenly, there was a loud commotion coming toward her. Em turned in horror to see a tremendous reptile smash through the vegetation, galloping full bore. It leapt over her striking her with its chest, and then its tail as it passed her, smashing Em into a tree trunk several feet away.

The tremendous lizard began thrashing to and fro. It had a giant snake, biting and coiling about its neck. The snake had a couple of coils constricting its neck and was trying to get the rest of its eighteen-foot body onto the reptile to finish it off. When the snake released its tail from the monster's foreleg, its tail flung into the lizard's gaping jaws. *Crunch!* He bit down on the snake's body. The anaconda released it biting jaws from the reptile to try to escape, uncoiling at the same time. The lizard shook its massive head back and forth like a terrier and flung the snake into the dense foliage, where it sounded as if it were slithering away.

The lizard turned to focus its attention on Emily who was slumped over. A young man was crouching over her. He had thick black hair and was bareback, wearing loose cotton pants that went to his calves. The man stood up and faced the megalania saying, "Chaca, you have done well! How did you know that snake was going to attack her?" The reptile dipped its head a bit and bent its neck, as if it were listening.

"Oh, you heard it slithering," Pedro said. Chaca stomped a foot and Pedro added, "Yes, I heard the twig snap too. Let's get her away from here in case that serpent has not had enough!"

Pedro bent down, gathered Emily's drawing materials, and lifted her up and over his shoulder. She moaned a bit but did not wake up. Pedro, followed by Chaca, set off in a new direction. After crossing several hills and gullies, they came to an ancient stone building concealed by the jungle. The building

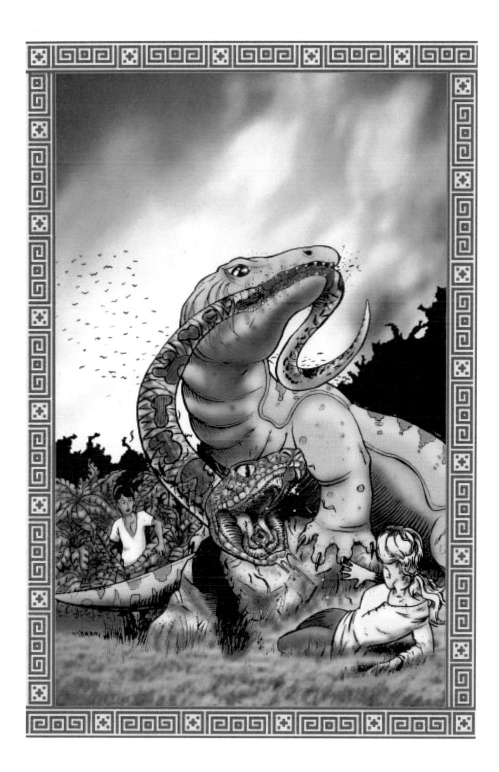

was some kind of temple, adorned with carvings. Plants, vines, even trees were growing out of the roof, window openings, and any cracks, which were numerous. They went around to the side of the temple, where it was shady and a bit cooler. Pedro gently set Emily down and propped her up in a corner.

"Chaca, you stay here and guard her while I go and get some water," Pedro ordered. The enormous lizard lay down about thirty feet away, facing the girl, much like a dog would.

Pedro ran off into the forest and was gone almost an hour. As he came to the forest edge, he saw Chaca rise up and look toward Emily, who was regaining consciousness. Pedro trotted over to them and heard Emily scream. "Aaaahhhh! Stay back!" she cried out, looking around for somewhere to run.

"Be still," Pedro called out, coming into her line of sight. "He's my friend. He won't hurt you. He actually saved you," Pedro continued.

Emily could not understand all of Pedro's words, but she did recognize the word *amigo* as friend and tried to compose herself. It also helped that Chaca had sat down again.

"Here is some water for you," Pedro said in English, holding out a two split coconuts that he had cut the tops off of.

Emily took one and drank it down. "Mmm, that's tasty," she said. "Thanks."

Pedro sat down on the patio, leaning against the wall, not far from where Emily had been resting. Emily followed his lead and sat down, too, still eyeing the lizard.

"Where am I? What happened back there, and how do you have a giant lizard as a friend?" Em asked, still having a difficult time understanding the surreal situation.

Pedro sighed, handing Em the other coconut. He tried to explain how he first came across the lizard as a young boy, but his accent made communication a bit difficult. Pedro said the temple was his secret hideout. Like the temple, Chaca was a great secret. No one, other than Pedro, had ever seen him before that day. Emily got the gist of his story and vowed not to tell anyone.

Pedro took out his knife to make a blood oath with Emily, but she motioned for him to put the knife away, and instead, showed him how to hook his pinky finger into hers, making a pinky promise instead. Chaca dutifully watched from nearby.

Pedro helped Emily get up, retrieved her art supplies from inside the building, and led her to a game trail that would lead her home. They said their goodbyes, and Emily turned to have one last look at Pedro and Chaca. She had to pinch herself to make sure it hadn't been a dream.

The walk took almost an hour. Emily began sweating on the way home and felt feverish and weak. She wondered if she was just fatigued from all the day's excitement. By the time she passed by the tarantula girl's hut, Em was stumbling and weaving. The terrain was predominately at a slight downhill grade, so she was able to stagger home. Dropping her things at the door, Em collapsed into her hammock. Her temperature was getting higher.

Juana eventually came along to make the evening meal. When she saw Em's things strewn about the floor, she went over to Em and saw that she was pale and her clothes were saturated with sweat. Juana felt her forehead. Having seen this before, she went over to their closest neighbor and had them send for the shaman, Don Octavio Pech.

The sky began to cloud up from the humidity and heat. Thunderclouds were forming and began rumbling menacingly. It began to grow dark, although sunset was still a couple of hours away. The wind picked up, and dead leaves and dust started blowing around. The tops of trees swayed, as the clouds rapidly festered into a storm. Large droplets of rain began falling from the sky, like small stones making mini-eruptions in the dusty dirt as they impacted. Em's doorway grew dark. Juana looked to see what the cause for this was and saw the shaman standing there holding a shoulder bag. Lightning flashed, causing his body to look like a dark, terrifying figure cast against the bright flash of light behind him.

"Taatich," Juana exclaimed, "You've arrived just in time. The girl is burning with fever." The shaman came to Em's side and opened her closed eyelid. Her eye was rolled back into her head. He had seen this many times before, so he began arranging some things from his bag to treat the sick girl.

First, he lit a candle. It had become as dark as night and the wind and rain were competing for dominance. Then, he took some incense out. He lit it and blew on the dried weeds, giving off a pungent smell and thick smoke, which he "bathed" Emily with. He moved the stuff over her body and head and chanted words to bind the spirits of sickness that harassed her. Then, he brought out a toad, which he kept in a miniature basket. Untying the lid, he tapped on the toad's back with a flat stick, causing the toad to excrete a whitish paste, which he scraped off. Mixing the goo with some water, he lifted Em's head so she could drink. He poured some of the solution into her mouth. She gagged and coughed, but she swallowed most of it.

Just as Emily choked the foul liquid down, the doorway darkened again. Dr. Scroggins was standing there, drenched, out of breath. He had been running most of the way home. He couldn't believe his eyes. There was the shaman, whom he had been told about, standing over his daughter, with smoldering leaves, chanting some foreign spell. He was so shocked, he didn't know what to do or say first. He ran to Emily and picked up her clammy hand. He felt her head, even as Juana was wiping the sweat from Em's brow. He looked at Juana and asked, "How long has she been like this?"

Juana replied, " Three hora." She motioned that she called for the shaman to come and help. With that, Dr. Scroggins looked at the shaman. "What is she sick from? What have you done?" Don Octavio did not understand his words exactly, but he knew what was being asked of him.

Don Octavio replied in Spanish that the girl had the water sickness, motioning toward his own mouth as if drinking from a bowl. Then, the shaman brought out the toad, and, while holding the amphibian, he motioned across its back and made the drinking motion again.

Dr. Scroggins was horrified. His mind raced to understand how he, a trained physician from a modern college, was at the bedside of his daughter in a remote jungle, as she was being treated by a mystic healer with smoke and toads. He told Juana that he was going back to his office to get some medicine. Juana grabbed Dr. Scroggins by his arm and pleaded with him not to leave. The storm was intense and night was falling. Dr. Scroggins felt he had to attempt the journey. He ran outside in the torrent, which was almost at gale force. He stopped a short way down the path under a large tree. He could not even see the next hut, which was only thirty or so yards from his position.

"Ahhh!" Dr. Scroggins yelled, looking up at the sky, as if cursing the clouds and the heavens. He stumbled back to his hut. Entering it, he looked at the shaman and panted, "I hope you know what you are doing."

The shaman replied in his native tongue that he would stay with them that night and pray with them, and the fever should break by morning. Dr. Scroggins sank into his chair beside Don Octavio as Juana built a small fire in the hut and prepared a maize drink from the crushed corn and supplies that she had brought with her. They were in for a long night.

Chapter 10

When Pedro and Chaca left Emily at the fork in the road, they headed in the opposite direction of the village. Moving along animal trails, the two walked side by side for about twenty minutes, until they came upon an impenetrable thicket of trees and bushes tangled with vines. It was not uncommon to the region, but Pedro rarely saw one so massive.

They came up to the perimeter of the thicket and turned to the side, entering the outskirts of the mass. They came to a solid wall of vines, hanging from the dense trees. Chaca lowered his head to the ground, like a peccary, and moved forward under the vines, lifting them off the ground like a curtain. Pedro only had to duck, as they both passed under at the same time. The foliage was very dense on the other side of the vine wall, but only for a distance of three paces, where the jungle stopped, and a wide open space lay before them. It looked like a tremendous crater in the ground, rimmed by solid limestone rock on all sides. The sun was not obstructed by a forest canopy there. There was an uneven grade that led down into the dry hole, which measured about three hundred feet across and fifty feet deep. Protruding rocky outcrops and gravelly sand made their footing a bit difficult at times during the descent. The heat from the rock was intense. It had become oven-like as it absorbed the sun's rays. Down, down they went, traversing almost half the inside edge of the grand hole. Eventually, they came to the bottom, which was mostly flat with rocky outcrops protruding from the ground like giant termite mounds. Vegetation was sparse due to the oppressive heat.

Both Chaca and Pedro sighed loudly as they made it to a cool shaded area. In that part of the crater, there were large underground tunnels that sometimes went for miles, large enough to accommodate Chaca's great girth.

Without stopping, they pressed on through the first large tunnel that became as dark as night. In the distance, they could see a speck of light which they headed toward. As Pedro's eyes grew accustomed to the darkness, it became a bit easier to navigate, but he relied mostly on his memory of the terrain. Before long, the tunnel gave way to another opening, which was just as deep, but the circumference was much smaller than the first crater. This hidden crater had been an underground cave; its ceiling had collapsed a millennium ago. Its ground was covered with giant ferns and avocado trees. It was also much cooler than the initial crater, and there was a small spring of water, which remained pooled up, providing life and moisture to the plant life there.

It was here that the two came and drank from the spring, before retiring in the shade onto a rocky area, which looked like forest furniture covered with ferns and moss.

Pedro said to Chaca, "That sure was some kind of morning!"

Chaca flicked his forked tongue as if recalling the snake encounter. Then, he yawned, and set his head down on a flat rock and closed his eyes. Pedro was more concerned about the girl and her discovery of the giant lizard than Chaca was. He pondered and muttered aloud what he would do if his companion were ever discovered by the villagers. Chaca opened one eye, and, in response to Pedro's query, he opened his large mouth, revealing his numerous serrated teeth, and slammed it shut with a loud clap.

"Oh, you'd just eat them? Huh!" Pedro replied to Chaca's response. "That's real mature." After a nice rest, Chaca got up and pulled several avocados off the trees, crunching them up and tossing one over to Pedro.

"Thanks, amigo," Pedro said, as he cut into the flesh of the fruit with his knife. He glanced up and saw that clouds were forming above them and knew what was happening.

"Chaca, it's going to storm soon, so I better head home," Pedro said.

Chaca rumbled a kind of reply in his throat, got his bulk up, and moved toward Pedro, who leaned forward and hugged him around his massive neck. Then, Chaca ambled into one of the caverns nearby, and Pedro began the ascent back to the top of the cenote.

The skies were increasingly ominous; Pedro moving along quickly to avoid the rain. His biggest concern, however, was not the weather. There had been an unforeseen complication in his otherwise predictable life, a beautiful girl . . . and she has seen Chaca. Like a chess master, he envisioned a variety of sequences involving Emily, Chaca, and others. Ultimately, he decided the best course of action was to take no action at all. Secrecy would prevail.

As Pedro walked up the road to his home, a nicely built traditional structure, his sister, Maria, was outside in the cooking hut. "Hello Maria," he said casually.

"Hi Pedro," Maria responded, "Where have you been? Mother wants you to bring us some firewood."

"I've been out exercising in the forest, building my muscles, you know," he said flexing his bicep and snickering.

"Well, you go get that wood next time if you want to build muscle."

Pedro went inside and sat down. He was hungry and tired, but he knew there was more work to be done. After resting a bit, he headed to his family's food plot to find his father and gather some wood.

Pedro's family was one of the few in the village who owned land. Long before his great grandfather was born, a Spanish official had deeded them a large parcel of the area, for reasons long forgotten. Other villagers would rent or lease land from his father, Andres, and would give a certain amount of produce or meat to him in return. This meant the Canek family did not have to work at the henequen factory. It also made life a bit easier for his mother, Victoria, who would use the extra money to create jewelry and other adornments that she would sell at the market.

Pedro soon saw his father working in the field. He was hoeing the soil among the maize. Pedro called out to him, "Taat" or father. Andres looked up and smiled. He was a gentle and caring man.

"Paal," Andres replied. This irked Pedro a bit, because the term meant child; he felt he was too old to be called that since he was seventeen years old. Andres raised his hand and waved for his son to come over. Pedro carefully walked through the garden, arriving at his father's side.

"Son, go over there and tie those bundles of wood and set them on the burro, so that we can have fire for the meals," Andres suggested.

Pedro smiled broadly at his father, wondering why he made the extra effort to help him whenever possible. Pedro admired his father and hoped that one day he would grow into being such a man of substance and character.

Andres explained, "Ernesto had an old tree fall down at his place, so he gathered up some of the extra wood and brought it here for us to have. I thought you might appreciate some help." Pedro sighed with relief. He wouldn't have to chop wood that day. Andres also said that he was finishing work for the day, because the sky was angry.

Together, they returned to their home. When they approached, Andres began singing a song. He was almost always in a merry mood. Pedro felt embarrassed by his father's merriment, even though there may not be any witnesses.

The wind blew violently as random raindrops fell like marbles. Pedro brought the burro inside their hut, and Maria hastily finished cooking the tamales on the grill as the storm blew in. Their mother, Victoria, also returned before the rain, more by chance than planning. She hadn't had many customers at the market, so she stored her crafts with a trusted friend near the market and left early.

The whole family arrived at their hut within twenty minutes of one another, just before the thunderstorm released its havoc on the community.

Victoria said, "I saw Don Octavio go over to Medico Ezra's hut on my way home."

"A strange coincidence maybe?" Andres replied. Pedro tried to hide any concern, but his surprise showed on his face. His expression did not escape Maria's notice.

Victoria said, "Maria, we need to talk about your upcoming quincinera celebration."

Andres added, "Is my baby already turning fifteen years old?"

"Yes, Taat, that is why you have gray hair on your head now," Pedro said, laughing at his own joke.

Maria objected, "Na, tell him to leave me alone." Maria resented that her time was always filled with work, while her brother was allowed to come and go as he pleased.

Victoria replied, "Now Pedro, don't make me remind you about your manners. Perhaps you should spend less time in the forest and more with me helping at the market."

"Aw, Na," he replied, "That's Maria's job. Taat is already teaching me the family business." He looked to his father for support, and Andres winked at him.

"Well, just mind yourself then, son," Victoria said, hoping to put an end to the discussion. "Maria, let's go over here away from prying ears, where we can discuss some ideas I have about what to wear that day."

Pedro turned in early and went to sleep listening to the sound of the rain, as the wind gently caused his hammock to sway back and forth, rocking him to sleep.

Meanwhile, at Medico Ezra's hut, the two doctors kept vigil over Emily that night, each doing what he'd been trained to do. They alternated watches so each could get a minimal amount of sleep.

At morning's first light, Dr. Scroggins noticed Emily awakening. He felt her forehead, which was no longer burning with fever. She opened her eyes at the touch of her father's hand.

"Oh, Father, I had the most horrible nightmares," Emily said. Don Octavio came to her side, and Emily was startled.

"The shaman was already here tending to you when I returned last night. A violent storm blew in, so Don Octavio spent the night with us, praying for you," Dr. Scroggins reported. Emily held out her hand to clasp the shaman's hand with a thankful, but tired smile.

The shaman turned to Juana and gave her some directions for Emily's care. He shook Dr. Scroggins's hand, and, taking his sack, departed from their choza. Emily rose to her feet, with her father and Juana's assistance. She went outside and asked Juana to take her to the bushes, which Juana did.

When they returned, Dr. Scroggins was readying the outside fire pit for the morning meal. Emily went inside and sat down, while Juana began her morning ritual of food preparation. The sun was now rising, and that set off a chorus of bird calls and songs, more vibrant than most mornings. Emily was moving about carefully, because her balance was still a bit shaky. Dr. Scroggins announced that he was going to get an early start that day, as he anticipated patients who had been injured by falling limbs in the storm. As he was leaving, Dr. Scroggins asked Juana what Don Octavio had said to her.

"He said that the girl should rest and not do any hard work," Juana replied.

"I think today is a good day to show the young lady how to make some of these meals she's been enjoying," Juana suggested.

"That is an excellent idea," Dr. Scroggins replied. "It will help to keep her occupied as well. Emily wasn't as enthusiastic about the idea as they were.

Emily went inside the choza and returned with her pad of paper. She paged through the stack, looking over each of the drawings that she had made. Juana would look over occasionally to see the sketching too. She saw that Emily had an eye for artwork, which was a valuable asset to a person from her community. Em stopped at the totem pole picture and added some detail to the background. She found herself penciling in the outline of the ruins where Pedro had taken her. Em daydreamed a bit about what had happened.

Em's dream was interrupted by the clip-clop of hooves. There was a man with a burro and wagon, hauling produce. He stopped and spoke to Juana, who came over to Em and said, "This is my cousin, Gerardo. He has offered to give me a ride to the market. Go, get ready to leave if you'd like to come."

Emily replied, "Okay, sounds like fun," as she was glad to have something to break up the monotony of hanging around the hut. Gerardo helped Juana get up onto the back of the cart, and Em hopped up by herself. Off they went, jostling side to side with their legs hanging down behind the cart. Along the way, they passed by other huts and plenty of children running about playing, many of whom waved to them. Emily was happy to have any interaction with her neighbors. She was also glad to see another side of Juana.

Before long, they were in town. Gerardo helped them down from the cart and went about his business. Like most of the shoppers, Juana was in no hurry. She stopped at many of the booths and tables just to chat with folks. She picked up crafts and examined them and thumped a melon or two. Emily enjoyed shopping with Juana. She was introduced by the matriarch many times to villagers who greeted Emily with warm smiles. One dealer even presented Em with an orange to eat.

After a while, Em said to Juana, "This has been so nice spending time with you. Would you mind if I went off by myself a bit for a while to look around?"

Juana said, "Go. Go enjoy yourself and meet some people your age."

Emily wandered off, peeled her orange, and ate the juicy pulp. She stopped at a nice looking booth that had all kinds of trinkets, necklaces, pins, and bracelets. They were made from shiny stones, copper, shells, even nuts. She was admiring one bracelet in particular, when a voice spoke to her from behind, "That would be a good choice for you because it repels snakes."

Emily recognized Pedro's voice and turned, saying, "It is pretty, but I don't think I will need it for that reason."

"Aren't you Medico Ezra's daughter?" the lady behind the booth asked.

"Why, yes, how did you know?" Emily queried.

"This village is not as large as you might think," the lady continued.

Pedro was anxiously waiting for a chance to speak. "Perhaps I could show

you around a bit. Would that be okay, Mother?" he said looking over at Victoria, and then, Emily.

Victoria said, "Yes, I suppose so, but don't forget to come back."

Pedro took Emily over to some benches under a giant cieba tree. "What are you doing here? I heard that the shaman came to see you last night. Are you okay?" he asked.

"Oh, Pedro, I had a most horrible night of fever and nightmares. My father and shaman Don Octavio stayed up the entire night, watching over me."

"I was worried about you, between the storm and hearing of the shaman at your choza," Pedro replied. Em smiled. It was nice having someone worry about her, she thought.

"When can I see Chaca again?" Emily asked.

Pedro winced, as she said those words, hoping it would not come up. "No one here even knows that Chaca exists!" he said in a firm hushed tone. "I don't think it's a good idea."

"Who am I going to tell? You are my only friend! Please let me see him again," Em pleaded.

"Oh, if I do, it must remain an absolute secret. We can't be seen alone together, or people will be suspicious of what we are doing," Pedro added.

"We can have a signal of some kind. That way, I'll know when to go there," Emily suggested.

The two of them sat there pondering what to do. Finally Pedro consented. "Do you know the fork in the path leading from your hut?"

Emily replied, "Yes."

"Well," Pedro continued, "there is an old forked tree on the side of the path surrounded by fan palms. I will break off a palm leaf, and tear it apart so that if I leave eleven points on the leaf, we meet at the ruins at eleven o'clock. I'll attach the stem in the crotch of the tree. Three points would be three o'clock."

"That's great!" Emily said, getting very excited. "How will I know if you mean morning or evening?" she continued.

"Morning will be the left fork, evening the right fork," Pedro replied.

"That makes sense," Em said, looking around to see if they were being watched. Pedro got up and said, "I'd better get back to work now. I'll set the palms later for ten tomorrow morning, so we can see how it works."

Emily waited for a few minutes before getting up and looking around for Juana. She did not notice Hector and Rolando spying on them from afar.

Emily found Juana and suggested they go together to visit the doctor's office. Juana agreed, so they set off in that direction. Em's strength seemed to be holding up, but when they stepped through the door of the office, Dr. Scroggins was a bit alarmed.

Jumping to his feet he asked, "Is everything okay? Are you all right, Em?"

Emily laughed a bit at his reaction and replied, "Yes, Father, I'm fine. Juana got us a ride to the market with her cousin, Gerardo. She's been showing me how to select food and stuff for cooking, just as you agreed."

"Well," he stammered, "It's just a bit soon for you to be out and about after last night's events."

Juana interjected, "We are returning home to rest now, Medico Ezra. She just wanted to show me your office. It's very nice."

Dr. Scroggins replied, "I see. Thank you, Juana. This place will do, if I can just get more of the sick folks to come here. I am beginning to see a pattern with this illness, but I need more evidence."

"We should be on our way, Juana," Emily said, hoping to ease her exhausted father's mind a bit.

"Yes, let us go," Juana replied. The two women left the doctor's office, just as Rocio was returning with some bottles.

"Oh! Hi, Rocio," Emily said.

"Hello," Rocio replied, a bit surprised to see Emily.

"What have you got there?"

"Some water samples that your father has requested."

"Interesting," Em quipped, "well, goodbye. It was nice seeing you again."

Rocio went inside with the bottles. "Here are the samples you asked for," he said.

"Ah, very good. Now, we can get started on the tests," he said, while unpacking the microscope from its case. "Where is that map of the village?"

"It should be here today, Doctor," Rocio replied. "It is to be delivered by Alcalde Tejada."

"Hmm, I wonder what else the alcalde will be bringing," Dr. Scroggins muttered.

Juana and Emily were walking around the square enjoying the cool clear weather when Hector and Rolando approached them. Hector greeted with a half bow and a polite nod.

"Hello Miss Juana—and Miss Emily, are you visiting your father this morning?"

"Yes, we did, and we're doing some shopping," Em replied.

"How nice, and how are your drawings progressing?" Rolando inquired. Hector shot him a glance indicating that he wanted to ask that question.

"Oh, I have only made a few drawing as of this time," Emily replied.

"Well, perhaps you might like to show them to me over tea sometime?" Hector invited.

"Perhaps," Emily replied coyly. "What is that you have there?" Rolando was holding a large rolled up paper of some sort.

"This is a map that my Uncle Tejada has sent to your father, the good doctor," Rolando replied, while sneaking a glance at Hector.

"I see. Well, goodbye for now," she said, abruptly ending the meeting. Juana leaned over to Emily and said, "Those two boys are always a bit too sure of themselves."

"Maybe, but they do dress well and are so well mannered, too," Em added.

Juana rolled her eyes, knowing the boys were already fooling Emily with their fancy talk and shallow advances.

The women soon returned to the market where Gerardo was waiting. He assisted the ladies with their groceries and helped them into the cart. As they were departing, Emily looked about to see if she could spot Pedro, which she did. She did not wave though, wanting to appear disinterested. Pedro glanced her way as he wondered what business she had with Hector and Rolando, who were not two of his favorite people.

After Emily and Juana departed, Pedro said to Victoria, "Na, can I go home now?"

Victoria replied, "Yes, son, you can go home and play." Pedro ran off quickly, before his mother could think of any more chores for him to do.

Maria grimaced. "Na, he always gets to do what he wants!"

"Do what?" asked Hector who, accompanied by Rolando, had eased up to her family's booth. He was smiling broadly at Maria. Maria was pleasantly surprised that Hector was there. Many of the village girls admired Hector's looks, as well as his family's position in town.

"Oh, never mind," Maria sighed.

"Will you be attending the tlachtli games this week?" Hector inquired.

"Yes, isn't everybody?" Maria replied.

"Probably; I was just wondering if you'd like to sit with my friends, that's all."

Maria blushed as she realized that she was being extended an invitation. "Well, that sounds nice. I'll have to ask my parents."

"Very well, let me know when you decide, please," Hector said, as he nodded to Victoria and left with Rolando.

"Na, can I— "

"We'll see," Victoria replied. "Come and help me sort beads for this necklace." Maria complied, but she began daydreaming about going for walks and watching the games with Hector. Victoria was thinking both of her children suddenly had newfound interests.

* * * * *

Dr. Scroggins set up his microscope on a desk near the back window where the sun's rays would enter the room. He adjusted the mirror on the tool to reflect light up through the stage, illuminating a slide he had prepared.

"Rocio, would you bring me that book I left out on the table?" Dr. Scroggins asked.

"Yes, isn't that one of the books Dr. Carlos delivered?"

"Yes," Dr. Scroggins replied, "I need to compare these microbes to the drawings in the illustrations."

Rocio brought the book over, opening it to the pages of drawings.

"What do you see, Medico Ezra?" he inquired.

"It will take time to tell," Dr. Scroggins replied. The doctor spent the remainder of the afternoon taking notes and drawing examples of the tiny creatures he observed in the water samples.

As the sun moved past its zenith, shade overtook the window, making the study of the water samples almost impossible. Dr. Scroggins secured the slides in a squat container of woven reeds after he marked them with a grease pen and entered the data on an evidence card. Rocio had left long ago to tend to his father's maize business.

As the sun waned, Dr. Scroggins realized he needed to get on the road or he would have to remain at the office all night. Emily would not know where he was until the next day. So, he closed up and departed for home at a quickened pace, delighted that his scientific theories could be valid—based on his preliminary studies.

Gerardo stopped the burro in front of Emily's choza, and the women hopped off and gathered their groceries. There was an abundance of fruit, herbs, salt, vegetables, and some woven cloth that they had to unload. Most of the supplies, except for the cloth bat, were put into the outbuilding where the food was prepared.

The burro slowly plodded away, as the women spent several minutes resting from the shopping spree. Emily was the first to say, "I am pretty tired."

Juana replied, "Me, too."

They both reclined for a considerable amount of time. Juana looked toward the sun and said, "It is time to prepare the evening meal."

"Ugh." Emily sat up and said she would help.

Luckily for Emily, Juana had acquired some corn paste that was almost ready for tortillas. All she needed to do was get the fire burning and toast the mash-like pancakes on a hot flat stone. Later, she would add other ingredients to a pot to simmer, before loading everything into the corn tortillas.

Emily was a willing student. Juana actually became more animated and vibrant with Em's participation.

Juana soon gave the grill over to Emily, who poured the corn paste onto the heated stone and promptly mangled it because it was not cooked enough. Juana steadied her hand and flat spoon, until just the right time to flip it. Then, after another minute or so she scooped it off and placed it on the awaiting pile of finished tortillas, which were separated by palm leaves so that they would not stick to one another.

While Emily was focused on grilling and flipping, Juana got the filler ready and placed it in a pot alongside the grill. It eventually began to bubble and boil. Juana added water and an extract to the mixture. Emily's nose tingled from the smell.

Dr. Scroggins arrived as the medley of cooking came to an end. He walked up and immediately noticed that Emily was out at the cooking hut with

Juana. "What is that wonderful smell?" he asked.

Juana looked over at Emily and nodded for her to reply. "Why Father, we are stewing hog's feet," she joked.

Dr. Scroggins replied, "Aye, lass, I know the odor of hog's feet, and that is not what is in the kettle."

"True, but you will have to wait until the food meets the plate, before you can decided what it is you are eating."

Emily and Juana served a delicious meal to the doctor. He was even more grateful than usual for the food, because he knew that Emily had a hand in the process. He was watching his daughter grow as a person. Em was maturing and growing up. Juana also knew that a small milestone had been met at the end of the day. Even though it was only one day of food preparation, she anticipated good things to come.

Dr. Scroggins said, "This tortilla is as good as any that I've had in town."

Emily replied, "Well, Juana did most of the work. I think, with her help, I could get good at this, eventually."

"I'm pretty tired, and am going to turn in," Dr. Scroggins said, retiring into their hut. The ladies cleaned up, and Emily also went to her hammock, after Juana left for her own home.

Emily awoke the following morning before her father and left for a short hike to check out the signal tree. She left a note saying that she would be back soon. She felt rested and was in a happy mood, even humming to herself as she walked. About ten minutes later, she approached the fork in the road next to the big tree. Wedged into the left fork was a palm leaf with only ten points at the tip of it. Em said to herself. "That means ten this morning." She pulled the leaf from its place so Pedro would know that she had seen it. Just then, Juana came into sight from the opposite direction.

"Good morning, Juana," Em said.

"Hola, Emily," Juana replied.

"Here, I want you to have these," Juana said, handing her a folded cloth. Emily opened the cloth, revealing two dolls as long as her hand, fashioned in the traditional Mayan way from corn husks. They also had doll outfits made of cloth, and the male doll had a sombrero. Emily gave Juana a big hug. Juana sang a tune that she learned as a child, teaching Emily the words as they went.

Emily giggled a lot while attempting to pronounce some of the words. Juana was very patient, repeating short phrases over and over. Emily was holding the dolls up in front of her, pretending that they were dancing at a fiesta.

Dr. Scroggins came out of the hut when he heard the singing. His heart was greatly lifted at what he was seeing and hearing, especially after such a wicked time two nights ago. Emily helped Juana with her tasks, continuing to try to learn the tune to *The Poll Parrot:*

> "My lady, your little parrot wants to take me to the river,
> I've told him I will not go there,
> I'd die with cold all a shiver!
> Peck, O peck, O peck, O poll parrot,
> O peck, O peck, O peck the sand crystal,
> Peck, O peck, O poll parrot,
> Peck, O peck, O peck at your sister.
> I should like to be a parrot, In the air shifting and veering,
> There to tell you all my secrets,
> Without anybody's hearing.
> Fly off, fly off, fly off poll parrot,
> Seek the hotter lands of the tropics,
> Flee then, flee then, flee then, poll parrot,
> Flee then, flee then from everybody."

After their morning meal, Dr. Scroggins announced that he was off to work. Emily hung around the hut, taking it easy until about nine o'clock. Then, she left to go to the ruins to meet Pedro.

"These ruins are farther than I thought," Em said to herself. She was deep in the jungle and was growing worried that she would not be able to find her way back to the old temple. Soon, she came upon the stone totem pole, and that encouraged her. It was a short time until she saw the ruins. She called out to Pedro, but he did not answer.

Emily went inside the dank old structure. The rooms were bare, but there were many carvings built into the walls and lots of leaf litter on the floor. Vines were cascading through the windows, down the walls, and across the ceiling. There was a stone bench in the main room, which was built into the structure against a wall. Emily went over to it, and after brushing it off a bit, she sat down to wait. The stone felt cool against her skin. After a short time, Em lay down on the bench to wait and relax. She closed her eyes and listened to the sounds of the jungle. As usual, there were birds calling out to one another and the occasional sounds of monkeys. While she was waiting, a small commotion began in the corner of the room among the leaf litter. She turned her head toward the sounds and saw a snake wrestling with an orange centipede. The snake gained the advantage and began swallowing the wriggling arthropod. She felt her skin get goose bumps, as she felt disgusted by the show.

Emily was so enthralled by the snake she did not notice Pedro, who had quietly come up to the window above her. He too saw the latter part of the battle and shouted, "Hey!" Startled, Emily jumped to her feet.

"Ha! Ha! Ha! Ha! Ha!" Pedro laughed, enjoying the joke he played on Emily. Emily reached through the window and poked Pedro's shoulder.

"That was not funny!"

Pedro laughed a bit more, which caused Emily to calm down and laugh at herself.

"Come on outside," Pedro said.

"I think I will," Emily replied, glad to leave that creepy old room.

"I see you found the signal palm," Pedro continued.

"Yes, I took it down so that you would know that I found it."

"Good idea. Did anyone see you come here?"

"No. Well, just some children at the edge of the village, but they weren't really paying attention to me,", she said.

"That's good. Let's go for a hike and see what we can find," Pedro suggested.

"All right," Em agreed.

"Where's Chaca? I thought you might bring him."

"I don't see him every day. Besides, I thought it would be better to just get to know one another by ourselves," Pedro replied.

"Oh, well. I see your point," Emily replied, a bit let down. They hiked around, climbed on stones, turned over rotten logs to see what was under them, and talked a lot as the hours passed.

Later that afternoon, the heat of the day set in. Pedro thought it would be a good idea to cool off at one of the remote cenotes or water holes. He told Emily to be very quiet so they could catch a glimpse of the wildlife that might be there for the same reason. Their delicate footsteps kept them from disturbing a female Morelet's crocodile guarding her nest.

Chapter 11

Doctor Scroggins came to his office and noticed a note tucked into the door jamb. He went inside and sat down at his desk to read it.

You are invited to attend the tlachtli games at Coba in three days as my guest. Please come by for the details at your convenience.
Regards,
Alcalde Tejada

Dr. Scroggins went over to the map and studied it. He had his water samples and notes spread out on the desk in front of him, as he searched for an answer to the medical riddle. "What do these things have in common?" he asked himself. Tapping his pencil on the table like a drummer, he was deep in his thoughts, not even noticing that Rocio had come inside the office.

"Medico Ezra, I was wondering if you would like to have any water samples from Muyil?" Rocio said, pointing to an area on the map just south of their position.

Dr. Scroggins smiled and replied, "Yes, I think that is an excellent idea."

"I will go there today with my friend, Alejandro. What jars do you want me to use?" he asked.

"Take these three. Juana cleaned them with boiling water this morning," the doctor replied.

"Okay, it will be tomorrow before I can bring them to you," Rocio added as he put the jars in a canvas satchel and left.

Dr. Scroggins gathered a few items together and left the office as well. He would check on a few families as he made his way over to the alcalde's residence. He strode up the road and was greeted by Hector's father, the beekeeper, as he went past their store.

"Medico Ezra," the owner, Martin Chan, yelled. "Please come inside for some tea and honey." Dr. Scroggins knew it would be rude to refuse an impromptu invitation like this, so he agreed and went up the steps. Martin gave him a warm greeting and a firm handshake, offering the doctor a seat at a nice wicker table on the porch. "I will be right back," he said, hurrying inside the store.

He came back with a cigar for each of them and got right to his point. "I would like to make my honey products available to you. They are useful in the making of salves and ointments."

"Yes, I suppose they would be. Thank you. Please do have several jars sent over when it is convenient," the doctor said.

Hector came out with a tray that held two rose colored tea glasses. He was not happy to be performing a domestic chore, but politely served them. Dr. Scroggins noticed that Hector was flustered, and after the boy went back inside, he asked about the situation.

"Do you not have any help today, Martin?"

Martin replied that his shopkeeper, a young Mayan girl, had a child who had come down with an illness and was not there that day. Dr. Scroggins interest was immediately piqued as he asked the girl's whereabouts. Martin told him she lived nearby and gave him directions as he smoked his cigar.

"Are you not a cigar man?" Martin asked the doctor.

"Not just now, thank you. Perhaps later after dinner," he said, slipping the sweet smelling cigar into his shirt pocket. He did finish the tea and thank Martin before setting out to visit the girl and her sick child. As he left, he noticed that there were several men loitering about behind the honey shop. There were also makeshift chairs, stools, and a few small round tables. He would later find out that this was an outdoor bar where Martin's staff served honey-based alcohol called xtabentún to the local men.

There seemed to be more activity on the streets than usual; there was almost a festive hum about the place. Dr. Scroggins stopped at Martin's worker's hut. She was speaking with the shaman when he arrived. The two men nodded a greeting to one another, but Dr. Scroggins felt a bit uncomfortable, due to the very different methods of healing the two healers practiced. However, after a few moments, Shaman Octavio motioned for Medico Ezra to enter. The shaman watched the doctor as he listened to the child's heart and looked into her eyes to see if her pupils were dilating properly. Then, he made some notes in his book and took a sample from the jug inside. It held the water the family used for bathing and cooking. He did not offer any prescriptions to the family since their traditional healer was already there.

The doctor departed and continued on his way to the mansion of Alcalde Tejada. There was lots of activity on the premises. Secretary Escobar noticed Dr. Scroggins arrival and hastily met him, bringing him inside to Tejada's office.

"Ah, Dr. Scroggins, I've been expecting you," Tejada cooed.

"As your unofficial envoy, I felt it would be prudent to inform you of the big contest our village is having with the Coba people. The contest takes place on a stone-paved field with a heavy rubber ball. Each team strives to bounce the ball through a round opening on top of the arena's angular walls without using their hands. It is a very spirited contest," Tejada explained.

"That sounds very interesting," Dr. Scroggins replied. "Do you have a part in this contest?" he asked.

Tejada laughed, looking over at Escobar. "My days of competing have long been gone. It is a young man's game. Our culture has done this for as long as I can remember." He continued, "I would like you and your daughter to be my guests, going with my transport for convenience and safety on the road."

Dr. Scroggins graciously accepted. Then, the three men went outside to the commons and they discussed the various banners, adornments, and supplies that would be sent to the arena. The doctor was impressed.

"Who are those men over there?" the doctor asked.

"Those are a few of the players practicing the game. Many more will be here later and tomorrow as well, in preparation for the contest," Tejada said.

"Interesting," Dr. Scroggins muttered. With that, he said his goodbyes and left.

On his way back to his office, Hector and Rolando ran past him, heading for Tejada's place. They had some kind of leather braces or armor tied in sizeable bundles tucked under their arms. "Now I can see why he was so glum a while ago," Dr. Scroggins thought.

When he reached his office, Dr. Scroggins took out the water sample and made a slide of it. He then studied the water under his microscope. This slide had something the other did not have. It was some kind of grub-like larva wiggling in the water. He made a drawing of it in his book, gathered up his things, and headed for home.

Arriving home earlier than normal, Dr. Scroggins decided to have a bath while no one was around. Afterward, he relaxed in a hammock, which he had strung outside in the breeze. He lit his cigar, pondering all the things that were on his mind, including how much he missed his wife Mary.

After a while, Juana arrived.

"Have you seen Em?" he asked.

"Not since this morning," she replied.

"Hmm, I wonder what she is up to now."

* * * * *

Pedro and Emily were just ten paces from the crocodile when Pedro noticed it. He motioned for Em to follow him, taking a wide berth past the reptile. They had not gotten far when the croc's eyelid opened. It swung its head directly at them, opened its mouth wide, and charged. Pedro and Emily turned and ran. Pedro leapt into some low tree branches and pulled Emily up out of the beast's way, just as its mouth clapped shut. It circled around the base of the tree looking up at them. They had no escape. They were trapped. The crocodile positioned itself between the two youths and her nest and lay down to rest. It would blink and close its eyes, only for a moment, but, after an hour or so, the moments became longer and longer.

Finally, Pedro whispered to Em, "Let's make a run for it that way." She nodded. "On the count of three. One . . . two . . . three!" They jumped down as swiftly and quietly as they could and ran as fast as their feet would carry them. After they went over the top of a hill, they jumped up into another tree and waited. They did not hear anything pursuing them, so Em said, "Let's go."

They walked away at a brisk pace, sweating and panting a bit. Every little sound and movement caused them to jump. Soon, they came to a fork in the path. The left path would take Pedro toward his home, and the right was Emily's way home. Pedro took Emily's hands in his and looked into her eyes. "That's the most fun I ever had . . . with a girl." Then he blushed a bit and retreated quickly, before Emily could think of something to say.

"I'll look for a signal tomorrow," she shouted into the forest, not knowing if her words were swallowed up by the dense foliage or not.

The sun was about to set by the time she made it home. Juana had finished cooking and was cleaning up. Emily joined her and began washing the utensils. She was humming that parrot tune to herself again. Juana looked over at Dr. Scroggins who returned her gaze with a look that implied, "What's with her? And, I'm not asking."

The next morning when Dr. Scroggins awoke, Emily was already up and outside. She had started the morning fire and was boiling some coffee. He came outside, yawning and stretching.

"Are you well rested, Daddy?" Em asked.

"Yes, dear, I slept like a rock!" he replied. "But I'm a bit stiff from all that walking," he added.

"I know what you mean," Em said.

"What's that you said?"

"Oh! Nothing," Em replied.

"What's this picture you've been drawing?" Dr. Scroggins asked.

"Oh, it's some kids playing with dolls, like the ones Juana gave me. She is so nice!" Em commented. "Are you going into town this morning?"

"Yes, I have a theory I'm considering, regarding the sickness in the village, and I need to run more tests," Dr. Scroggins said.

"May I go with you? I'd like to see what you've been doing."

"Sure you can come along," he said with a smirk, knowing that Emily wasn't revealing all of her intentions. Juana came, as always, but this time, half of her job was already done. She looked around to see if there was somebody else around the hut before coming to the conclusion that Emily had done the work. Emily was adding some details to her drawing, when Juana came over to her and admired it.

"You are good at pictures," she said to Em. Em just smiled.

Juana enjoyed some coffee while she finished making the morning meal. She didn't mind that there were coffee grounds in it.

Soon, Em and her father were headed to town. As they passed by the signal tree, Em noticed that there were not any leaves wedged into the bark.

As they went along the path, Dr. Scroggins told Emily of the water analysis tests he'd been conducting. He explained the microbes that he'd been observing through the microscope and told her how he thought they might help him determine the cause of the fever that was plaguing the village.

They went past the market area. Emily looked over to where Pedro's family booth usually was. Victoria and Maria were there getting things ready, but she did not see Pedro.

"Dad, could I walk around for a little while and meet you at the office later?" Emily asked. "Oh, and I need some money, too."

The doctor's ears perked up quickly, but before he could ask why she needed money, Emily said, "Pleeeease," blinking at him with the cutest face she could make.

"Very well, here are a few pesos. Spend it wisely," he added.

"Thank you, Daddy," Em said grabbing the money and hugging her father. Dr. Scroggins resumed his walk to his office, and Emily went over to Victoria's booth.

"Good morning," Emily said to the women.

"Good morning to you, too," Victoria replied. Maria was trying hard to appear too busy to notice Emily. Maria suspected that her privileged brother might be befriending this foreigner, and she resented Emily for it.

"I would like to buy a gift for someone, but I don't know what to get."

"Perhaps a necklace made of those pretty purple and pink shells." She looked around some more and spied some woven sandals that had the same shells sewn to the top straps. Victoria noticed her interest and reacted as a skilled saleswoman would. "Those things go well together; would you like to see them closer?" She took out the sandals and handed them to Em.

"Yes, I think these will do nicely," Em said. Maria saw the money and noted that Em had much more than what she would need to pay for the sandals. "Perhaps this bracelet would match, too?"

"Do I have enough for all that?" Em asked, handing the money to Maria.

"Just enough," Maria said, taking the coins from her. Victoria wrapped the items and placed them in a sack. "Here is some change," Victoria said. Maria's eyes squinted a bit as Emily put her hand out for the change, but she forced a smile when she noticed her mother staring at her harshly.

"Bye now. Do come again," Maria said with a false tone of sincerity.

"Oh, where is Pedro this morning?" Emily innocently inquired. Before Maria could say something unwarranted, Victoria replied. "He's off to the alcalde's field to practice for the ball games in two days."

"Ball games? Well, tell him I said hello, please." As she turned to leave, Em made a face at Maria, who returned a grimace back at her.

When Emily reached her father's office, she saw Rocio and Alejandro coming down the road with a sack of some kind.

"Hi, Rocio!" Emily said warmly.

"Hello, Miss Emily! I'd like you to meet my friend, Alejandro."

"Hello, Miss Emily," he said.

"Oh, you boys stop with that Miss stuff. Okay?"

"Well, sure then. What do you have there?" Rocio asked.

"I was going to ask you the same thing." They all giggled a bit.

"Well, we went to this ruins south of here to get water samples for your father," Rocio said.

"And we think we saw some kind of dinosaur in the bushes, too," Alejandro hastily added.

"Really?" Em said, wondering if they had seen Chaca.

"All we saw was a really big tail and bunches of bushes and trees getting shoved aside as the thing retreated."

Rocio thumped his friend on the chest and said, "Quit exaggerating. We don't even know what it was. It could have been a crocodile or something."

"More like or something," Alejandro retorted.

"Well, I did some shopping and bought some nice lady things," Em said.

Rocio looked at his friend, then Em, and said, "We have to get these to your father."

"Perhaps we can have lunch later?" Em asked.

"No time today, we are going over to the tlachtli practice soon. Bye."

The two boys went into the doctor's office, leaving her standing there outside.

"Here are those water samples we collected," Rocio reported.

Alejandro was "all eyes," looking around at the office.

"This used to be a storage room for coffee," he said aloud, not realizing that he was speaking his thoughts.

"Yes, it was, I am told," the doctor said. "Now show me on the map where you collected these samples," he said to Rocio. Alejandro was wandering about the place, touching things and was quite engrossed.

Rocio pointed to the areas he thought they had visited. The map was not very detailed. Dr. Scroggins made pencil notations on the points of interest and added numbers to them that corresponded with the numbers on the collection jars.

"Is there anything else you need from me today, Doctor?" Rocio asked.

"No, that will be all. You may go now. Thank you, boys. You've been a great help."

"Thank you, sir." We are heading over to the ball game practices now. Have you heard of it yet?"

"Yes, yes, I have. Alcalde Tejada has invited me to go along with his group."

"That is good. Sometimes foreigners don't fare so well at these games," Rocio said as he motioned for Alejandro to put down the book and leave with him.

The boys left his office and the doctor, who was already deep in thought, looked up from the map and wondered what Rocio meant by that.

Rocio said goodbye as he passed Emily on his way out.

"Father, what is this ball game everyone is talking about?" Em asked.

"Well, from what I've been told, it is a contest between two villages. The players try to put a heavy rubber ball through a hoop. Whichever team does that first wins," the doctor said.

"It sounds exciting. Can we go?" Em asked.

"As a matter of fact, we have been invited by the alcalde himself to join his group."

Emily began thinking about the many possibilities that lay before her.

"Father, I'd like to go watch them practice today. Do you mind?"

Dr. Scroggins was already looking into the microscope and studying. He looked up at Em and said, "Fine, fine, just be home way before dark so I do not have to worry about you."

Emily thanked her father, scooped up her packages, and headed over to the practice area. When she arrived, she was surprised. There were wagons being decorated. Jugs of drinks were accumulating under the ciebo trees in the courtyard. All kinds of cut flowers and palm leaves were being brought in and staged for decorating. Horses and mules were being washed and groomed. Toward the back of the property, Em could see the men gathering and running about.

Emily found her way closer to the field of practice. She was still fifty yards away but could recognize some of the men's faces. She saw Rocio and Alejandro, Hector, and Rolando, as well as other men and boys from the village, but she did not see Pedro. Then, some other men fitted with leather pads and headdresses went out to the practice area. Pedro was among this group. These men looked fierce, and they chanted loudly at times. She could see them passing a large ball around and doing various exercises and running drills.

She climbed up to sit on the fence railing, and one of the men spotted her. "Hey you! Get out of here!" he yelled.

Emily looked behind her to see who he was yelling at. "You, lady! No women allowed. Get lost!" Of course, all the men stopped what they were doing and turned to see what the commotion was about. Emily then realized she was the problem. Her face turned red, and she ran off for home, almost forgetting her packages.

It took her a while, but she made it back to her choza.

She sat down and ate an orange. Then, she got out her art paper and began a new drawing. It wasn't going well, so she paged through her other drawings and settled on the one with the dolls, finishing it with detail. She turned the picture over and wrote on the back: *To Juana, from Emily.* She rolled it up, tied the roll with a string, and took it to the outside stove shelter where she had placed the other gifts.

Emily then went out to the path and stuck a palm leaf in the fork with two points on it. Having done that, she hummed the song she had just learned and went around the jungle nearby looking for flowers to pick.

She had brought a small knife which came in handy when she spied some birds of paradise, an exotic blossom. She cut a few of those, as well as some geraniums, Mexican sage, senecio, and petunias.

She returned home, found two jars, and made two flower arrangements. She looked them over and decided they needed some greenery to hide the stems, so she walked out back and gathered some banana leaves and skirted the flowers with them.

About this time, Juana came along. She immediately saw the flower arrangements and said, "Those are so pretty. Why did you make two of them?"

Emily replied, "One is for you, and the other is for my father."

"How sweet," Juana said, bending over to smell them. "Thank you so much!" she went on, showing Emily her beautiful smile.

Emily slid her art pad over and began working on her new drawing. She was so excited and could barely wait for Juana to find her surprise.

"Oh, my! What is this?" Juana exclaimed.

"Oh, just a little something I got for you," Emily said. Juana tried to refuse the presents, but Emily insisted. Juana unwrapped the bigger package first and admired the sandals.

"They are so pretty," Juana said.

"There's more," Emily said, motioning toward the other packages.

Juana opened those too. She looked at Emily with tears in her eyes. "Why did you do all this?" Emily hadn't a reason. She just wanted to do it, but, fearing a wrong reply might offend Juana, she simply said, "I didn't know when your birthday was, so I chose today. I hope you don't mind."

Juana laughed and scooped Emily up into a loving hug and rocked her back and forth a bit. Then, after a short time they began the process of getting the evening meal ready.

When Dr. Scroggins arrived, the two women recounted the surprise to him.

"Dad, I gathered these flowers for you to thank you for taking such good care of me," Emily said. That evening was a joyous one. After dinner, Ezra took his hammock outside and smoked the remainder of his cigar. He listened to the birds chattering and wished for his Mary to be at his side. He missed her tremendously. While relaxing, he entered a dream-like state and remembered a happy time with his sweetheart Mary.

While they were courting, young Ezra was busy with his studies, while Mary had her obligations to the family farm. They both looked forward to Sundays when their schedules would be suspended long enough to go into Charleston for a church service in the morning, followed by some free time.

They had feigned formality when speaking to one another in town, especially on the church property. A scandal would result if they were to sit on the same pew during a worship service without having publicly proclaimed an engagement to be married. They could, however, sneak glances at one another amid the preacher's best efforts to deliver a heartfelt message.

One Sunday, as the congregation filed out, Ezra was one of the first to exit. He waited on the far edge of the lawn under one of the poplar trees for

Mary. She usually came with her parents, and after the service, she would ask to take a walk with her girlfriends and catch up with them later.

"Hello, Miss Mary," Ezra said, bursting with excitement.

"Why hello, Mister Ezra. Fancy meeting you here," she replied, batting her eyelashes and keeping the charade going a bit longer.

Ezra held out his bent elbow for her to take a hold of, and they headed to the park. They savored those precious hours, knowing they probably would not see one another again for seven days.

Spring was in the air. Trees were budding, birds were singing and gathering sticks and grass for their nests. Soon, they came to the pond where ducks were quacking and splashing as if they were putting on a show. Ezra let Mary's arm go and gently grasped her hand.

"Why don't we sit for a few minutes?" he suggested.

They sat on a nearby bench, enjoying the beautiful scenery. A perturbed heron squawked loudly and flapped its wings, slowly gaining altitude as it flew away.

"I just remembered. I brought a sandwich for us to share and a drink too," Mary said, opening her purse. Ezra watched her withdraw a folded napkin and a small whiskey flask. Mary was waiting for his reaction, and the look on his face was exactly what she had expected. She laughed, saying, "It's not what you think, you silly thing."

"What is it, then?"

"I made honey tea and had to use Papa's flask because it was the only container that would fit in my purse."

They had a good long laugh at that.

"Look, I made you liverwurst on rye."

"Mmm, my favorite," Ezra said reaching for a half. She slapped his hand reminding him, "Ladies first." It was all in good fun.

They sat there eating and sipping, from the same bottle, passing the time.

After lunch, they walked along the water's edge, knowing that their time together would soon be drawing to a close. They discussed their schedules for the coming week. Mary asked Ezra where he was going to be for Easter and said perhaps he could join her family if he didn't have plans.

They were so enthralled in conversation, they didn't realize they had gone around the entire pond, and it was time to head back into town. Stopping under a cherry tree, Ezra reached up and plucked a pink blossom for Mary. She sniffed it and twirled it in her fingers like a miniature parasol.

With that, Dr. Ezra Scroggins got out of his hammock and headed into the hut. He would return to his memories the next night.

* * * *

In the morning, Dr. Ezra went into town. He had spent a lot of mental energy, contemplating factors that could be contributing to the sicknesses in the area. When he was crossing the market square, which was relatively empty early in the day, he watched a group of about two dozen people proceed along the road. They were obviously grieving. A man pulled a homemade cart behind him at the front of the line of people. The cart was adorned with flowers and had lit candles attached to it. Then, Dr. Scroggins saw what they were carrying in the cart: a small human body wrapped in sackcloth. Dr. Scroggins removed his hat and bowed his head in reverence for the family.

After they had gone, presumably to the outskirts of the village to bury the child's remains, he hurried on to his office to look through his notes. He found the entry that he had noted a week earlier regarding that child's problems. His frustration mounted, and he paced back and forth, stopping often to look at the map on the wall or to flip through pages of notes. He stopped in front of the map again and began to visualize an informal pattern revealing itself to him for the first time. The dots on the map that had water samples that seemed contaminated began to line up in a zig zag pattern.

Dr. Scroggins took out a blank sheet of parchment paper and began drawing another map on it that was a close up of one of the quadrants of his wall map of the area. Then, he circled an area they had not visited yet—an area that had no reports of sickness. He weighed down the corners of the paper with four flat stones. As he was placing the last stone on a corner, the office door opened and in strolled Dr. Carlos.

"My friend!" Dr. Carlos exclaimed, "I have returned!" Carlos's enthusiasm quickly waned as he read his friend's face.

"Welcome home, Carlos!" Dr. Scroggins crossed the room, and the two men briefly embraced, patting one another on the back.

"I have gained the government's support from the city of Valladolid. All we have to do is submit a detailed report of our findings, along with the suggestions for a cure, and they will use their workers to spread the knowledge and help rid the area of this scourge."

"That is fantastic!" Dr. Scroggins replied. "It is good that you have made the proper contacts over the years you've spent practicing there."

"Yes, that's true, but have you found a solution to the riddle yet?" Carlos asked.

"I think so. Just this morning, I realized that this area seems to be worth investigating," he said, making a circular motion over the map with his pencil. "These numbers indicate water samples that we have collected."

"We?" Dr. Carlos asked.

"Yes, I have enlisted the help of a local boy to help me with the field research," Dr Scroggins said. Then, he pulled up a chair and began telling Dr. Carlos of all that had transpired during his absence.

It was late morning by the time the two doctors had reviewed the notes, slides, and maps. They were oblivious of the increased traffic on the road outside, as the buzz of the ball games was in full force. People moved about, readying themselves and the village for the march to the festival.

Rocio stopped by to see if his services were needed that day. Dr. Scroggins asked if he would accompany them over to the area circled on the map.

"Medico Ezra, that is a swamp full of biting insects and dangerous snakes and spiders," Rocio replied.

The men stared at one another, each waiting for the other to speak first.

Then, Rocio said, "I need to practice for the games today, but I can lead you to the trail that will take you to that area."

Dr. Carlos jumped up and said, "Young Rocio, you go enjoy the practice. I can find our way to this place. I seem to remember exploring in that vicinity as a youth."

Rocio was relieved. He did not want to let down his doctor friends, but he really wanted to go play with his friends. Ballgames were not held frequently in his village.

"Thank you, thank you," he said and fled out the door. Alejandro was waiting outside for him, and they took off running, not looking back.

The two doctors made plans to go to the field, each packing a sack with supplies. Then, they went to the market, which was bustling with activity, and bought some food that would sustain them during their field research. Dr. Scroggins stopped at Victoria's booth and spoke to her.

"The sandals and jewelry you sold Emily are quite beautiful," he said.

A bit surprised, Victoria replied, "Are they gifts for your spouse when you return home?"

Dr. Scroggins replied, "No, Emily gave them to our house servant, Juana, for her birthday."

Victoria showed her surprise at such lavish gifts, but she was also touched by what Emily had done for Juana.

"If you see my daughter today, will you give her this note?" he asked.

"Yes, of course. Is it very important?"

"Kind of. We are going to the jungle for research, and I want her to know in case we don't return tonight."

"Very well, I will see to it that she gets the note today, even if my son, Pedro, has to deliver it himself."

"You are too kind," Dr. Scroggins said with a smile.

After the doctors departed, Maria said, "Let me see that." Victoria handed her the note, but Maria was unable to read much of it because it was in English.

"That was a very nice thing the girl did for Juana," Victoria said. Maria just huffed in reply, wondering why her brother fancied Emily to begin with. "Perhaps she is a good person and I've misjudged her," Maria thought.

Chapter 12

Emily stayed around their choza for most of the morning. She had been noticing that other families had plants and flowers around their dwellings, so she decided to do the same for theirs. She got the shovel they used for cleaning the ashes out of the fireplace and looked around for things to dig up. Not too far away, she found some plants growing knee high, which looked like dark green tongues edged with yellow. She dug up about a dozen of them, brought them back to her hut, and planted them in a line across the front. She went back out and located some oregano plants. Em recognized them from watching Juana cook.

All the digging and planting was fun. She felt strong and healthier from the walking, running, and digging that she had recently been doing. She went to the fork tree and put a two-leaf palm in the right side. Then, she headed off into the jungle, but this time, she went toward Pedro's hut and followed that path down into the woods. Most of the people were in town busy with activity, so no one noticed her. Emily tried to imagine what Pedro would be thinking as she walked the trail that he had walked countless times.

That route had more hills than her usual pathway. Suddenly, Em heard snorting and plants rustling. A peccary with five piglets raced across the path not twenty feet in front of her, squealing and making lots of noise as they went. The last piglet saw Em out of the corner of its eye and whirled around staring at her. It charged Em, who was completely caught off guard, but, before she could even look for a tree to climb up into, the pint sized piglet stopped, snorted, and raced through the underbrush, following its siblings.

"Whew, that was a close call," Emily sighed, wiping some sweat from her brow. As she walked, Em saw gray squirrels racing through the canopy. They chirped at her furiously, twitching their bushy tails until she left their territory. Soon, Em happened upon a stone ruin. It resembled the others she had seen, but this one was the size of a gazebo. She thought she would take a rest in the cool shady interior. Em sat down with her back against a wall. As her eyes adjusted to the lack of light inside, she spied an opossum hiding on the far side in the dry leaves. It remained perfectly still like a statue. It looked cute and furry with round black ears tipped with white. She leaned her head back and shut her eyes for a moment and listened for any movement from the marsupial. She may have even dozed off for a minute or two. Feeling refreshed, and not wanting her body to stiffen up, Em got to her feet. That caused the creature to reveal its sinister looking teeth, which matched its awful hiss. Em promptly left, looking for signs of the path leading off in other directions less travelled.

Emily felt alive and free. Even the hooded oriole seemed to agree with her as it sang a melodious tune while it flitted from the top of one tree to another. She was looking up into the trees and noticed some small exotic pineapple-looking plants with red flowers called bromeliads. There were also frequent butterfly sightings. She saw an orange monarch, two brilliant metallic blue morpho butterflies, and a dark kite swallowtail, as well as others. Undoubtedly, the pretty yellow and orange lantana flowers lining the edges of the path were attracting the aerial beauties with their fragrant blossoms.

When Emily crested the next hill, the forest was less dense, and she felt as if she had been to that place before. It took her a few minutes to decipher the puzzle. Yes, she had been here the other day, but she had been travelling from the opposite direction. After going farther along the path, Emily saw the large ruins where Pedro had brought her after the giant snake attack. She made her way over to the structure and slowly circled the building, admiring its design. She wondered why nobody lived in it. She also wondered where all the people were who had obviously lived there long ago.

Emily was busy pondering, when all of a sudden a fast moving reddish blur vaulted past her, coming to a sliding stop. It was Chaca, and Pedro was on his back, riding him like a cowboy!

"Hola, amiga! Hello, Emily!" Pedro said as he dismounted the great lizard, sliding down its side and landing on his feet.

"I've never seen anything like that before, ever!" Emily said incredulously.

Pedro laughed knowing that his dramatic entrance would evoke such a response. Chaca watched the two youngsters for a minute before going over to a nearby papaya tree to eat some fruit.

"So, what have you been up to lately?" Em asked.

"We've been real busy practicing for the tlachtli games tomorrow. Are you coming?"

"Yes, Dad's been invited by the alcalde to go with his entourage."

"Wow, that's good! I hope to get some playing time on the ball court," Pedro said.

"Are you good?" she asked.

"Pretty good. I've been playing since I was twelve years old. I don't have a lot of time today because of all the packing and stuff. What do you want to do?" Pedro asked Em.

"Well, we never got to go swimming," Em said.

"That's a great idea, Chaca!" Pedro called out. The lizard shuffled over to them, still chewing the fruits with juice and pulp running out the edges of his mouth.

"Chaca, will you take us to the ocean beach near Muyil?"

Chaca lowered his head and raised his front leg up so that Pedro could climb aboard. Pedro leapt up like an acrobat and reached his hand down for Emily to grasp. Pedro swung her up onto Chaca's back just behind him.

"Hold on!" Pedro said. Then, he undid a rope he had wrapped around his waist and slung one end of it under Chaca's neck and grabbed it with his other hand.

"Ffff!" Pedro said, causing the lizard to move ahead. Chaca knew the way to that beach area because he had spent a fair amount of time around the isolated ruins nearby. Chaca would speed up or slow down as needed. Along the way, tree branches and leaves would swat the riders. One time, a large banana spider landed on Pedro's face. He was able to grab and sling it off before the arachnid had time to bite him. Nevertheless, it was unnerving, and Emily almost fell off from his contortions.

They passed through a marshy area, splashing their way as they went. A tapir was disturbed by their sudden presence and galloped away, making funny faces with its trunk-like nose. They smelled the salt water in the air now. Chaca slowed way down, as there were at times, humans around fishing or combing the shoreline for seashells. He stopped close to where the jungle met the sandy beach. He flicked his long pink forked tongue several times, tasting the air. Satisfied that they were alone, Chaca dropped his head down and Emily and Pedro took turns sliding off his back. Pedro kept his eyes on the beach as they stalked a bit closer. Emily stood next to the magnificent lizard and whispered, "Thank you," to him, rubbing the side of his still panting neck.

The three trotted across the sand and went into the turquoise waters. Em and Pedro took off some of their clothes and sandals as they went. The sky was clear and the waves gently broke on the white sands. There were crabs scurrying about, and seaweed was strewn across the beach.

"Stay away from those things," Pedro said, pointing to a clear gelatinous glob.

"What is it?" Em inquired.

"It is a stinger," he replied. "It will burn you like fire if it touches you."

"Ew, it's gross!" Emily said.

"They show up during the storms. It must've washed up the other night."

"Look! A turtle!" Em exclaimed, looking out into the sea.

"That's a big one," Pedro said.

"Let's go to it," Em suggested, wading out into the surf.

Pedro glanced over at Chaca who turned to watch Em when she began splashing in the water. Pedro followed Em.

"Do you see that line of waves out there?"

"Yes, I do," Em replied.

"Don't go past them because the coral ends and the deep ocean starts."

Em looked out and saw the color of the water was several shades darker. They were up to their chests in the water, a long way from shore. Pedro dove under the water and swam holding his breath. Emily copied him. Their eyes were open, and they were seeing beautifully colored fish. Some were in pairs and others in schools. There was a fat looking parrotfish that was chomping at the coral and releasing sand from its port near the tail. They had forgotten about the turtle when it swam past them, stopping to pluck sponges off the rocks. It had a dark green shell and was the size of a rowboat, but much wider. The turtle turned to look at them but swam on.

Emily and Pedro would come up for air and talk about what they were seeing. She dove back under and picked up a starfish to show Pedro. Its hundreds of sticky little feet stuck to her hand. Then, she reached for a conch shell. Pedro yelled underwater at her, bubbles boiling out of his mouth, as he waved his hands, "No-o-o-o!"

Emily was startled by his reaction and stopped just inches before she grasped the conch. Pedro surfaced and explained to her that the shell's animal had a spear that it would shoot in self defense. Anyone stung by one would die after much pain and suffering.

While they were talking and bobbing on the surface, they heard a loud splash. It was Chaca smashing his powerful tail into the water. Pedro turned to look at what Chaca's head was pointed toward and saw a silver triangle-shaped fin coming in their direction. Emily's eyes widened in horror, as she gauged how far the shark was from them. They began swimming for the shore, knowing they couldn't reach it in time. Pedro climbed up on a cauliflower coral and helped Emily up. They watched from their precarious perch, just two feet above the surface of the water, as the shark patrolled the reef for a meal. Eventually, it thrashed about, and blood spread across the water. Some unfortunate fish had lost its life.

Emily and Pedro slipped back into the water and raced for the shore. They fell onto the wet sand and laughed off their excitement and nervous energy.

"Thanks, Chaca! You saved us!" Emily said.

"He doesn't like ocean water," Pedro said. "Hey, there's a lagoon around the point over there. Let's go to it and rest for a while."

"Okay," Emily said. Gathering their clothes, they all strode over to the point where a small cove was nestled. Several coconut palms leaned out over the sand making shady benches. They sat down across from one another, and Chaca curled up at the tree line in the shade. The rhythmic splashing on the shore, combined with the swaying of the trees, lulled them to sleep.

"Ouch!" Emily said, shaking a crab's claw off her toe.

Pedro rose up to see what the commotion was. "Girls," he laughed. The wind shifted after a while which meant the onset of evening. Chaca was the first to notice, lifting his head and smelling the air. Suddenly, he jumped to his feet and ran across the cove. They saw an armadillo waddling along the beach. Chaca snatched it up and ate it with an awful crunching sound.

"Lizard tacos," Pedro said as if not concerned. Emily gagged at the thought of having such a meal. Chaca returned, quite pleased with himself, and rolled Pedro off his resting place.

"Hey, what was that for?" Pedro complained. Chaca didn't answer but did lower his head. Emily understood what he wanted and ran up his snout onto the great lizard's back. Pedro's mouth fell open as he looked over to his friend as if to say, "She did not just run up your face!" Chaca didn't mind though.

He enjoyed Emily's antics.

Pedro climbed up the dignified way, using Chaca's bent leg as a step. He again tossed the rope under his neck and off they went, disappearing into the jungle's wall of foliage. They saw a flock of scarlet macaws fly overhead, during the return trip. The gregarious birds sounded like loud crumpled horns, as they announced themselves to the forest. They were, however, a beautiful sight, having a multicolored bodies with white faces, red heads, yellow shoulders, blue wings, long flowing red and blue tail feathers.

The only noteworthy action was when Chaca jumped over a large fallen tree trunk, dislodging Emily, causing her to slide down his back. She stopped at the base of his tail.

Pedro guided Chaca to the fork where he and Emily usually parted.

"Do you think he can take us farther up the path toward your choza? I'm tired," Emily said, hugging Pedro a bit tighter and pressing closer to him.

Pedro's ears perked at the mere idea of someone seeing his beloved lizard. He was also thinking of the taunting he would have to endure, if he were seen in the village with Emily.

He really liked having the young lady holding him for protection, but he could not selfishly ask Chaca to risk revealing himself. Pedro decided to leave it up to Chaca.

"Do you want to go home or go farther today?" Chaca continued for another mile or so, lying down at the base of the last large hill that separated the woods from the village's outskirts.

"So long, my friend," Pedro said to the lizard, as he rubbed his scaly snout.

Emily also thanked him, but as he crept away, she ran her fingernails down the lizard's rough body, causing him to quiver. He swooshed his tail a bit, making Emily jump over it. Although the scratching felt good, Chaca did not want Em to be so familiar with him.

Pedro was deep in thought trying to come up with an explanation as to why he was walking out of the jungle with Emily. He knew they'd have only a few minutes before a relative or neighbor would spot them. Pedro stopped Emily and told her, "We have to think of an excuse as to why we are coming out of the woods together."

Emily had not been thinking about their excursion from that perspective. She replied, "Oh yes, I see what you mean." Pedro continued to think of a variety of excuses or reasons, play acting the conversation he would later have with his parents later. They had been gone all day, and he didn't know what time he was actually missed by his family. Frustrated, Pedro said to Emily, "We just have to tell them the truth."

"The truth?" Emily blurted out shocked.

"Yes, the truth is always best. I'll say that I was out running on the trails for exercise when I happened up on you, and you had gotten lost while you were exploring."

"That's it? And why do I have to be lost?" Em replied.

"Because I am escorting you out of the woods from an area that is not very close to your family's hut, silly," he said in a triumphant manner. "Besides, I'm not sure if my family is ready for us to become close friends."

"Oh, I get it," Em said.

"Just leave anything about Chaca out of the story!" Pedro chided.

They paused at the edge of the clearing and steeled themselves for the unknown. Pedro was thinking that fibbing to his family was as dangerous as the shark episode earlier. They passed by several huts and milpas as they went, not seeing a soul. Pedro's hut was just ahead of them. He relaxed as they approached its entrance. He said, "Wait here for a moment," as he went into his hut.

"Pedro! Good, you're home. I was getting worried about you," his mother said.

Pedro just stood there for a prolonged moment. Victoria sensed something was amiss. She looked around the corner of the choza and saw Emily nervously standing there. Realizing that the two were together, Victoria handed Pedro the note and said, "Medico Ezra requested you give this note to his daughter." Avoiding the usage of Emily's name, Pedro switched the paper from one hand to the other and held his arm out and said, "Here, it's for you." He wondered what terrible consequence his mother would think of for him. He even imagined for a moment that he would not be permitted to participate in the games the next day and felt his world caving in around him—all because of a girl!

Emily took the note and read it. "My father's in the field collecting more samples, and may not return tonight," she reported to them.

Victoria said, "You should stay with us then so that you are fed and not alone." Pedro's heart sank, dreading how he would deflect an entire evening's questioning about Emily from his family.

"That's all right," Emily began, "Juana will be there to look after me."

"Yes, I will walk her to her hut," Pedro valiantly offered.

Victoria studied her son carefully and was pleased. She said, "That will be fine, but don't delay, because your father will be home soon, and we have more chores to do."

"Yes, Na." Pedro said, motioning for Emily to follow him.

Victoria wondered what other surprises lay in store for her family. Just then, Maria came out from behind their cooking shelter with an armload of kindling. She saw her brother leaving with "that girl." Her mouth dropped open as the fire wood tumbled out of her grasp, and she said, "What'd I miss?"

The two walked with purpose, but not hurriedly as to arouse suspicion.

"That was close!" Pedro sighed heavily, wiping his brow.

"You handled it very well," Emily remarked, smiling at him.

Pedro felt like a wet, wrung out cleaning towel. He was so ready to put the day behind him. They came to the fork tree.

"I can see myself home from here," Emily announced.

"Are you sure? I promised Na."

Emily interrupted him and said, "I had the grandest time today. Goodnight." Then she stepped forward and kissed Pedro on the cheek.

Pedro was stunned. Emily spun on her heel and skipped toward home, calling back over her shoulder, "I'll see you tomorrow. Good luck!"

Pedro stood at the base of the signal tree that had meant absolutely nothing to him his entire life, but now seemed to control his movements. He felt like a fish out of water enduring all these new situations. Alas, he was a happy fish, though. He turned and headed back home, holding one hand on his cheek.

Emily skipped on home where Juana was relaxing. Emily showed her the note. Then, she asked Juana many questions about Mayan boys and about the ball games the next day. They talked for a long time before settling in for the night.

Like many families in the region, Pedro's parents grew a plot of food to teach their children the basics of gardening, as well as the benefits of doing

chores on a daily basis. As the seasons passed, the level of responsibility increased, along with Pedro and his sister Maria's size and abilities.

This past season, they had ample rain, and under their father's guidance, the milpa produced an abundance of squash, corn, tomatoes, beans, and peppers. They did not relish the pulling of weeds or loosening the soil, but when it came time to pick the produce, spending time there was more enjoyable.

Once the crops were in, Pedro's father had his son train with some of the village's men who were fishermen by trade. This way, the boys were taught to provide for themselves and eventually, when grown, their families. As a matter of fact, Andres had already been teaching the fishermen's children for years. This benefited the whole village and strengthened relationships as well.

Pedro would accompany his mother and sister to their market booth where he would meet other boys in his age group. Omar, who was a senior fisherman, would accompany them down to the shore where they learned to catch bait, mend nets, bait hooks, and surf fish.

Two or three of the boys would be permitted to board a boat for the day based on their ability and an informal rotation so that all the lads would eventually have the experience. When Pedro got to go on a boat, he was quick to learn what was expected of him. He fell into the rhythm of the fishing life so well, he usually did not need reminding to fetch a net or bait a hook. Occasionally, a line would get snagged on the corals below. The men would curse in frustration when this happened because their line would snap or have to be cut.

One day, when the hook was taken by a fish, but entangled in the coral, Pedro leapt overboard, much to the dismay of his guardians, and dove down twenty feet untangling the line and bringing the fish back up to the boat. Omar was amazed, a bit angry, but more joyous with the impromptu success and initiative Pedro had shown.

His popularity rose greatly among his peers, but Pedro dismissed their congratulations in favor of the excitement of the adventure.

One day, Omar brought several of the boys to a large inland cenote. It was a collecting pool full of rain that had fallen in the area and rarely, if ever, completely dried up. A different fishing tactic was used here than in the ocean. Omar showed the boys how to walk through the reeds on the shallow swampy end collecting grasshoppers and insects from the reeds and grass stalks. He would then show them how to bait the line with live bait and wait silently on the shore, hidden for long periods of time, until the wary fish below would be tricked into believing the people had gone and only a tasty meal remained. Most of the others had difficulty being still for any length of time, but Pedro had a calmness about him that came naturally. That, and his keen eye and reflexes, usually were rewarded with a catch.

As time passed, and Pedro's love of the jungle increased, he ventured farther more frequently into the woods behind his home under the relaxed supervision of his father. Andres and Pedro would go on hikes along the animal trails, where his father would instruct him about all the things a lover of nature would need to know. Pedro learned how to walk with stealth like the jaguar and to use his eyes to methodically scan the forest leaves for movement or color changes. He learned how to recognize many of the sounds, often by painstakingly tracking the source of the buzz or click until he observed the animal creating the sound.

Pedro was not a slave to time. He woke when he was rested, slept when tired, ate when hungry, and the rest was not of much importance to him, including chores. By the time he was ten years of age, it was not uncommon for him to be gone in the jungle for half the day after accompanying his Dad to the farm in the morning. Andres did not mind because he had plenty of farmhands. He also rather enjoyed Pedro's tales of discovery as they returned to their home for the evening meal.

Andres recognized that his own childhood friends, now grown, were bent over from years of working too hard, and their hands were gnarled and scarred from the abuse they had taken. Even he was a bit achy, although he had a lighter workload than most. Andres wanted something better for his son. He hoped that the freedom he permitted, along with Pedro's natural abilities, would somehow come together for a purpose that would benefit the lad— and the village, too.

In Pedro's immature mind, he thought of himself as being "crafty." He would go to the far end of the field, tossing away a stone or two from the soil, pretending he was tending to the crops; then, he would crouch down out of sight and slip through the wall of forest leaves bordering the field. Of course, the men noticed his absence day after day, but said nothing to him, only occasionally jesting to his father about it. More often than not, there were other eyes and ears noticing him crunching the forest floor and moving through the growth. Most perceived Pedro as a predator, others as competition, and all as an intruder, except for one.

This one exception had outgrown all others in this primeval forest in both size and wisdom, having lived far beyond a normal lifespan. He was so old that trees had sprouted, grown to maturity, died, and rotted, during his reign. He was so large that a person could walk five paces to his one making it very difficult to easily see a pattern of his footprints. This animal would use its tail at times to disguise the ground where it had been.

Pedro's stalker enjoyed trailing the boy, watching his antics, and noticing how he never hurt any of the forest dwellers, even though he would capture them or try to. At times, Pedro felt as if something were watching him. He would stare into the thick foliage, perceiving yellow eyes staring back at him, which could mean certain death.

One day, soon after the fishing lesson at the watering hole, Pedro decided he would go back and catch some fish for his family. The weather was sunny and there was a refreshing breeze blowing. When he reached the marsh, his ears were assaulted by the sounds of the long blades of grass rubbing against one another and the ever present clicking noise from the insects' legs sending out messages like Morse Code.

He made his way through the reeds, collecting a dozen or so of the jumping, crawling hoppers and stuffing them into a sack. Then, Pedro went to the edge of the pond and tied off a long string to an overhanging tree branch. He went back into the shade to wait for a bite.

He watched as the insect struggled on the water's surface causing it to ripple. Nothing happened. Again, the insect attempted escape causing a small commotion. This time, he heard a sucking sound as the hopper disappeared below the surface and the line went taut. Pedro waited for just the right moment, and then, with one long gentle, but steady heave, he pulled the fish from the shallows onto the shore. Pedro removed the line from it and ran a stick through it, catching it through the mouth over the outside of its gill. He put it back in the water twenty paces away where it could breathe but not escape.

Over the next hour and a half, this sequence occurred four more times.

Pedro thought he had enough fish to feed his family, but it was too early in the day to return because everyone was still working. He decided to stay longer and try to catch more fish for the village shaman and a neighbor or two. He sat down and hummed a tune to himself, shading his eyes with his hands, thinking of how he could mimic the hoppers' noise somehow to attract birds. He was daydreaming of being a quetzal bird, zooming around in the air, spying the ground with super keen eyes for delicious bugs to eat.

What he did not realize is that he has been the focus of a crocodile that was only forty feet behind him. Guarding her nest of eggs near the edge of the jungle, the twelve- foot Morelet's croc moved slowly at first, sliding along on her belly. Thirty feet, twenty feet . . . Then, she rose off the ground like a dog and began running. The rasping sound of the reeds turned to crunching. Pedro knew it was too late to turn his head to look! He planted his right foot into the soft ground and pushed as hard as he could, leaping to his right in an arc, rolling across the ground a full eight feet away. The move startled the crocodile, but she was determined.

The croc turned quickly and opened her horrific jaws and hissed a sound that could cause a person to faint. Pedro's mind raced and sweat poured from his brow. He was shaking badly. He knew he had to make a run for it and get into the trees. It was too far. The dragon-like creature surely would catch him, but he had to try. He said to himself, "On three. One . . . two . . . three!"

He took off like a cat with all the quickness he could muster. The crocodile turned to pursue him, slashing her tail through the reeds. In one second, she had closed half the distance between herself and her two-legged prey. One more second is all she would need to crunch his soft flesh in her pulverizing jaws. The croc leapt forward with her gaping jaws ready to attack.

Pedro knew that he was out of time. Even though the distance to the trees was only a few paces away, he did not have that luxury. If only he could fly like the quetzal bird! His eyes trained on the branches in front, and his ears focused on the croc behind. Pedro sensed something moving across the reeds behind him like a horse. He heard a loud thud accompanied by hissing and scrapping and thrashing. He leapt for the trees and clambered as high as he could and crouched there like a monkey, trembling.

Pedro stared in disbelief. He was looking at a monstrous lizard, so large that the crocodile appeared to be the size of a hatchling in comparison to it!

"Quetzalcoatl!" Pedro gasped.

The lizard slipped its tail under the crocodile's belly and flung it through the air out into the pond where it landed with a big splash on the far side. The croc surfaced a moment later, swimming in a tight circle getting her bearings before submerging and staying out of sight. Satisfied the crocodile had been dispatched, the lizard turned its attention to the boy.

Pedro was beside himself watching the two titans battle. He has seen prey become the hunted before like when a frog that is eating an insect gets eaten by a snake; but why would this behemoth discard its meal like that? Even worse, now the horrid creature turned its gaze upon him and was flicking its tongue right at him.

Pedro's heart sank as the giant lizard casually came straight toward him. He looked around for somewhere to go, or hide, or something to defend himself with. The situation was hopeless. He would have to accept whatever came next. The monster came halfway to him and then lay down looking at Pedro. It bobbed its head up and down a few times and waited. Pedro was feeling numb. His mind was overloaded. He felt his arms and legs shaking. The tree branches were too thin to support his weight. He climbed down a few feet to the thicker secondary branches.

The lizard took this as a positive sign and nodded his head again several times. Pedro was beginning to think that if the creature were going to eat him, it already would have, so taking a risk, he nodded his head back. The lizard stood up, which sent Pedro scrambling back up toward the twigs. The lizard lay back down and waited. More head bobbing. Finally, it lay its head down on the ground between its front feet. Pedro had seen dogs and cats do this before. He decided to try and talk to the creature.

"What do you want?" he said calmly.

The lizard cocked its head sideways a bit and began to get up but caught itself and remained on the reeds in a prone position. Pedro was encouraged by its response; he was beginning to think that he might survive the encounter. Growing a bit bolder, Pedro began thinking that the lizard might be a god since it had obviously saved him. He decided to offer an exchange or a deal.

Pedro said while pointing at his catch, "I have several tasty fish over there, which I will gladly give you in exchange for my life," Pedro said in his best businessman's tone of voice.

Pedro waited for an answer of sorts.

"Well?" he demanded.

With that, the lizard stood up. Pedro's face drained of its color as the tall animal strode over to his tree and stretched its neck out long enough to bump Pedro's butt off of his perch and onto the top of the reptile head. Then, it raised its nose up toward the sky, and Pedro slid down its neck until his feet caught against its shoulders and legs. He was facing backward toward its tail. It strolled over to where the fish were hidden in the water on the broken branch and lay down again, turning its head toward the boy and looking him in the eye.

Pedro and the lizard stayed there eye to eye for perhaps a minute. Each had a lot to lose; both had to trust as never before. Pedro kicked his leg over the back and slid off and looked around for the crocodile. Not seeing it, he got the fish and moved inland a bit. Pedro got them off the stick, lined them up on the ground, and stood back. The lizard flicked its tongue over them and clicked its teeth excitedly.

It reached down and slurped up three of the five fish, crunching them like roasted nuts in a most enjoyable manner. Pedro waited for it to finish them off. He even thought about attempting to slink away while the reptile was distracted.

"Are you going to finish them?" Pedro politely asked.

The lizard sat down on its back haunches licking its mouth. Pedro cocked his head a bit and mirrored him. He was realizing that that animal had chosen to save him for some unknown reason and was befriending him, too. But to what degree? Would he be pounced upon like a cat does a mouse when tired of it? There was no way to be sure.

Pedro pushed the fish toward the lizard with his feet, knowing that a goliath such as it could eat a hundred fish if it wanted to do so. It just nosed the fish back to where Pedro was standing, and then, it did the oddest thing. The creature took its big head and nuzzled it into Pedro's belly, rubbing up and down a bit while emitting a rumbling, purring sound. Then, it sat again and blinked at the boy, waiting for him to make the next move.

"Well, if you don't want these fish, I'm bringing them home to my family." Pedro put them on the stick and began walking away. His heart beat faster

177

and faster the farther away he went.

"I'm leaving now," he said over his shoulder. There was no response, no hiss, nothing. As Pedro was about to make the first turn into the jungle, he looked back to the reeds, but the giant lizard had vanished.

When Pedro returned to his father's fields, he found him resting in the shade of a seibo tree. Together, they went home to prepare the fish for dinner as Pedro told his father as much of the fantastic tale as he could remember. Andres could not recall having chuckled inwardly so many times during their homeward walk before, but he was impressed with his son's vivid imagination and his ability to catch fish.

* * * * *

Doctors Carlos and Ezra set in a westerly heading. There seemed to be a pattern developing of water holes that tested positive for microorganisms, which were consistent with some of the illnesses and deaths in the region.

The men had easy going at first, but after the first few hours, the terrain had become marshy and flying insects and ticks became numerous. Large shade trees gave way to smaller thorny trees and large plants. Vines hung in the grotesquely shaped trees, creating an exhausting tangle of impediments.

The path long ago had given way to narrow animal trails only a foot wide. They were constantly smacking their faces, necks, and wrists, and brushing off voracious ticks that could crawl up their clothing at an alarming rate. The men had to pause frequently to check one another for the parasites, as if they were monkeys grooming one another.

The plague of insects was so profound that they lost focus at times and dropped their guard. They also had to be wary of serpents and crocodiles, which undoubtedly shared the terrain. More than once, they saw a snake's tail slither into the dense underbrush. There were also many small lizards scattered about. Frogs, whose shadows could be seen on translucent leaves, hopped away when disturbed.

The misery tested their resolve, but years of training and discipline kept the men on task. Dr. Carlos filled several jars with water from several water holes. Dr. Scroggins made detailed sketches of the cenotes' proximity, size, and distinguishing landmarks if any, matching the numbers on the jars to the locations.

They had a near miss when Dr. Carlos had his hand submerged in the muddy water and an animal struck at him from beneath the surface. Almost dropping the jar, Dr. Carlos watched as a sizeable snapping turtle maneuvered below.

As the afternoon gave way to evening, the men realized they were not going to be able to return to Tulum before nightfall. Having misgauged their position, they found themselves on the northwestern side of a very wide water hole. They decided to press due north and hope to intersect a well-travelled road. This plan greatly lifted Dr. Scroggins's spirits, as he was not looking forward to a night in the jungle swamp.

Although the jars weighed only two or three pounds in total, they felt like twenty or thirty pounds to the fatigued men. They stopped for a rest when they exited the marsh, coming across a fallen tree under some shade. A light breeze would waft through periodically as they rested and ate the last of their food.

"Do you think we will find a place to stay before dark?" Dr. Scroggins asked.

"Well, the main road is not too far ahead of us. We should just get to it around dusk, and perhaps a family can put us up for the night," Dr. Carlos replied.

"I hope so. I feel as if I have stones tied to my feet after all of that sloshing around in the mud."

"I know well how you feel, my friend. Your efforts have been valiant thus far. Let us get on our feet and complete the task." The pep talk worked. Dr. Scroggins struggled to an upright position, and off they went, hoping for the best.

They reached the main road before twilight. Surprisingly, there were many travellers with carts and mules either moving along or in some stage of setting up a roadside camp for the night. One such family even offered the men a meal and hammock, having recognized Dr. Carlos from their village.

Dr. Carlos accepted two tortillas from them and said, "Let's press on. I believe there is an outpost ahead where we can have a roof over our head." They did just that, arriving there as the sun slipped into darkness. There were a couple of other travellers there who had a small fire going.

The doctors found a wide bench and flopped onto it, sitting upright just long enough to eat their sparse meal and sip some xtabentún, which the men offered to share. It was not long before the doctors found rest and then peaceful sleep, while the other travellers laughed and sang songs into the night.

In the morning, Emily and Juana were sleeping in a bit. Juana did not have to do her daily walk to Em's hut, and Em was stiff and sore from the previous day's ride. The ladies moseyed around, stirring the coals, and getting a morning drink of cocoa and chilies heated up. There were a few corn cakes left over from the previous night that went well with their lazy breakfast.

They noticed more activity than usual around them in the woods and village.

"Oh! Today we have to go to the next village for that ball game!" Em exclaimed.

"I am too old for such a walk," Juana replied, clearing the table.

"No, Juana, you must come along. We have been invited to ride along on the alcalde's wagons."

"Really?" Juana replied a bit surprised.

"Yes, Father told me yesterday, and he is not here today to be with me. Won't you come?" Em pleaded.

Juana agreed, and they made their way to the market for a few fruits to eat while on the road, before heading to the alcalde's residence.

There were already many carts and a few wagons on the roadway heading toward Coba. People were joyous, shaking maracas and playing flutes. Children were running about, playing with anything round like coconuts and oranges, pretending to be tlachtli players.

Emily was surprised by the number of people, wagons, horses, and ponies. She sought out Tejada, who assigned them their seats on a wagon, after he had inquired as to the whereabouts of Dr. Scroggins.

Soon, a loud deep belltone rang out, and the procession began the long trek to the opposing city to play the tlachtli ball game.

The players themselves went ahead of all the other villagers. Emily recognized several of them including Shaman Octavio, Hector, Rolando, Rocio, Alejandro, and yes, Pedro, among others. The players' families would cheer and chant when their particular son or spouse passed by, encouraging the men greatly.

Finally, Em's wagon, which was full of people and supplies, lurched forward to depart. Juana smiled broadly. It had been a long time since she had known this type of involvement and excitement with family.

Very soon, their wagon passed Victoria and Maria's cart, which was mule-led. Emily waved to them. Victoria waved back, mainly at Juana, whose radiance could be noticed. Victoria's parents had once been friends with Juana and her spouse, but things changed after Juana's husband, Uriel, died. He was bitten by a rattlesnake while working their milpa. The convoy moved at a steady pace. After a couple of hours, they went by the shelter where the doctors had slept.

"Emily!" Dr. Scroggins shouted. He was keeping a lookout for them. He and Dr. Carlos jumped into the back of the wagon. They looked a mess, despite efforts to get cleaned up in the morning. The reunion was a happy one. They all shared their adventures with each other and the other listening ears too, but Emily left out the Pedro and Chaca parts.

When they arrived at the entrance to the other town, there was a formal greeting. The alcalde and his men, along with Tulum's tlachtli men, were greeted by Coba's politicians and prominent people of status; all were wearing their finest outfits. The reception was brief but nice. Coba's leaders obviously knew Tulum's people were in need of food and rest, so they invited them to proceed to the great field next to the ball courts to make camp. Coba also had jugs of fresh water, firewood, fruits, and nuts there for their guests.

The two doctors were afforded a place to bathe, and someone offered to wash their clothes. Before sundown, Coba put on a show with musicians and dancers for entertainment. The activity ended early that night, so the visitors could rest. The next day promised to be full of excitement!

Fog shrouded the great field at dawn. This was not entirely unusual. Clouds often settled on open areas when the ground was a bit cooler than the air. Carlos was the first to stir in the Scroggins camp. He smelled the air that was heavy with smoldering smoke from the campfires at their temporary quarters. He stretched, and his back made a few popping sounds as he raised his strong arms over his head and flexed his muscles. Dr. Carlos could have easily been in the player's compound, but he sacrificed his natural talent for a higher cause—that of medical knowledge for the betterment of society.

Emily woke next and gazed on her father's slumbering face next to her. Dr. Carlos smiled at her and set out for a walk, and Juana remained in a peaceful slumber a while longer.

Emily went over to the food wagon. She was not the first female there. A few others also heeded the morning's call. Emily silently fell into place, assisting the others as they stoked embers and prepared a morning drink. She handed out several cups of the liquid before taking one for herself. Emily leaned against a wagon wheel, relishing her hot drink. Her thoughts turned to Pedro, as well as to her father. She got up and found another vessel and poured in some of the confection.

Emily squatted next to her father and held the steaming drink close to his nose. His nostrils began to quiver. She had to stifle a laugh. Dr. Scroggins wiped his face with his hand and brushed back his hair. Emily noticed for the first time the man that he was, as opposed to the father figure he had always been. He seemed vulnerable, yet strong. She noticed the wrinkles at the corners of his eyes and was profoundly proud of him in that moment. She nudged his shoulder and said, "Dad, I have your morning drink."

He lay there and yawned a great big yawn, stretching his arms and legs, and completing the wake-up process with a *Brrrrb* exhale. Dr. Scroggins propped himself up on an elbow and took the warm cup from Emily. His blue eyes met hers and showed appreciation without words. He pursed his lips and sipped from the cup. For Dr. Scroggins, it was like nectar. To Emily, it was healing and satisfying that she was able to provide a small thing for her father in this foreign and exotic land.

At the first sign of the sunrise, the fog lifted a bit and began to disperse from the great field. Two drums began to beat in unison, somewhat softly, but noticeable nevertheless. Then, from one end zone, a group of men appeared. They were the Coba players. They did not have their equipment on as of yet, but they were in two rows. They clapped their hands and chanted a prayer to the sun for her favor as they progressed up the field toward the ball court.

After they had passed, the Tulum people answered with a tune that their own home players knew well. The Tulum men rushed forth from their family areas and met amidst the rising fog. They gathered themselves under the guidance of Shaman Octavio and formed a circle in the center of the great field.

The shaman had a deerskin drum which he began to beat slowly, several times a minute. The drum was also ringed with small bells. Don Octavio gave it a few good shakes and began the steps of their villages dance. The dance was not designed to intimidate other villages but to show their competition how united and disciplined they were.

Hundreds of visitors heard the call, as their youth silently assembled on the manicured lawn of the great field. The most experienced men were already there when the younger ones arrived. Within five minutes, the three lines were moving in unison, forward and backward, as the tone of the drum dictated.

As the fog lifted, the visitors were able to see and appreciate their men's skills. They moved forward and chanted, "Ha!" Then, they took several steps back and yelled, "Ho!" This was repeated several times. The players went through their morning exercise and assembled on the eastern side of the court, while their families prepared their equipment and medical salves. Few participants were able to withstand the rigors of the highly competitive game unscathed.

Coba's officials rang a bell at the tenth hour. This was the prearranged signal that the two villages were to assemble on their respective sides of the ball court. Within the hour, all the people of both the home and visiting teams were gathered. They waved colorful banners, chanted, and played instruments. They could barely wait for the contest to begin.

From the western side of the court, the Coba players trotted out and formed a large circle. They clapped their hands and slapped them against their thick leather pads. Some of the players also wore arm bands above the elbows that had colorful parrot feathers attached to them, featuring brilliant blue and yellow designs.

The Tulum players formed three rows. They bowed down, then stood erect, and bowed again, repeating the movements as they entered, chanting "Ha! Ho!" These men also had leather armbands, but their identifying colors were displayed with red and green parrot feathers. It was a tradition that the teams kept several mascot parrots or macaws which were highly valued and well taken care of. It is from these mascots that the plumes were obtained, as they molted or shed their feathers.

The respective sides cheered wildly for their teams. Having done their introductions, the starting team stayed on the ball court as the alternate players withdrew to the bottom of the stands, out of the field of play.

Everyone was ready. The place went silent for a moment before the ball was put into play, as was the custom.

Coba launched the ball into the air to begin the contest. A teammate thrust his waist forward sending the ball, which was about the size of a basketball, but much heavier, into the air. The ball had to cross the midline with each player's contact, or the opposition would score a point. The rubber ball, which weighed six pounds, could also hit either the stone side wall that was part of the field or be struck and returned to the opposition. The wall was built at a thirty-three degree angle. The men had a difficult time anticipating where the ball would go. They held their positions and smacked their armbands with enthusiasm.

The contest was evenly matched. Despite their uniforms, skills, and supporting chants from the onlookers, success in the game of tlachtli was very difficult. The players were not allowed to kick the ball or strike it with their hands. A game would be won when eight points were accumulated or when a team managed to actually send the ball through one of two carved rings at the top of the stone side walls.

An hour passed with only three points scored. The ball went over the end line on Tulum's end, so Coba was awarded a point. Tulum came back with two points when they struck one of the six stone markers that were on top of the stone walls.

"That was an amazing strike," Rocio said, after Hector directed a skillful shot at the marker. Hector backpedaled to his defensive position, appreciating the acknowledgement.

Each team had to obey the rule of each man striking the ball when it was his turn, or they'd lose a point. So, the teams had to constantly rotate their players to be in position to return the ball. Coba scored two more points when they struck the round hoop, although the ball did not pass through. Coba was ahead three to two.

The onlooker's energy hardly waned. They would periodically take up chanting or shaking their maracas and waving banners. The substitute players would look up into the stands and hope that their time would come to be on the court.

Two Tulum players had been injured. One wrenched his ankle, and the other had sacrificed his body, slamming it into the stone wall. Their bruises and sprains would heal, but both had to be replaced in the game. That's when Rolando and Pedro were called onto the field. They were absolutely ready to play.

Martin set the order of their performance. Don Octavio was first in the sequence. The serve came to Rolando who met it with a standard hip bump. The ball easily crossed over the mid line to their opponent's side. The Coba man returned the pass to Tulum. Don Octavio gave an enormous hip bump to the ball, which went high into the air and landed deep in his opponents' territory. Another Coba man countered, as the Tulum men advanced.

Alejandro was next to strike the ball. He had a good strike and sent the ball back into the air where the next Coba player could barely return it as he crashed to the ground. Then, Tulum's Ernesto struck the ball and it went high into the air. As the ball came down, Pedro ran up the side embankment and shoved it through the hoop.

It all happened so fast. Tulum had come from behind and won the game!

The Tulum side of the court erupted with cheers. Many of them had thought the long journey alone would put their men at too much of a disadvantage to win. Their players rushed about the ball court, jumping up and down, shouting with glee, and pounding their fists against their chests. The winning players looked up into the stands for the approval of their families. Rocio and Alejandro saw their parents and raised their hands in victory. Hector and Rolando also sought the approval of their parents, who were celebrating. Shaman Octavio danced a wide circle around his team's half of the court. Pedro also looked up into the audience. He first looked over to where the commoners were seated near the periphery. He saw his mother and sister and waved to them in excitement. They waved back, but his eyes continued to scan for another. He found that person under the alcalde's banner. He spotted Emily and nodded to her. She gazed down upon him in wonderment. Pedro knew that it was a freak accident that he was able to direct the ball through the stone hoop. He felt embarrassed—but he also felt like a hero.

Alejandro and Rocio lifted Pedro to their shoulders and went down the

visitors' side of the ball court, parading him in front of the fans, along with the rest of his teammates. They exited the way they had entered, and the stadium emptied out onto the grassy field where they were encamped. The Coba officials ordered the feast to be brought out to both the east and west fields.

While everyone was celebrating and enjoying the food and drink, Alcalde Tejada asked for the two doctors to come sit with him. He was interested in their progress, especially after Coba's alcalde informed him of Dr. Carlos's request for assistance from Valladolid. They joined him at his area that was complete with portable verandas and seating.

"Ah, doctors. Isn't this victory satisfying?" Tejada asked.

Dr. Carlos said, "Yes, a well played match."

"Please, come, sit and tell me of your latest exploits."

Dr. Carlos looked over to his friend and indicated to Dr. Scroggins that he should explain their theories. He told the alcalde that their latest batch of water samples might hold the answer. Tejada leaned back in his chair digesting the information. He appeared somber as he thanked the men for their efforts and excused himself to rejoin the festivities. The event was a perfect opportunity for him to bolster his public image.

"How do you think that went?" Dr. Scroggins asked Dr. Carlos.

"I'm not sure. That man is an experienced politician and will probably take the course of action that benefits him the most. The people are pawns in his chess game of life."

The men sought out their respective loved ones. Dr. Carlos went to spend time with Tomas and Ana. Dr. Scroggins found Juana relaxing with her friends who included the Caneks, Pedro's family.

"Have you seen Emily?"

"Not lately," Juana replied.

"I saw her walking with my brother a little while ago," Maria quipped.

Andres and Dr. Scroggins looked at each other, wondering what to make of this relationship that was developing. It was new ground for both families. He found a place to sit and did his best to participate in conversation.

Meanwhile, Pedro and Emily went for a walk and found themselves near the base of the Coba pyramid. They sat on a short wall of stone and talked for some time. After laughing about Pedro's miraculous shot that won the game, they recounted their day at the beach and how they had first met.

Emily took the time to explain what life was like back home in Charleston, and about the town she came from. Reluctant at first, she also told Pedro about the fine plantation home that she lived in. Her story seemed as fantastic and unbelievable as Pedro's account of his friendship with Chaca.

There they were, two youths from distinctly different cultures and backgrounds. One was isolated by distance and almost alone, the other isolated by a fantastic secret that prohibited closer interaction with his family and friends. They shared a common bond, however, that of trust by necessity. They heard the camps playing music and the joyous attitude still prevailed. The heat of the day had become oppressive with only an occasional breeze for relief, as the sun began setting behind the forest.

"Hey, why don't we climb the pyramid? There must be a better breeze way up there above the trees," Pedro suggested.

"All right, but it looks steep and dangerous," Em replied.

"We will just have to be careful," Pedro said, leading Em by the hand over to the steeply stepped Nohoch Mul pyramid, which stood 130 feet tall. They began climbing the stone structure. Each step was over two feet high, so they couldn't walk up the block steps. They had to crawl like toddlers going up household stairs. They stopped to rest halfway up, already higher than the jungle's canopy. One false move or mistake, and the tumble would be fatal.

"Come on, let's go," Pedro encouraged. Emily looked up to count the remaining steps. She realized that there would be no real rest until they got to the top, which had a flat patio around a small stone temple. Her knees felt weak, and they trembled a bit. They finally clamored over the last blocks and strode the twenty or so feet to the temple's base, and sat down with their backs leaning against it.

The view was magnificent. They could see above and over the jungle in every direction.

"I feel like I am on top of the world," Em said, flipping her hair, so the steady breeze would dry it off.

"You are!" Pedro said. Neither of them had ever been so high off the ground before.

"Look, there's a lake," Em said.

"That is Lake Macanxoc," Pedro told her. Emily got up and wandered around looking out at the amazing scenery.

"There's another lake!" she exclaimed.

"That is Lake Coba. It's known as the waters stirred by the wind, although it actually means ash gray water."

"I like *wind stirred water* better," she replied.

The sun was setting, and Pedro realized they would be stuck up there until dawn if he didn't leave. His family would be worried, and Dr. Scroggins would undoubtedly be furious. Then, Pedro noticed the moon was rising already. What luck! The tall structure would be illuminated by the moon god himself.

Pedro relaxed because he was not pressed to leave immediately. The constant wind was refreshing as it altered from warm to cool breezes. The setting sun's rays gave an orange hue to the off-white stone. Pedro looked over at Emily who seemed to be glowing. One side appeared silver, and the other looked gold from the reflections of the sky's magnificent orbs.

Emily had also noticed how the light made Pedro's muscles and strong facial features gleam like burnished bronze. There was almost a mystical aura about them. Pedro could no longer hold back. His heart beat loudly in his chest. He looked into Emily's awaiting eyes, took her about the waist, held her close, and kissed her.

Emily returned his passion. She felt as if she were lost in time. She had no idea how long their embrace had lasted when a hawk screeched overhead. They separated a bit and watched the raptor soar into the dipping sun and disappear.

No words needed to be spoken. They just held hands and wandered about the patio. They were one with the world and with each other. The birds serenaded them, as they sat down and fell into a trance-like state, content to be in one another's arms. Even as night fell, the moon's rays kept the place illuminated. Pedro noticed that some of the campfires were burning down and realized that they had better go. He started to get up, but Emily pulled at his arm.

"Do we have to go?" she whimpered.

"It would be best," Pedro replied, resisting the temptation to stay and tempt fate.

They slowly descended the pyramid, stopping two-thirds of the way down

to gaze at the magnificent moon still peeking over the trees. Pedro quietly uttered a prayer of thanks to it.

They held hands, descending slowly, knowing that the magical moment would cease when they arrived at camp.

They ambled into the quiet gathering and let their hands go just before entering the firelight, although the moon's glow had betrayed their silhouettes.

Dr. Scroggins got to his feet with a small groan and said, "Let's go, Em."

Pedro looked sheepishly at his folks, who were at a loss for words, as the Scroggins and Juana headed to their camp.

"I'm going to see what the team is up to," he announced, hoping to escape without questioning.

"It's a good thing he scored the winning goal," Victoria finally murmured.

That brought a broad grin to his dad's face. Maria got up with a huff and groaned, "I can't believe this!"

His parents knew something about their son had been forever changed.

Dr. Scroggins asked Emily, "Do you want to talk about anything?"

Em replied, "No, not really." That was enough for her father. They entered their rest area and settled in for the night. Emily went to sleep wondering if Pedro could somehow hear her thoughts about him, like he could with Chaca.

Most of the crowd dispersed shortly after nightfall. There were, however, areas of merriment that persisted into the night. It was healing to the people to go to sleep with laughter and music around them, after the sickness and death that hovered over them for more than two years.

Dawn arrived early in a cloudless azure sky. It was already warm, but the humidity was low. The Tulum visitors did not need much time to repack their things and take to the long road home. The ball players went with their respective families. The alcalde's entourage was the last unit to finish packing, and they brought up the rear of the column.

Dr. Scroggins and Emily were riding with strangers, that is, without Dr. Carlos and Juana, who returned with old friends. They sat quietly, lost in their own thoughts, rocking along the road in the back of the wagon. Although there was still good cheer among the visitors, their enthusiasm had surrendered to the practicality of the trip, which promised to be long and hot.

By evening, they were approaching Tulum. Shaman Octavio and Tejada sent runners ahead to spread the word that the village was to assemble for a brief gathering to thank the gods for their tlachtli victory.

The weary travellers assembled around the market area, and gradually they were greeted by cheering friends and family members, who had not attended the game. Some of the men found their way over to the cantina behind Martin's honey shop for a drink or two of xtabentún. It seemed most of them were revitalized.

Soon, Tejada and Shaman Octavio arrived at the temple. The religious group of people lit torches and candles, and the area was adorned with the flowers that were weaved into ropes or made into bouquets. Two priests began the ceremony with the blowing of the conch shells. That hushed the crowd and drew them onto the plaza. More priests, who were understudies of the shaman, proceeded up the walkway shaking rattles, and chanting a traditional song of blessing.

The tlachtli players came next. Pedro had been honored with a place at the front of the line. They had changed into their playing gear of leather pads and feathers. They strode with dignity, realizing the importance of the moment. Once they had ascended the wide terraces, they halted in formation. The shaman loudly spoke a prayer, and the priests came forth with the lit torches of dried taje and smudged the men's cheeks with it.

Tejada stepped forth from inside the temple. He was adorned in a ceremonial gown. He thanked the people for their support and informed them that the gods had heard their prayers, especially the prayers of those who had lost loved ones to the sickness. He dismissed them and bade them well as the activity of the ballgame was officially closed.

Most of the people went home at that point. Some of the men returned to the cantina, planning to have a day of rest the next day. Emily looked for Pedro, but he was surrounded by well wishers, and she lost sight of him in the crowd.

Gerardo offered Juana and the Scroggins a ride home on his cart. Dr. Scroggins saw that there was limited room on the cart, so he sent Emily with them and said he would get back to the hut after he and Dr. Carlos had tested the new water samples.

"All right, Father, I'll see you later," Emily said, mustering a smile.

Chapter 13

The two doctors entered their office and immediately set to work. Scroggins prepared the slides, while Carlos got out their drawings and transposed the information onto the larger area map.

"Carlos, come look at this."

Looking into the eyepiece, Dr. Carlos said, "Your theory is correct. The tainted water samples are mostly coming from this area where there is marsh land surrounding the water source."

"I knew it," Dr. Scroggins exclaimed. The men were exuberant despite their level of exhaustion. Sitting back in their chairs, they began considering their next step.

Dr. Carlos suggested, "Why don't we take the night off and go have a drink with the others? Tomorrow, we will assess our findings and postulate remedies."

"The last several days have indeed been difficult," Dr. Scroggins replied. "Yes, let's go unwind a bit with the others."

They put away their things and set out to cover the short distance to the cantina. They were pleasantly surprised to see lots of men still celebrating. There were several bottles of honey liquor setting on the tables, and it was freely poured.

Some of the men began leaving for their homes, knowing that their spouses and children would be expecting them. Others, with less responsibility or reasoning, stayed on, thinking the full moon would light their way home well enough.

Dr. Scroggins was peering through the elixir's bottle. He felt a bit dizzy and wondered if the others were feeling that way. He looked around and saw Dr. Carlos speaking with Shaman Octavio. The two came over to him, and Carlos indicated he had told the shaman they had found a possible cause of the sickness.

The cantina fell silent. The men were no longer smiling. Dr. Scroggins thought the liquor might be affecting them as well. Some rose to their feet and put their arms out unsteadily. Then, there was a loud groan that seemed to come from the earth itself. They looked around in disbelief. Trees began swaying back and forth, as if a gale force wind were blowing, but there had been only a gentle breeze that night.

They could hear things crashing to the earth. The ground was vibrating, and the groaning seemed to be growing louder and closer. Then, from across the market square they heard and felt a terrifying rumble. *Crack!*

Those who rushed outside could see the ground itself heaving upward and moving toward them. Trees broke at the roots and fell. Birds took to the air, calling in panic. Dogs began barking and howling, and the men looked at one another in disbelief. They felt as though they were in a boat on a rocky sea as the earth rolled underneath them, throwing them to the ground. The houses and huts nearby were shaking, and many of them collapsed. Screaming and wailing filled the air as frightened families fled the collapsing buildings. Others were caught, smashed, or killed beneath the toppled structures.

Dr. Carlos had the presence of mind to try to save their work. He shouted to Dr. Scroggins, "I'm going back for the map and the book!"

Dr. Scroggins stumbled to his feet and replied, "I'll go with you."

They half ran, half stumbled in a zigzag pattern, falling to the ground more than once. People were running amuck. Some were holding crying children. Others were wandering around like zombies overcome by shock. Fires began to break out, as wooden buildings collapsed onto their stoves and cooking pits.

The ground continued to shake for several minutes. Unnerving cracking sounds and hisses could be heard all around. Shaman Octavio climbed to the top of El Castillo. He could see over top of the forest, and in the distance, he saw a large brownish-gray plume of smoke, much larger than any fire he'd ever seen. It glowed orange and red. He fell to his knees and prayed for mercy, wondering if the ceremony earlier had upset the gods. Some of the priests noticed where he was and came to his side. They marveled at the sight of the erupting volcano. They looked to their leader for direction. He told them to tend to their families first and return to aid the other villagers.

Half an hour after the first earthquake, a tremendous *boom* sounded over the village. People fell to the ground, covering their heads. Yellow clouds of noxious gasses seeped from a great crack in the ground. Those who were unfortunate enough to encounter these gasses experienced horrific deaths.

Their lungs breathed in toxic sulfuric acid, and their bodies melted from the inside out. Their skin dissolved, and the inscrutable pain subsided only with death.

A mound of dirt began to swell on the south side of the village. As the evening turned into night, the horrid glows of fiery embers continued to launch from the fissures, splattering their molten mass onto the tinder of the jungle floor.

Anyone who was capable of helping others seemed to be bandaging the injured villagers. Martin brought out honey salves to help comfort those who had been badly burned. Tejada and Escobar beat a hasty retreat to the alcade's compound which was just outside the zone of destruction.

Emily, bewildered and alone, was very close to the rising mound of earth. She had just gone outside to water the beautiful plants she had nurtured beside the hut and to gather some firewood for the next morning when the chaos erupted. She dropped her water jug when she was thrown to the ground. She managed to scramble to the path that led to her choza, but a gaping hole had replaced the ground she had tread so many times. On the other side of the chasm was a mountain of fallen trees. Just then, she remembered Juana, who lived alone. Emily ran toward the area where Juana lived, but she had never actually been to her hut. She called Juana's name over and over again, but Juana did not answer. Emily saw Tomas outside his fallen choza. He was yelling for help and tugging at the wooden posts and beams. Emily went over and saw Ana pinned under the wreckage. She grabbed a tree post that had fallen clear off the hut and used it like a fulcrum to lift the roofing beam just enough for Tomas to pull his spouse clear from the debris.

"Have you seen Juana?" Emily shouted.

"No, not since we came to our homes," he replied.

Emily ran to the hut that Tomas said belonged to Juana. It was damaged but not crushed, and no one was there. She ran around the area, trying to spot her friend, but finally, she had to hope that Juana was safe and resign herself to looking for her later. Emily staggered toward town.

Em came upon a family on the path. The mother had four children with her; only one was old enough to go the distance on her own strength. Emily scooped up the second oldest and placed him on her hip the same way the mother was holding the third child while she cradled an infant in her arms.

The two ladies could see the clearing of the plaza and market ahead of them, but the ground had ruptured. Trees were blocking the way. There was an awful smell. People were lying on the ground, groaning and suffering.

"We have to go around," Emily yelled, motioning so the woman would understand. The mother was desperately seeking a safe route, but there was none visible in the darkness. Just then, a priest appeared and took the child off her mother's hip. "Follow me," he said. "There is a way over there."

They went with the man who helped them scurry across a tangle of trees. He led them to the plaza where dozens of villagers had made their way to the open area. There were many hurt people wandering about. Emily saw Rocio passing through.

"Rocio, have you seen my father?"

"Not for some time now."

"What in all the heavens is happening?" Emily asked.

Rocio began to reply, but, when words failed him, he ran off to find his family. As time went on, there were hundreds of people on the plaza. The sound of screaming and crying filled the night. Emily made her way to her father's office, but no one was there.

Emily's thoughts turned to Pedro and his family. Where were they? Why had they not come to the plaza? There were so many hurt or injured. She remained busy for hours giving them first aid. She finally sat down, exhausted.

Her relief was only temporary as she awoke to the terrible scene again. First light was dawning over the eastern horizon. There was an eerie silence in the jungle. Not even the armies of insects that surrounded them could be heard buzzing or clicking.

In the distance, back toward Emily's hut, a deep reverberation, like stones sliding over one another, emitted from the earth. There was a sound like the door of an old house moaning in protest as it opened. That sound was followed by a rumbling roar, and finally, a sickening *pop!*

The ground that had already cracked, lifted several feet, shook terribly, and rose another five feet, splitting southward. A new fissure had opened, and the mound split open. Molten lava began running out of the opening across the ground, instantly incinerating everything it touched. Boiling sap and exploding tree trunks resounded through the jungle like cannon fire.

Emily felt obligated to go back into the hellish forest to look for Juana. As she left through the western wall of the city, she made her way south. Soon, she came to the watchtower on the corner of the stone wall. There, the wall turned toward to ocean. The two gates in the wall were useless, due to the corrosive gas and fissures that were just beyond it, at the edge of the woods.

She ran up the steps of the two-story structure. Through the smoke and haze, she saw a small band of people making for the plaza. She ran down to intercept them, hoping desperately that Juana was one of them. Meeting the people about fifty yards from the plaza, Em recognized Tomas and Ana. They were with Victoria and her family, but Pedro was not among them.

"Have you seen Juana?" Em asked.

"We have not. The underworld fire was all around us, and we barely could find a way out in the darkness," Andres said.

"Where is Pedro?" Victoria asked with great trepidation.

"I have not seen him," Em replied. Her heart dropped, but she could only hope the boy she knew to be so resourceful had found safety with the mighty Chaca. Juana was the one she had to help.

"I must go and look for Juana," Em said, bolting into the jungle like a gazelle before they had time to dissuade her.

The Caneks continued the short distance to the plaza. They were finally safe, for the moment.

* * * * *

Back in Charleston, Mary saddled her horse and went for a ride. As she passed Cletus's place, she yelled, "I'm going to the village. Keep an eye on things while I'm gone."

Cletus tipped his hat and replied, "I sure will, ma'am."

Mary nudged the horse and said, "Giddyap!" They took off at a gallop, crossing the meadow to the forest. Mary followed the path, slowing the pace for a while to rest her horse.

Mary had spent her childhood in those woods, just as Emily had. The Scroggins' house had originally belonged to her family. The farm and the horses kept her busy, but the solitude of her empty house left her feeling empty. Maybell helped ease her solitude, but on that day, she felt particularly lonely and anxious. Mary thought that a ride would brighten her day.

The smells and sounds of the forest greatly improved her spirits. Memories of her childhood came alive as she passed familiar landmarks. Mary recognized a large rock on which made she and her childhood friends had scratched pictures or silly sayings.

Mary came to the stream that bordered the Indian village. Her horse forded the waters, and soon she was at Ah-ti-yah's cabin. She had not even made it to the door when Ah-ti came running out and gave her a big hug.

"It's so good to see you!" Ah-ti exclaimed. "What are you doing way out here?"

"I received a letter from a ship in port, and I thought I'd come by and let you know that Emily and Mr. Ezra are all right."

"Really? That's great news. Where are they?" Ah-ti asked.

"They have gone to Mexico on some kind of medical mission," Mary replied.

"Oh my, that is far! Did they say when they would be back?"

"No, that's the troubling part. Ezra said they were headed for Dr. Carlos's village and that he would send word when he could."

"I'm sorry. This surely has been very hard on you."

"Yes, quite frankly, it has, but at least there's something positive to hold on to. They'll come home, Ah-ti. I'm sure they will," Mary said.

"Thank you for sharing this news with me. Please let me know if you hear from them again." Ah-ti said.

"Certainly," Mary said. She set out for home feeling much better.

* * * * *

Earlier, Pedro had been overwhelmed. All of the attention and praise had been a little much for a boy from a humble family who had grown accustomed to spending hours alone in the forest, with the enigmatic Chaca as his sometime companion.

After the ceremony, he had shaken more hands and received more back slaps than he had in his entire life. He could not locate his family among the throngs of people, and he did not want to follow his teammates to the cantina, so he slipped away through the western gate to head home.

Along the way, he decided to take a detour and visit with Chaca. He would have enough time to find his beloved reptile, and then Chaca could carry him back to the village's edge.

Pedro had almost reached the entrance to Chaca's abode when the ground began to shake. He reached up and took hold of the vines that shrouded the entrance. The trees that supported the vines swayed wildly, and Pedro flailed in the air like a fish on a line.

He heard the ground moaning and tearing apart. Boulders smashed to the ground. Pedro's stomach churned as he imagined the caverns below collapsing, crushing his beloved Chaca. Several trees that bordered the top of the cenote's rim uprooted and fell down into the sinkhole, smashing with a thud that ordinarily would be profound, but amid the tumult, Pedro could not absorb it.

The shaking subsided. Pedro made his way down the ramp strewn with fallen rocks and debris, down to the cenote's floor. He jogged past the stalagmites which had not been damaged by the tremors.

Entering the mouth of the tunnel that led to Chaca's hideaway, Pedro called out as loudly as he could, "Chaaaacaaaa!"

He stood motionless, filtering the noises of the disaster, and listened for signs of his friend from inside the tunnel. Nothing! He repeated the call, facing the open cylindrical walls of the cenote. "Chaaaacaaaaa!"

Pedro was torn between going back up to the surface and going into the tunnel. Calming himself for a moment, Pedro looked on the ground for indications that the reptile had passed in either direction. The clean hard limestone on the cavern's floor did not offer any clues. He strained his eyes for footprints or tail impressions.

Pedro had no choice but to enter the tunnel. There were signs of structural damage. Sections of the roof had fallen down, and a wall was compromised and disintegrated onto the floor. The sharp stones cut his hand as he crawled on all fours over the damaged wall in the darkness, counting on the moonlight at the end of the tunnel to lead him to his friend.

He entered the area where he had spent much time. Chaca was not there, but Pedro had anticipated that.

"Thank the gods, there's no blood," Pedro thought.

Pedro paused before entering a cavern into which he had never been invited. His relationship with Chaca had always ended there. With trepidation, he crept into the tunnel.

The darkness quickly enveloped him and the musty stench of stagnant air entered his nostrils. Stalactites, protruding from the tunnel's ceiling, and stalagmites, countering from the floor, made the way even more difficult.

"I'd hate to be a blind man doing this," Pedro said aloud.

He fumbled his way deeper into the chasm. He tried to move a bit faster, but he tripped and faltered a few times. He came to another area where the roof had collapsed. Pedro tried to squeeze his way past the stones, but the gap between the fallen conical rocks was too tight.

"Chaaacaaa!" he called in a loud whisper, fearing that a louder noise might dislodge more stones.

"Chaca, are you in there?" he said with more confidence.

He heard some stones roll. Taking this as a sign, Pedro doubled his efforts and rolled a few larger stones away with determination. The more he moved, the quicker he worked. Within a few minutes, he opened a space large enough to crawl through. On the other side, he could hear the sound of Chaca's breathing in shallow gasps.

Pedro went to Chaca's side and saw his giant head on the cavern's floor. He whispered to his friend, "I am here, I am here." In the dim reflective light of the rocks, Pedro was able to see that Chaca had been pinned by the debris from the roof.

Pedro was bewildered. The only thing he could think to do was embrace Chaca's tremendous head and stroke his scaly brow.

"You'll be okay," he promised, fearing the worst. Tears fell from Pedro's eyes. Chaca was more important to him than anything else in the world.

Pedro went down the left side of the behemoth, feeling his skin along the way. Luckily there were no shards piercing his hide. There was however a mass of stone pressing against his abdomen, restricting his breathing.

Pedro said to his friend, "I have to get this rock off of you. It's gonna hurt."

Chaca huffed in compliance. Pedro stepped across his tail and set his body for the push. Placing his back against the wall, Pedro pushed the boulder off using his legs and feet. Then, he moved up Chaca's side, feeling his scales along the way. When he approached Chaca's abdomen, there was stone rubble squashing his ribs. Pedro flung several of the stones off of him. Chaca drew in a heavy breath. As he did so, a few remaining stones rolled off, allowing his ribcage to expand normally. Pedro rested against the side of his friend, feeling his gut expand and contract. They lay there together for some time.

Then, Chaca rose like a slow but formidable eruption. He pressed his tail to the ground and pushed up from his hind legs. The stones around him bruised his leg as they fell away. Chaca knew that he had to stand to escape. Pedro heard the sound of the rubble giving way to the determination of the reptile.

Chaca stepped forward and stood tall.

Pedro was relieved and said, "Are you all right, my friend?"

After a moment or so, Chaca turned his massive head and licked Pedro with his forked tongue.

"We have to get out of here," Pedro urged.

Chaca drew several deep breaths and waited. Pedro also waited. He had been with the giant reptile for years and knew that Chaca could not be rushed or forced to do anything he did not want to.

Chaca clamored down the tunnel. He groaned as he moved. Pedro realized that the lizard was in pain and was grumpy. He loved Chaca, but he had a fleeting fear of the animal's mauling him in his discomfort. After all, Chaca was a wild and fierce anomaly, a creature that other people had never encountered.

They soon encountered the obstructions of the collapsed cavern. "We cannot get past this," Pedro said.

Chaca turned his head and looked at Pedro as if replying, "Yes, we will."

Not fully understanding Chaca's intentions, Pedro opted to remain close to his friend's side. Chaca, in turn, looked back at him as if to say, "Hang on!" Pedro complied and ran behind Chaca as he smashed through the stones.

On the other side, Pedro asked, "Are we okay?"

Chaca swept his left foreleg forward and brought Pedro to the front of his head. Chaca extended his tongue to smell the air. He determined that advancement was in order. They came to the entrance of Chaca's private domain. Pedro saw the area in front of him and said, 'Let's rest here a moment."

Chaca agreed. He had better night vision than Pedro and plainly saw that his tunnel was blocked. Pushing Pedro to the side, Chaca leapt forward with all his might. He smashed through the obstructions, scattering them to either side of the tunnel. Pedro ran to him and exclaimed, "That was incredible!"

Chaca's scales had many abrasions, and he had also endured heavy bruising and a fractured rib.

You can never go in there again, Chaca implied.

Understanding his look, Pedro said, "Who would want to?"

The two moved toward the surface.

They waited and listened. Pedro suggested that they move away from the big hole just in case it fell in on itself. Chaca agreed. They moved away with Pedro riding on Chaca's back toward the village.

The route they would normally take was impeded by the refuse of the earthquake. Gases were still emanating from the fissures in the ground. Chaca had to proceed with caution, and progress was slow. They had to double back time and time again when their route was blocked. Pedro noticed that, when Chaca had to move his right leg higher than he normally would, a groan would escape his mouth. Pedro was concerned for his friend, but they had to push ahead. They made it to the normal drop-off point just after night had fallen.

They could hear the commotion of scared and injured people. Pedro said, "Wait here until I come back." Then, he trotted down the path to his home. When he got there, it was empty. He called out for his family. He looked around a bit and saw that many of the chozas had fallen. Pedro ran back to Chaca and said, "We need to get closer to the city to help, but you can't risk being seen."

Chaca lowered his head and lifted his left leg for Pedro to scurry aboard. They set off again but kept a wide berth from the village's perimeter. The earthquake had not done much damage out that way. For Pedro, this terrain was unfamiliar, but Chaca knew it from a lifetime of hunting and avoiding contact with people. It took several hours to traverse the distance. They came to a place where they could hear the discord. Pedro got down to creep ahead to see what could be done, if anything.

As he was about to go beyond Chaca's line of sight, Pedro heard a thud behind him. He turned, and what he saw sent a cold shiver of fear down his spine. His beloved friend was lying on his side, with his tongue hanging out the side of his mouth.

Pedro ran back to his side and put his hand under Chaca's nostrils. He felt air still moving through them. "Thank the gods," he uttered with relief, although the beast's eyes were shut. Pedro looked about for a place to hide his companion. There! Just over a hundred feet away, there was a thick wall of brush and reeds, which often meant a water hole. Pedro ran over to the area and was grateful that there was water and cover there. He came back to Chaca, who had rolled over on his belly. He lifted his head as Pedro approached to look at him.

Pedro said, "There is a cenote over there with reeds to lie upon."

Chaca remembered that place; he knew it well. Groaning and rising to his feet, Chaca labored over to the marsh and quickly found a suitable place in the shallow water, resting his head on the dry edge. Chaca drank his fill of the clear cool water and lay down and went to sleep.

Pedro sat near his friend and kept watch. He was torn between his desire to make sure his family was okay and his need to stay with Chaca. He blamed himself for bringing his friend out in the open when he should be at home resting. He sat and thought about what to do, but he also fell asleep.

Pedro awoke a couple of hours later with a start. His mind had been reeling as he slept. "Maguey," he said. The shaman had told him that some of the plants that were known for their medicinal value. People extracted juice from the maguey plant to treat bruises and pain.

He got up to look for the plant, which grew six feet tall and had knife-shaped leaves protruding from a common point at the base.

"How am I going to find one of those in the dark?" he muttered.

Pedro knew those plants preferred dry soil and full light. He walked away from the cenote, scanning about the drier shrubs for a maguey. After half an hour passed, he mumbled, "It's no use," and began returning to the cenote. Pedro looked up at the moon, as if praying for help, and, blocking his view of the moon was a massive flower, the rare flower of the maguey! He trotted over to it and cut off a few of the long succulent leaves. He stacked them and looked for a couple of stones to smash them to a pulp. He brought his discovery back over to the pool, sat down and began pulverizing the fleshy leaves. It took about fifteen minutes to mash up enough of them to create a gob about the size of a tlachtli ball.

The noise woke Chaca, who was feeling a bit better. Pedro took the ball of leaves over to Chaca and said, "Here, eat this. I made it for you because it will help you with the pain." Chaca opened his mouth. Pedro was about to stuff the medicine in when he saw those large, triangular, razor-sharp teeth shimmer in the moonlight. He thought he would toss the food, in case Chaca should close his jaws upon his arm and sever it. Instead, he placed it on the back of Chaca's tongue where it would be easiest to swallow. Chaca swallowed the glob without incident, drank some more water, and lay back down to rest.

Since Pedro was awake, he scouted around for something to eat. He found some papaya, knocked several out of the trees, and ate. He then decided to survey the damage in the city while Chaca slept. He made his way through the forest, coming to the edge of the clearing opposite the western wall. He could only see a sliver inside the plaza, but to the south, he could plainly see broken ground and smoldering fires. He even saw bodies lying on the ground. Whatever happened next, he feared the day would be horrible.

Retreating to the swamp, Pedro had to make a decision as to whether he needed Chaca's help or not. He decided to keep his friend's existence a secret, especially since the lizard was injured. Pedro walked to the western wall. As he was halfway between the forest and the city, the ground began to shake again. He had a most difficult time staying on his feet. The ground swayed and undulated and split and hissed. Pedro was no longer a witness to the horror, but a victim. He watched as the southern area heaved and broke. The ground rose several feet right before his eyes, and a yellowish-green cloud rose from the depths.

He had almost made it to the gate when the lava erupted from the mound with a gush. Pedro was terrified, as were all the others who heard and saw the calamity. He observed the survivors on the plaza and quickly scanned them for his family. Not seeing them, he was hesitant to enter.

Once again, Pedro went back to tend to his friend. He made his way back without being seen. When he arrived, Chaca was no longer resting in the water but peering through the reeds in a crouching position. As Pedro approached, Chaca bobbed his head in confirmation that he felt up to par. Pedro was almost overcome with emotion. He hugged his friend about the neck and scratched his scales above his eyes. Chaca's familiar purr rumbled.

"Are you okay?" Pedro asked looking into the eyes of the reptile.

Chaca blinked.

Pedro encouraged him to stand and follow. They went south, circumventing the city's perimeter. There they were, ready to assist, but unable to expose themselves as a team. Just then, the ground erupted and spewed toxic gas and magma into the air. The subterranean fire leapt thirty feet into the air and began to ooze steadily from the depths. The ground moaned and yawed, cracking from the pressures of the tectonic plates below.

The magma first ran across the surface, but after breaching the fissure near the city, it puddled into a smoldering pool of death. It bubbled and spat and sent globs of fiery molten mass into the area nearby. The pool continued to rise, and the magma began to flow at an astonishing rate, running downhill from the forest quagmire toward the city walls.

Again the magma pooled, but for a brief period due to the shallowness of the area. A priest stood in the southern watchtower and surmised that the liquid fire would soon roll in through his position. He blew his conch. The survivors and peoples of the jungle perked up when they heard the alarm. They knew that the conch meant something important, and they moved away from that wall. A few young men went to the tower to assess the danger.

The men quickly returned, telling of the impending doom of the encroaching molten mass. The situation seemed hopeless. The flat grade of the plaza could not keep the earth's fury from consuming all of the buildings and the people who had taken shelter there.

The villagers began to leave out the northern gate. They swarmed the narrow gate and a crowd amassed as they tried to exit all at once. Panic set in, and people desperately tried to get their injured loved ones beyond the city walls.

Pedro saw this from their hiding place. He looked up at Chaca, and said, "If you ever want to help, the time is now."

Chaca raised his leg and Pedro scurried onto his back. They hurtled through the forest toward the people.

Pedro and Chaca observed that the lava was consuming the dead bodies. The molten river poured faster from the depths and rushed toward the first southern gate.

They were still hidden in the woods as the people ran away. Pedro prompted him to move toward some fallen trees. Together, they went across the clearing in plain sight of everyone. Chaca was no longer a secret. Chaca lowered his head like an anvil and pushed the trees across the clearing against the western most section of the southern wall. The five thick tree trunks created a temporary barrier that would most likely redirect the liquid fire. Standing there for a moment, Chaca observed a gap underneath the logs of half a foot. He ran over, and using his powerful feet and claws, scraped and dug the earth, flinging it against the wood. His giant feet dislodged massive amounts of dirt, quickly burying the tree trunks to a height of four feet.

The magma gushed toward the makeshift barrier, pooling up on the wood and dirt. Then it flowed along the outer wall toward the ocean.

"Chaca! The other gate! We have to block that gate, too!" Pedro yelled. They went over to the other gates closest to the ocean. The terrain inside would allow the lava to turn and go into the plaza also. Pedro looked around for a solution. Across the clearing, he noticed a thick tree on the edge of the open chasm. The tree had been rocked about so violently that the trunk had snapped.

Pedro yelled, "There, go there!"

Chaca dashed over to it and awaited instructions.

"Go up to it and make it fall over," Pedro commanded, as he jumped off. Chaca climbed up the leaning tree. It moved a bit but wouldn't fall. He went to the top and pushed down against it as it teeter-tottered. Finally, the roots gave way and snapped. The tree came crashing down and Chaca did a somersault from the crash. The lava was closing in on the gate. The heat from it was intense and over a thousand degrees. Pedro clamored back onto Chaca's neck, and, with his feet, he directed the behemoth which way to push the trunk and large flat root ball. At first, he rolled the tree, like a wheel on an axle. It made a semicircular path as it went. When the trunk was facing toward the wall, Pedro had him move to the bottom of the root ball and use his head, like a bulldozer to shove the tree trunk through the gate.

Pedro was so focused on completing the task that he did not hear the people calling out to him. Finally, they got his attention, pointing behind him. Pedro turned to see what they were warning him about. The magma had circumvented around him, trapping them. The heat was singeing Pedro's clothes, and he held his breath, so the fumes would not burn his lungs.

Chaca looked up and saw that they had little time left. Chaca backed up a stride or two and vaulted forward jumping up onto the root ball and then on top of the stone wall. He could not jump over the wall because a crowd had gathered and he would squash the very onlookers they were trying to save. Chaca ran west along the top of the wall. When he came to the corner, he bridged across the gate onto the watchtower and let out a mighty roar!

If anyone had not noticed the giant lizard yet, they certainly did then. Chaca swooshed his mighty tail back and forth, dislodging some of the tower's stones. He pointed his head up at the rising sun and roared again, like a dragon. Pedro perilously clung to his back and squeezed his legs around the lizard's neck as tight as he could to keep from falling off.

Pedro looked out into the throng of people. He scanned them looking for his family. Finally, he saw his mother, father, and sister. Their mouths were hanging open with disbelief.

Pedro waved to them. The crowd cheered loudly as they began to understand that the monster or god was not there to devour them in wrath— but to save them. He had pictured Chaca grabbing Emily with his tail and lifting her to safety, but Emily was not among the crowd. Pedro looked over to the temple and saw Shaman Octavio on the roof, waving palms at him with one hand and an incense torch in the other.

Just then, Hector and Rolando returned with a wagonload of bandages, salves, and supplies for the wounded. They were looking forward to the praise they should receive from their endeavor, but when they looked up and saw the jungle boy atop of the great lizard, they felt rather small and insignificant.

The last people to see Pedro and Chaca were Dr. Carlos and Dr. Scroggins. They had been concentrating on the injured. Dr. Carlos smiled broadly. Dr. Scroggins just blinked with wonder.

Pedro did not want to face all of their questions. The lava had been averted, so he decided to get out of there.

"To the jungle, Chaca!" he commanded.

The lizard ran across the top of the western wall and leapt off it. Chaca and Pedro disappeared into the jungle.

The magma continued to ooze from the ground for several days, slowing down greatly after its initial outpour. The blocked southern gates diverted the mass down the cliff into the ocean.

Emily ran off, trying to retrace her steps to get back to the path fork. It was more by luck than intent that she eventually made it to the area. Most of

the chaos had subsided, and the overpowering noises had greatly diminished. Em looked like a bee, buzzing from flower to flower, as she went from one collapsed choza to another, calling out to Juana. She would dig through the thatched roofs or duck and crawl under them to make sure that no one was trapped and unconscious.

Emily called and called, "Juaaanaa, Juaanaa!" Then, she heard a faint reply. Looking behind her, Em saw yet another wooden structure that had collapsed. She went over to it and got down on her elbows and knees and called out again, "Juana, are you in there?"

A small weak voice replied, "Yes, I'm here."

Em's heart leapt as she had finally located her friend, but she feared the worst. Emily got on her belly and wiggled a bit under the roofing. As her eyes adjusted, she saw that Juana was pinned under both a wall and the roof, with the weight of building materials on her stomach and legs. She was twisted, lying on her right side. Em's heart sank with despair.

Tears welled in Em's eyes.

"I'm going to get you out of there!" Em said assertively. She reached down and began to tear away the thatching to expose the posts and beams. Each action she took caused Juana to groan.

"Stop, stop!" Juana begged. Emily did just a bit more, getting the thatching off of Juana's head and shoulders. Juana looked up at Emily and said, "You are such a sweet girl."

Emily replied, "Please don't talk. Save your strength. I will go for help." Em tried one last time to lift the wood, and Juana let out an agonizing cry.

Juana motioned with her hand to come closer.

"I have something to tell you."

Tears rolled down Emily's cheeks. She bit her lip hard causing it to bleed. Juana reached her free arm up with determination and brushed Em's hair back from her face. She winced and took a shallow breath and said, "I have grown very fond of you, dear. I never had children of my own—that is, until you came along."

Emily was trembling, but she held Juana's hand against her heart.

"I am going to the afterlife now."

Emily interrupted, "No, no, you can't. Please. Don't leave me."

Juana continued, her voice growing weaker. "Here, take my shawl. It's called a reboza. When you wear it, think of me happily, like the day we sang the parrot song." Em took the shawl.

"Sing the parrot song for me, would you, dear?"

Emily forced a smile to her face and took a long deep breath, shaking as she exhaled. Then, she began to sing the tune, her voice trembling with sorrow.

"My lady, your little parrot wants to take me to the river . . . "

Juana's hand went limp as it slipped from Emily's grasp. Emily held the shawl to her chest and continued singing gently, sending Juana on her dream walk to the chorus of the song they had shared.

Emily placed Juana's hand under her cheek as if she were pleasantly sleeping in her bed. She knelt there for a long time. Emily recounted the day Juana had given her the traditional dolls. She thought of the joy she felt learning to cook and of shopping at the market. She thought of Juana's smiling eyes and they way her beauty shone in them and pushed past her old and tired body. Em had witnessed Juana growing to love again after so many years of mundane existence since her husband had passed. "That is how I will remember you," Emily said to Juana as if she were still listening. "Your joy will go with me always."

Em got to her feet. She had to leave but would return later after the crisis was over to do what needed to be done. Still sobbing, she reluctantly turned away to go see what had become of her own choza.

Pedro and Chaca stopped to rest at the marsh nearby. They also got into the cooling fresh water and soaked for a bit, relaxing, and drinking. A short time later, they knew it was time to leave before someone followed their trail and caught up with them.

Pedro took Chaca past the area where he had obtained the maguey leaves and showed the plant to Chaca, who licked it with his tongue. Recognizing the odor, Chaca ate a bunch of them and looked rather sloppy while doing so. Pedro laughed as green ooze dripped from his jaws.

They made their way back to Pedro's place, taking the long way around. Chaca stopped at the small valley just beyond the hill. Pedro dismounted and said, "There is much to do in town with all the injured people and damaged huts. It may be several days until I can see you again."

Pedro gave his friend a big hug around his neck and scratched his scaly face gently. Chaca closed his eyelids, enjoying the affection, and sighed. Their bond was stronger than ever, and would need to be, to withstand long periods apart from each other in the future. With a final slap on his friend's shoulder, Pedro said, "Go on, now. I'll see you later, my friend. You are a hero, you know." The lizard ambled off with his waddling gait, not looking back.

Chaca went back to his secluded hideaway. He paused on the cenote's brim, peering down to look at what had changed. He licked the air, checking for unfamiliar scents. Satisfied, he went down the ramp. He took a drink from his private watering hole and lay down in the shade, not returning to the tunnel.

When Pedro got home, he felt a sadness that he did not have time to feel during the crises. He sat alone and missed his family greatly. He wondered if Em had felt the same loneliness being away from her own village. Pedro steeled himself for the walk back to the plaza. He went down the path, stopping to look at the fork tree for a moment.

Meanwhile, Emily had just left her beloved Juana and was in a zombie-like trance. She was fatigued, and her feet plodded along as she walked. She didn't even know where she was going. Emily looked up, and to her amazement, she saw Pedro in front of her with two palm leaves. He had not seen or heard her coming yet through the smoky haze.

"You don't need to do that. I'm right here," Emily said, startling Pedro.

Pedro turned and ran to Emily and gave her a big hug, lifting her off her feet. Then, they put their heads onto each other's shoulders and embraced for a long time, neither wanting to be the first to let go.

"Juana's gone," Emily finally stammered, her throat choking up with emotion. Pedro did not reply. He just looked into her eyes, consoling her hurting spirit. Then, he brushed back her hair and gently kissed Em on her cheek, knowing that whatever words he spoke would not be sufficient.

Emily took a deep breath and composed herself, sniffling and wiping away her tears. "So, what were you planning to do with those leaves?" she asked, mustering a little smile.

Pedro remembered he still was holding the fronds and said, "I don't know, I hadn't gotten that far yet." He tossed them to the ground and took Emily by the hand. "Let's go," he said. "I'm sure your father is wondering where you are by now." They headed toward Em's choza, each taking turns sharing their tales of the last day's events. They had something special between them now. Their bond would also prove to be vital for their futures.

When they came within sight, they saw that the hut had been destroyed by the earthquakes. Emily ran up to it in disdain. The roof and walls had collapsed. Pedro got down and crawled inside, returning with Em's drawing pad, two dolls, and a few of their clothes. They went over to the bench outside and sat. Emily tried to come to terms with the fact that her home was wrecked and that she needed to find her father. They gathered her possessions and departed for the plaza.

Dr. Scroggins treated dozens of wounded people out on the plaza during the night. The villagers were more like refugees in their own town, since many of their homes had fallen down or burnt. Once the tremors subsided and the molten magma was averted, attention was directed toward setting up suitable shelter for those who had nowhere to go. The badly injured were brought to Dr. Scroggins's office, and when that place was filled, they were lined up against the wall outside in the shade.

The supplies that Alcalde Tejada sent were quickly put to use. Hector and Rolando made a good team obtaining water, food, and other necessities as needed. Dr. Carlos would tell them what they were in short supply of, and the two young men consistently brought those things back.

After securing his father's warehouse, Rocio finally came by and helped put out a fire that had erupted when a nearby hut collapsed on its kitchen's fireplace. Dr. Carlos, after conferring with Dr. Scroggins, asked Rocio to go out with a map and make notations on it, showing where the ground had split and where the lava had covered the forest. He took some supplies with him for the trek, found Alejandro, and went toward the outskirts of the village.

Rocio and Alejandro departed out the western gates near the shrines and went through the market area, which was populated with merchants and their wares. The merchants' goal was not to seek profit but to help their fellow villagers. Passing through the market, they encountered Pedro and Emily. They were all glad to see their friends were safe and uninjured. Alejandro had to ask Pedro, "What is going on with that monster?"

Pedro, at a loss for words, skirted the truth, using his people's lore to protect Chaca. "That was Chac, the god of rain, coming to our aid to stop

215

the earth fire from destroying us."

Alejandro and Rocio's eyes got so large, he thought they would fall out of their heads. They were afraid to ask anything else and went on their way.

After walking a bit more with the city wall just ahead of them, Emily asked, "Is that true?"

Pedro replied, "If I offered any other explanation, more questions would follow. This is the best way to keep Chaca safe." The answer made sense to Emily. Her mind quickly forgot that problem after they went through the gates, and everyone turned to see them, still holding hands. A momentary silence fell over the people as their hometown hero re-emerged. Some people even feared him, thinking he might be a god, too. The women were the first to begin whispering, and some pointed to Emily's shawl. They knew something had happened to Juana.

Emily said, "I have to go see my father."

Pedro said that he was going to go talk to the shaman.

"I need to get his support regarding Chaca."

Em headed to the office and Pedro to the temple, where many of the villagers were opting for traditional healing.

Emily hurried along to see her father. Her steps quickened, the closer she got to his office. When she arrived, she saw her father and Dr. Carlos wrapping a splint around a boy's arm.

"Daddy!" Em exclaimed, crossing the room and hugging her father.

"Emily. Thank God. Oh, I'm so glad you're okay!" Dr. Scroggins embraced his daughter as he choked back tears.

Emily looked around at the many patients they were treating. She was suddenly aware of the role her father and Dr. Carlos had after the crisis, and she felt great admiration for both of them. Then, she remembered she had to give her father some terrible news.

"Juana's gone, Daddy. She's dead!"

Dr. Scroggins took Em by the shoulders and asked, "How? How did it happen?"

Em replied, "A hut fell in on her. I went to find her, and, I couldn't get her out. She had so many broken bones, I'm sure. She talked with me for a few minutes and even asked me to sing to her. It was too late, Daddy. She died right there in front of me." Em bawled uncontrollably.

Dr. Scroggins hung his head as the gravity of Em's statement sank in. His body was there, but his mind was not. Just the day before, he was watching Juana laugh with her friends after the tlachtli victory. His mind returned, but he felt weakened by their loss.

"I need to get some air," he told Dr. Carlos. He walked outside with Emily following him.

"Our choza has collapsed," Em said, as they walked over to the market. They got some fruit there and sat down under the trees to eat. Doctor Scroggins said, "Did you hear about Pedro and the giant lizard?" Emily knew that the topic would come up sooner or later, but she preferred later.

"Could we not talk about that right now?" she asked.

Pedro headed across the plaza to the temple. There were people sitting on its steps and leaning against its stone walls. They would have to move periodically to stay out of the sunny areas.

The people that had exalted Pedro the day before now cowered with trepidation as he approached. They had many legends of ordinary people interacting with the gods, and most of the time, the person did not fare well. They scurried to the side, despite their injuries, like bugs attempting to escape being devoured by a bird. Pedro did not know how to react, but he was truly relieved that the praise and adoration had finally ceased.

He observed the shaman administering a balm to Enrique, who had a milpa adjacent to his own. He saw a priest arrive with a large basket of herbs from the minor temple, where the shaman usually stayed when not at his choza. This other temple was adjacent to the southern wall, and its entrance was the same one that Chaca had plugged with the tree root ball. The priests were concentrated about this other temple during the crisis, moving their extensive collection of plants and remedies into the upper level. They did not realize that, while they were attempting to secure the items from the magma, they were trapping themselves in a place from which there would be no escape—if the lava poured in.

Pedro ascended the steps to the main temple in the center of the plaza. He was recounting his story to himself, about the giant reptile's manifestation, so the story would be believable to the shaman. He got to the top step and Octavio wheeled about, as if an unseen hand had landed on his shoulder and startled him.

"Salvador Pedro!" Octavio spoke with reverence, bowing low to the ground. Pedro was uncomfortable with the title but was afraid to object to the greeting that Octavio offered him.

"I need to speak with you, sir," Pedro replied.

Shaman Octavio, along with the others who were present, backed away with reverence. The shaman clapped his hands, and two priests emerged with special torches of incense that they had recently prepared for this occasion. All eyes were upon Pedro. The shaman waved his hands, and the priests, who were Pedro's teammates, spun the torches in circles sending aromatic smoke into the air. When he got to the top step, Shaman Octavio who had been uttering a prayer, knelt before him and raised his arms and hands in full view of the people and said, "We honor the warrior who rides with the gods and rescues his people!"

Then, Octavio placed a necklace of turquoise and gold around Pedro's neck. When he did this, two more priests, who were waiting nearby, blew into their conch shells, and all the villagers in the immediate area fell to their knees and bowed low to the ground. Pedro was not expecting or wanting this adoration, but he adapted quickly. "Arise, I am one of you, privileged with the gift of agility and service," Pedro said. Shaman Octavio rephrased his statement announcing, "Let us look after one another, whether neighbor or stranger in these difficult times." The crowd cheered again for Pedro and for the words of the shaman, which they held close to their hearts.

Pedro went inside the temple and spoke at length to Octavio about his experiences of the last two days. Of course, Octavio was extremely keen on hearing the details pertaining to Chaca.

Pedro altered his account by avoiding his longtime relationship with Chaca and starting the tale with the sudden manifestation of their rain god just as the quake tore open the earth. Octavio hung on Pedro's every word. Believing that Chaca was indeed Chac, their god of rain, he reached out and touched Pedro on the forearm, to be sure that he was still in the presence of a man and not a god.

While they were talking, several priests came and went as their duties required.

"Will you stay with us, Salvador Pedro?" Octavio asked.

"I cannot. I must return to my family and people to minister to them,"

Pedro said, speaking elegantly.

"Keep this necklace as a tribute for your favor and mercy to our peoples," Octavio said.

Pedro, not wanting to offend the shaman said, "I will wear this gift with honor, on occasion, as required." This statement was perplexing to those around him who considered him to be a god-man.

"You shall further your ways in the art of traditional healing, soon."

"I will learn the ways, Shaman," Pedro replied with pride.

Victoria, Andres, and Maria had entered just before Pedro's brief speech. His parents were bursting with pride. They did not quite understand how he had accomplished these things, but they were pleased not only with his heroics, but also by his humility. After leaving the shaman, he made his way over to the area where they had been patiently waiting for his attention. When the conch shells blew, and the villagers assembled, Victoria and Andres were just as curious as everyone else as to what was happening. They were astonished when they saw their son standing in front of the shaman, being doused with ceremonial smoke. They had stood in awe as Pedro received honors that no one else in modern memory had received. Andres drew his wife and daughter close to his side, wrapping his strong weathered arms around them.

Andres was the first to speak. "Look at your son. He has the gift of mercy." Then, Andres squeezed Maria a bit and said, "Your brother has been chosen to save the people."

Maria had been moved by her brother's actions and finally relented. "Yes, I can see now that the freedom you gave him was warranted. I thought that all he was good at was evading chores, but he has also been becoming strong in body and heart," she said.

Pedro stood in front of his father not knowing how the man would respond. After all, he was still the same boy who shucked responsibility and played in the forest. Andres did not bow before his son as the others had. Instead, he said to him, "The days have been long and your deeds have been great. Let us go home and rest."

Pedro smiled and relaxed a bit. Then, Victoria said, "You have done great things, but you will always be my Pedro." She hugged him warmly, as only a mother can. After that, Pedro looked over to Maria, who had pardoned him for their disagreements. She rushed forward and held her older brother close.

When she relinquished her embrace, she said, "You are pretty great!"

* * * * *

The tremors had ceased, and the fires had burned out, mostly due to a heavenly rainstorm a few days after the disaster. Alcalde Tejada and Escobar were busy organizing the community into groups of five to seven volunteers. Each group member would help the others repair or rebuild their chozas.

The people who had lived closest to the path fork had to relocate due to the unstable broken ground, the lava, and the burned-out forest. Pedro showed them the little known cenote west of the city and many resettled there.

Tejada, upon Dr. Carlos's recommendation, appointed Rocio to be in charge of assigning ample space for chozas and milpas for the people. Alejandro assisted his friend by tying cloth flags to trees or stakes, outlining each family's new area.

Pedro's family remained on the outskirts of town, preferring to be close to their milpa, which was mostly unharmed. Dr. Scroggins chose to live out of his office area in town beneath the maize warehouse. The injured patients had new shelters to return to within a couple of weeks.

When the village and its occupants' lives returned to normal, the two doctors returned to their task of determining the cause of the mysterious sickness and its connection to the tainted water sources. Upon the doctors' request, Tejada held a conference to listen to the their findings. Shaman Octavio, the priests, Pedro, and other notables were invited to sit in. On the appointed day, they gathered at Tejada's residence in a grand meeting room.

Tejada said, "Thank you all for coming today. There is a renewed sense of community among our people, beginning with the tlachtli victory, and then later, after the disaster, with the subsequent rebuilding efforts. The purpose of this meeting is to address the sickness that has been in Tulum for years. You have by now met or heard of Dr. Scroggins, who has come here all the way from America, at the invitation of Dr. Carlos Caamal."

The two doctors stood when introduced.

Tejada continued, "They have reason to believe that the sickness is coming from our water supply, so let's listen to what they have to say."

Dr. Carlos brought out the large map that Tejada had supplied them with and placed it on a tripod. He used a pointer stick to show the areas that Dr. Scroggins was describing. Dr. Carlos would also translate into Mayan or Spanish as needed.

Having discussed their theory, Dr. Carlos offered a solution. "We feel that the mosquito is responsible for the sickness and propose that fish be brought to these waters to eat their larvae before they hatch and fly."

Escobar objected saying, "What kind of fish could rid us of this scourge?"

Dr. Carlos replied, "I was just getting to that. In the water samples that did not have the mosquito present, there were many molly fish, which are only three inches long and greenish-gray in color. They are too small for eating and were found in shallow pools that could not support larger game fish."

The men looked around at each other, taking in this new information. Then, Shaman Octavio stood and walked over to the map. He pointed to an area where most of the destruction from fire had occurred and said in his Mayan tongue, which Carlos translated, "There are trees here that, when the bark is boiled, fever is healed."

The doctors looked at one another, astonished.

Dr. Carlos said, "Rocio, you will go with Octavio to this place and mark the map with the locations of these trees."

"What are these trees called?" Carlos asked Octavio.

"Cinchona," he replied, taking his seat.

"How are we to acquire the fish for the water pools?" Tejada asked.

Dr. Scroggins said, "Hector has a talent for getting and delivering supplies, and he is smart. Perhaps he would like this assignment."

Hector seemed surprised but pleased with this unsolicited referral.

Tejada said, "Well, Hector, here's your chance to become a man. What will you do?"

Hector said, "I will do this thing, as long as I have Rolando to help me."

"It is agreed then, you boys, rather, men, get started on this as soon as you are able. Dr. Carlos, after the meeting, you report to me, and we will discuss how our sister town beyond Coba, Valladolid, will contribute to the cause. I am sure that they will be most appreciative of these findings!"

With that, the meeting was adjourned. The men went outside under the shade of the trees to talk and enjoyed refreshments.

Octavio came over to Pedro and said, "Will you assist me with the gathering of the Cinchona bark?" Pedro was jubilant. He would no longer have to "escape" to the woods but would now learn how to gather plants and help people at the same time.

"Yes, I would like that very much," Pedro replied. Octavio reached his hand out to Andres, who accepted his grasp, thus sealing the deal with his paternal approval.

The next few weeks were incredibly busy for the healing team, as they were called by the villagers, once the plan had been explained to them.

Pedro had few opportunities to spend time with Emily, who had taken over for Juana and also as Dr. Scroggins's secretary. Emily would visit with Pedro's folks either at the market or their home. She also developed a friendship with Maria.

Victoria took up planning for Maria's quinceanera, her "coming of age" celebration for turning fifteen years old. The three ladies had great fun acquiring Maria's dress and planning the food and festivities. On the rare occasion that Pedro would come home to find Emily at his choza, he had difficulty wresting her away from her two new "girlfriends." However, Emily would be sure to let him know how special he was to her.

Maria's celebration would be grand. She had always been popular with the other girls, but her status had been raised even further, thanks to Pedro. They were so enthralled with planning and gathering supplies, Pedro's family had not even noticed that a sailing ship was putting into Tulum's port—but Pedro had.

The ship's cargo would soon be unloaded, and the provisions that Tulum had collected would be dispensed to the ship for export. The infusion of foreign supplies, coupled with the money gained for the sale of their local crops and goods, would help the village to recover and return to prosperity.

Chapter 14

It was midday when the brass bell rang, indicating that a ship was setting anchor off shore. People collected near the port to assist in unloading the cargo. Emily left the doctor's office and made the short walk to the shore to see the commotion, along with the other onlookers. Everyone was excited by the ship's arrival. There would undoubtedly be a fiesta for the captain and his sailors.

Tejada made his obligatory greeting, welcoming the captain for refreshments at Martin's cantina. They discussed the ship's contents and negotiated exchanges of quantities and value. Toward the end of their discussion, Dr. Scroggins appeared before them.

"Ah, Dr. Scroggins, what brings you to the cantina today?" Tejada cooed.

Dr. Scroggins introduced himself to the captain and asked if he had room for two passengers. He also inquired as to whether the ship would be sailing for the Americas.

Captain Stephan replied, "Aye! I sails for Philadelphia on the morrow. Be on the dock at first light, and I'll bring ye there. What has ye to pay for passage?"

Tejada said, "I will cover the passage fees for them." Dr. Scroggins nodded a *thank you* to Tejada and left to make arrangements for their departure.

He spotted Emily near the harbor.

"Emily, have you seen Rocio today?"

"Yes, he is supposed to give Dr. Carlos an update on the extended map toward Rancho Viejo."

"Good! Go catch him and ask him to tell Dr. Carlos that I need to speak with him tonight about an urgent matter."

Emily obediently left to relay the message. She caught up to Rocio who was about to head up to Dr. Carlos's place. She then went by Victoria's booth.

Victoria said, "You look worried, Chan Chiich," which was a nickname they gave Emily at the celebration; it meant "little bird."

"There is a ship in port, and my father just asked Dr. Carlos to meet with him, and he said it was urgent!" Em said with her lip beginning to tremble.

Victoria and Maria knew what must be happening. No one had wanted to think of a day when the good doctor and Emily would leave. They had become part of the village.

Emily ran off practically in tears and said, "I have to find Pedro!"

Pedro informed Shaman Octavio that he needed the day off. Seeing the lad was distraught, Octavio asked if he could do anything to help. Pedro declined his offer and ran into the jungle to think. He ran and ran until he came to the ruins. There, he sat down and just stared out into space. He couldn't think rationally.

"Stupid! Stupid! Stupid!" he cursed himself. "How could I be so stupid?" Pedro had realized that, with the arrival of the ship, Dr. Scroggins would be leaving with Emily. He had found the cause of the illness, so there was no reason to stay.

Pedro picked up a stout branch and beat the side of the ruins with it, until the branch disintegrated in his hands. He pulled on his hair and yelled again, not caring who or what might hear his tantrum.

He left that place and thought that he would go see Chaca. It had been over a month since their glorious day together. Pedro kicked the ground and flung stones from the path. Then, a short branch landed at his feet while he was walking. Angrily, Pedro picked up the branch to fling it back at the offending monkey. He looked up and standing there, not twenty paces away, was Emily. His arm already was cocked to throw, but the stick slipped and fell from his grasp.

He ran to Emily and picked her up off her feet, swirling her around in circles. "I didn't know if I'd ever see you again!" He put her down and hugged her close.

Emily felt as if she were being torn from the place she had come to think of as her home, unexpectedly and unfairly. She was so confused. She wanted to return home to see her mother and Ah-ti-yah and Caramel, those she had loved all of her life. She struggled while thinking about her newfound friendships in this beautiful paradise, comparing it to her privileged upbringing.

Emily and Pedro walked and walked, not saying much; each was trying to think of a way to avoid the inevitable. Soon, they came to the wall of vines. Pedro had not even noticed where they were until right then.

He said, "I have not seen Chaca since the day of earth-fire. Will you go with me to see if he is here?"

"Of course I will!"

They went down the cenote's ramp. Coming to the bottom, Pedro went over to the dark tunnel and called out, "Chaca! Chaca, are you in there?" Nothing stirred.

Emily said, "Why don't we just wait here for a while and see if he comes back?" They waited down at the water pool. Pedro climbed a tree and shook a few avocados out for them to eat. As time passed, Emily and Pedro slowly, in small painful increments, began to accept that this would be their last day together. It felt strange. First, she had experienced the loss of a close friend like Juana, and now she felt an incredible sense of loss, although the person she cared for was alive and well, and sitting next to her.

Emily suddenly jumped to her feet. "Why don't you come back with me?" she said with delight. She thought she had found a solution.

"What? Come with you? Your city is much bigger than this place! I am a simple country boy," Pedro muttered while trying to fathom leaving his home and family.

"Where would I stay? And what about my shaman learning and Chaca?"

The glad expression left Em's face as the reality of separation returned.

"It's no use," Em whimpered.

"Let's go back to the ruins and watch the sun set," Pedro suggested.

They left the sanctuary with heavy feet and heavy hearts. Arriving at the ruins, Em asked, "What kind of moon is it tonight?" Pedro had to think about it and replied, "It is almost a full moon."

At least they would have moonlight to illuminate their trip back to the village.

Pedro said, "Let's go down to the beach."

"That's a great idea! That way, I can check in with my father, and he won't worry."

"Great," Pedro uttered, not wanting to see the man who was wrenching his love away from his grasp.

"Wait, stop!" Pedro said abruptly.

"What is it?"

The bushes shook and out leapt . . . Chaca.

"Chaca!" they said in unison. There the giant reptile stood in front of them. He lowered his head as if to attack, and then he scurried forward licking Pedro and Emily in one, sudden, disgusting slurp. They each went to a side of his head and hugged Chaca's neck and scratched his scales.

Chaca sat down on his buttocks and panted like a pet dog. He had been following them even before they arrived at his dried cenote, unsure if they were being followed by others. He could not risk being discovered! Pedro gave him a good lookover and was glad to see that he had healed well.

Em and Pedro played with Chaca, teasing him a bit by playing keep-away with some oranges. It seemed like old times, rather, the not-too-long-ago times of fun and frolic. Soon, they knew it was time to go.

"Chaca, will you take us back, one last time?"

Chaca raised his foreleg up for them to clamber aboard, even though he didn't understand the "one last time" words. Up they scampered. Pedro took off his belt which was doubled-up, slung it around his friend's neck, and made the "ffftt" sound. Chaca took off running.

The ride was exhilarating. He stopped just prior to the last ridge as usual. Pedro let Emily down first, before jumping off. Emily gave the megalania one last hug, and as she did, she recalled the day she had done the same thing to Caramel. She sighed deeply and turned to meet her fate. Pedro remained a few moments longer and nodded his head several times, communicating with his old friend.

Dr. Scroggins had a lot to do and not a whole lot of time to do it. His possessions were at the office, which had doubled for his residence since the earthquakes. He looked over the medical supplies, which had grown considerably due to Hector's diligence. There were even a few natural remedies in the jars that he had adopted from his colleague, Octavio.

Perez, Dr. Scroggins's landlord, gave him a travel trunk made of wicker. They shared a drink of chocolate coffee together. Perez thanked Dr. Scroggins not only for all his help with the village's illness, but also for the support and training of his son, Rocio. Tejada had put Rocio in charge of land surveying, maps, and road construction.

Dr. Scroggins later strolled past Martin's honey shop and declined the offers of a drink in the cantina. There was a fresh bunch of "salty dogs" there, and he desired no more additional stimulation. He thought about the many experiences he had had, and the way it had all begun with the waylay from Charleston. He chuckled to himself about the swampy excursion he and Carlos undertook. He marveled at the tlachtli games and thought the most magnificent part of it all had been witnessing Emily's transformation from innocent Carolina girl to a mature young woman. He promised himself that he would spend more time with family when he returned home.

"Ezra!" Dr. Carlos called out.

He turned and greeted his friend warmly.

"You sent for me?" Dr. Carlos asked.

"Yes, Carlos, there is a ship in port, and I mean to depart on it in the morning."

Dr. Carlos was completely caught off guard. His mind raced as he considered the progress they had made toward eradicating the sickness which had been deemed malaria.

"Really? Truly? Are you to leave tomorrow? What of the medical team?"

Dr. Scroggins smiled and placed his hand on his friend's shoulder stating, "The medical team is under proper counsel. Your counsel!"

Carlos grinned broadly, knowing that indeed their task had been accomplished. He replied, "So it is definite then? Will you not stay until the next vessel arrives?"

"That would be asking the impossible. Have you forgotten that we left my office in Charleston to mend some injured sailors?"

Dr. Carlos certainly recalled that situation and understood Ezra's longing to return home.

"Let's go back to the office and go over a few things," Ezra suggested.

Along the way, they bantered back and forth just as they had done on their walks home during their college days.

"I'm leaving everything here so you can establish a clinic for the villagers," Ezra said. "You'll need this too," he continued as he handed his close friend the microscope box.

Opening the box, Carlos jested, "Let's make sure the instrument is inside."

"I think you should research Shaman Octavio's remedies as well, if he is open to it."

Carlos laughed out loud and said, "So there is room for modern science and traditional healing to work hand-in-hand!"

"Who are we to judge what science is proper or accurate without doing the research first?" Ezra replied.

While they were enjoying the revelation, Emily entered the room. They greeted her warmly and Dr. Carlos said, "I'll bet you are excited to be returning home."

Emily replied, "Yes, I do miss Mother and my friends."

Dr. Carlos said, "Well, I'd better be going now. I'll see you off tomorrow."

Dr. Carlos left, closing the door as he went out. Dr. Scroggins said to Em, "Here is a trunk for you to pack your things.

"Yes, Father, I will later, but Pedro is meeting me down at the beach soon to say goodbye."

"Oh, I see. Well then, please give him my regards and thank him for me. He is a fine young man."

"Thank you, Daddy," Emily replied.

Emily and her father hugged. He rubbed her back and looked lovingly into her eyes.

"My dear precious girl," he said softly, "it's going to be all right."

Em looked up into her daddy's eyes. She drew a deep breath and said, "I have to go," and left the office.

* * * * *

Pedro had gone home before heading to the beach. His mother and Maria were getting the evening meal started.

"What have you been doing today?" Victoria innocently inquired.

"I spent part of the day with Emily. She's leaving for America in the morning," Pedro replied.

Andres, Maria, and Victoria stopped what they were doing.

"So it's true, then," Andres said.

"Yes, it's true, and I don't want her to go! I am going to the beach to be with her now!" Pedro lamented.

He ran out the door. Victoria began to call out to him and Andres said, "Let him go, Na. Just let him go."

Pedro ran almost all the way to the beach. The reality of Em's departure worsened when he had to discuss it with his family. When he came to the city wall, he paused for a moment. He looked upon the temple watchtower and remembered how he and Chaca had triumphed. He calmed down, recognizing that some things in life just have to be endured.

Then, Pedro saw Emily standing on the beach. He watched her from afar for a moment before climbing down the solidified magma which descended to the water.

Emily was pleasantly surprised when she saw Pedro approaching her from the cliffs. He had changed clothes and was wearing his cotton pants and shirt and sandals. He was a vision of manhood, confidently striding toward her. His jet black hair was blowing in the wind.

Emily had been thinking about their time together. The chances of meeting a young man her age for whom she had developed feelings were remote in a foreign country. The odds of the same person's having a giant reptile for a best friend, scoring the winning goal at a major sporting event, and saving the village from the aftermath of an earthquake were incalculable. The most amazing part, to Emily, was that he returned her feeelings.

Pedro and Emily walked toward one another. A sandpiper objected to their intrusion. As it flew away, Emily stopped and playfully turned away prompting Pedro to chase her in the shallow surf. He caught her just as a wave rolled in, and they got wet from their thighs down.

Pedro grasped her and said, "I never want to let you go!"

They embraced in the surf. Waves gently crashed on the white sand beach. The sun was close to setting. They stood there watching it peek out from the clouds on the horizon. A line of pelicans soared by in a single file formation. They were just above the swells of the ocean's waves, gliding and occasionally flapping their wings.

Dr. Scroggins came to the cliffs and watched his daughter for a moment. He liked Pedro and wished there were something he could do about the pain the two would experience when he and Emily sailed—and the sadness they were likely to feel for some time after that.

Seaweed washed up onto Emily's foot and she stamped her feet, trying to rid herself of the gooey green plants.

Pedro said, "Let's go sit on the sand."

They did just that, and then, he remembered that there would be a late moon rise that night and thought he should get Emily back to the safer plaza area.

"Let's go up to the watchtower," Pedro suggested. Emily thought that was a good idea and agreed. They walked along the beach, trying to prolong that beautiful moment.

"I want to take you to the temple roof," he said.

Em said, "Okay, great, let's go!"

Pedro guided Emily to the roof of El Castillo. There was just enough time for them, once they were on the roof, to watch the orangey-red orb sink beyond the ocean, its gorgeous colors reflecting across the water before settling into its nighttime hideaway.

Pedro seized the opportunity to say to Em, "You can sail the ocean's vastness, but you will not ever know someone who cares for you as deeply as the sea flows, except for me."

Emily was moved by his declaration. She gazed upon her bronze companion and kissed him, not knowing nor caring how long they were engaged, as their two silhouettes merged into one.

The sun sank, and the darkness was evident as they attempted to go down the steps.

Emily said, "I must go home now before my father worries too much."

Pedro knew he had to let her go. His heart and mind objected, as he escorted Em across the plaza toward her father's office. His mind raced to think of something—anything that would dissuade her from leaving.

Coming to her father's office door, Pedro looked in Emily's green eyes, burning them into his memory. She was leaving, and he had to accept it. Emily looked upon her boyfriend in the darkness and kissed him one last time.

Chapter 15

When morning arrived, the villagers turned out to finish loading the ship. Captain Stephan boarded his vessel and hoisted the anchor. A party of canoe-men tugged the ship back out beyond the treacherous coral reef.

Dr. Carlos, Tejada, and Escobar bade Emily and Dr. Scroggins well and waved from atop the cliff. Hector, Rolando, Rocio, and Alejandro waved too. The priests chanted a song of blessing and protection over their honored guests.

It was somewhat of a painful separation for all, as they said goodbye to two people who had invested much of themselves in the village.

Andres, Victoria, Maria, and Pedro were there too. Tears streamed down Maria and Victoria's cheeks. They knew their sorrow must have been nothing compared to the anguish Pedro was experiencing. Andres rested his hand on Pedro's shoulder and felt it rise and fall as Pedro began to breathe heavily. They watched the canoes getting smaller and smaller. Panic was setting in as Pedro grappled with his emotions. His mother heard his belabored breathing and turned to him. Their eyes met, and at that moment, he understood the depth of her love for him.

Emily was standing at the rear of the ship, as was Dr. Scroggins. Time had seemed to stand still for them at times in the jungle paradise, and now, they felt as if there were not enough time to get used to the idea of leaving. The crew was scuttling about, setting the sails and adjusting the riggings.

Pedro could no longer stand idly by. He slipped from his father's hand and bolted toward the dock, which was not very close.

Maria called out to him, "Pedro, don't go!"

He glanced back at her and mumbled, "I must!"

He ran to the top of the staircase but could see that the ship was already too far away for him to reach, even if he found a canoe that was ready for the taking. Remembering the inlet cove on the far side of the city, Pedro ran off across the courtyard making for the entrance to the city wall. His sudden departure in full sight of his fellow villagers caused a commotion. His ears heard their voices, but his brain did not process the sounds. All of his focus was on closing the distance between himself and Em's ship. He ran like a deer, amazing all who could see him go. When he came to the far embankment, he did not even slow down to consider how he was going to scale the giant stones and twenty to thirty-foot drops. Over the precipice he went, bounding down the cliff like a jaguar. One false step would be devastating. He came to an insurmountable drop, and over it he leapt. Hitting the soft sand at the bottom, he rolled across it head first, landing on his face and chest.

The impact had knocked the wind from him. Pedro lay there for a moment as his body struggled to pump oxygen to his brain. His sight was blurry, almost foggy. He became aware that he had sand all over his face, up his nose, and even in his mouth. Undeterred, he rose to his feet and scampered into the ocean.

Dr. Scroggins had turned away to get settled on board. He was making his way to his chambers when he heard Emily shout, "Pedro!" He followed her line of sight and saw Pedro navigating the steep rocks. Just then, he fell, crumpling to the ground.

Emily shrieked in dismay. Her heart sank with dread. Dr. Scroggins rushed to her side at the rail. Emily was looking about for a way to get a rowboat.

Dr. Scroggins called out, "Em, he's getting up!"

Emily turned her attention back toward the shoreline and watched Pedro charge into the surf. She knew he was a strong swimmer, but the distance seemed too far. The ship was leaving a wake as the tropical breeze pushed the vessel forward. Pedro was like a fish, even a sea turtle, carving through the water and gaining on the ship. He swam out through a gap in the reef into the open water, closing the distance.

Emily called for him to continue with encouraging words. Pedro swam as hard as he could, heading for a point in front of the ship to intersect. Emily beckoned the captain to turn around. Captain Stephan denied her request, citing that a maneuver like that, with a fully laden ship, would cause it to flounder and sink.

"Set the anchor. Let him catch up; he can make it," Em continued.

"Aye, lass, we've not enough cordage to weigh anchor out here in the deep," the captain replied.

Emily looked at her father for an answer. Surely, he could think of something. While they were talking, a deckhand cast out a long rope with a barrel tied to it. Pedro stopped swimming to catch his breath. He saw the lifeline and made for it. The temperature of the water suddenly became a lot colder. He was out in the ocean current now, and it began to sweep him farther and farther from the ship.

Pedro knew that his Herculean effort had fallen short. Calmness came over Pedro that he had not thought he could feel. He summoned the courage to call out to Emily, "I will find you! We will meet again!" The barrel grew small like a glint on the sea.

Realizing that Pedro could not get aboard the ship, Emily cried out to him, "I love you!"

Pedro bobbed in the swells until he disappeared like a glint on the sea.

The onlookers on land watched the ship disappear from sight. Pedro's fisherman friends came out to retrieve him from the sea. They pulled him into a canoe, and he leaned against the back of the dugout and let his head fall back. He was spent. He closed his eyes and thought of his last swim with Emily and Chaca while his friends paddled back to shore.

Emily wandered about the ship's deck for a long time. She tried not to think of Pedro's anguished attempt to catch up with the ship. She began to think about how life would be different for her with him by her side. It was all very confusing. She ambled about on board watching the sailors work. The shoreline grew smaller and smaller until it could not be seen anymore.

Emily knew the voyage would take many days. She passed the time, as her father did, patiently waiting for Charleston, helping out here and there as opportunities arose. She helped Dr. Scroggins while he gave the crew medical exams. One day, while helping him pull a rotten tooth from an ailing seaman's mouth, Emily asked, "Dad, do you think we will ever go back?"

"That's hard to say, dear. I suppose it's possible," he replied.

"I feel like I'm losing friendships that mean so much to me," Em continued.

"Yes, as do I. Just remember that physical distance does not mean that those you care about will be forgotten. You should be able to send a letter to Pedro through the postal service or with a ship's captain who does trade with that area from our home port."

"That's a great idea!" Em agreed. "Are we done here yet?"

"Yes, you can go," Dr. Scroggins replied, seeing the excitement in his daughter's eyes.

Em left the galley and headed for their cabin. She opened her luggage to get out her drawing and writing supplies. She sat down at the table and began writing a letter.

Dear Pedro . . .

Within the hour, Dr. Scroggins returned to the cabin.

"Hi Em. I see you didn't waste any time getting started."

"Well, I figure now is a good time to write, so that when we get to Charleston, I can find a ship to send the letter back to Pedro."

"I see. Before this trip, it might have taken you a week or two to get around to it," her dad said with a hint of a smile.

Em looked up from her writing.

"Daddy, how did you handle being away from Mom for so long?'

"That's a tough question. I think we need to have faith that things will turn out all right and keep our feelings alive in our hearts. Besides, your mother is a strong woman. She can get things done on her own."

"I think I understand. You have to not let your emotions get you all confused, so that you are unable to get things done," Em said.

"That's right. Look at how you helped Juana with the cooking, and you learned a new language. You've even become a good assistant to me. This trip has changed you, Em. You're more grown up now."

Emily got up from the desk and hugged her father. They rocked back and forth a bit being thankful for one other.

Captain Stephan did not sail too close to land. It was best to stay far enough out to sea where miscreants would not be tempted to carry out acts of piracy. The weather held up while they navigated up the coast by Florida, but gray skies set in as they neared Savannah, Georgia. A hard steady rain resulted, and the wind picked up as the ship tossed about in the rougher seas.

The weather brought back some bad memories for Emily and Dr. Scroggins. They did not speak of the horrific beginning of the journey, but they both thought of Em's head injury and the way she had been detained in a pig sty.

Em had finished her letter. She needed to know how to send it.

"Dad, how do I get this letter to Pedro?"

"Let's think about that. Perhaps it might be better to send it to Dr. Carlos, since he has an office in town, and he can make arrangements to get it to

Pedro."

Em said, "That's a great idea." She wrote *Dr. Carlos Caamal, Tulum, Mexico, att: Pedro Canul Canek.*

Meanwhile, back in Tulum, Pedro continued his training with Shaman Octavio. Together, they explored the jungle, and Octavio showed Pedro how to find different roots, bark, flowers, and fruits. He let his protégé do most of the digging or climbing, and when they returned from the jungle each time, he showed him how to use the items for their medicinal values.

One day, Dr. Carlos paid Pedro a visit at his choza. Carlos knew of Pedro's aspirations to become a healer and wanted to see how his education was progressing. Pedro's family was there, and they had a nice visit. While having some refreshments, Dr. Carlos said, "Pedro, how do you feel about Emily leaving this place?"

The air fell silent as everyone turned to see what Pedro's reaction would be.

Pedro said, "I miss her very much. I have been hoping I can find a way to go and see her again someday."

"I thought you might," Dr. Carlos replied. "I studied medicine in America and lived there for several years. That, of course, is how Medico Ezra and I became friends, at college. I'd like to tell you about how things are where Emily lives." Dr. Carlos stayed a while, talking with Pedro and his family about America.

Outside in front of their choza, Carlos said, "If it is all right with your parents and Shaman Octavio, I would like you to assist me one day a week at my office and learn how to keep a journal and get acquainted with more modern ways of medicine."

Pedro was pleased with the offer and wanted to agree immediately but replied, "I will have to ask Octavio for his approval. I'm not sure that he will agree."

Dr. Carlos replied, "I understand. You just let me know when you get it sorted out."

The lighthouse in Charleston was spotted deep in the night, while the crew was asleep. Captain Stephan sailed a large circular course so he would be able to approach the port from a favorable wind direction when daybreak occurred. It was going to be a long day, so he wanted his crew to get as much rest as possible, before the difficult work began of off-loading their cargo.

He rang the bell himself, calling his men to muster at the first light of dawn. They made their way onto deck and received orders to make ready for putting in to shore after breakfast. Both Emily and Dr. Scroggins moved quickly to the deck rail to gaze upon their homeland.

The ship came in close to the port, and the first mate gave the order to drop the anchor. Emily smiled at her dad when they heard the *sploosh*! The next hour seemed like an eternity. Captain Stephan was good enough to have a rowboat lowered for the Scroggins to de-boat first with their belongings. The short row to the dock seemed to take forever as well.

"I can't wait to see Mother again!" Em said, bursting with excitement.

"Oh, I know what you mean, Em. I can hardly believe this day has come!" her dad replied with pent-up emotion.

The sailor pulled up alongside the docks steps, and they got out. He helped shove their meager luggage out onto the wooden planks. After tying the boat off, he went about his business seeking out the harbor master.

Emily and Dr. Scroggins set out at a fast pace carrying their own belongings.

Due to the early hour of the day, the port was devoid of people and activity. It had been raining steadily for two days as well, so commerce had slowed to a standstill. They crossed the dock area rather quickly. Dr. Scroggins was relieved that there were no townspeople there asking for explanations of his departure and journey. They walked all the way to his office. Stopping at the front door, Dr. Scroggins read a note that had been tacked onto it. "No appointments until further notice. Dr. Scroggins is away." He tried the doorknob; it turned, but the deadbolt was locked.

Emily said, "I'll go around back and try the windows." She did so, but they were locked also. She returned to find her dad sitting on the porch in one of the rocking chairs that patients' family members could use while waiting. Em plopped down in one. Their excitement had worn off a bit from their hurried walk back, and they were tired.

"Let's go to the livery," Dr. Scroggins offered. The sun had begun to rise. Roosters were crowing about town. Soon, the place would awaken with activity. The doctor, still wanting to avoid contact with curious townsfolk, took Emily by the hand and led her down the porch steps.

Emily noticed the smell of the air. She felt glad to recognize the familiar odor of her hometown. She noticed the streets and houses and how different they were from those in Tulum. The trees and bushes were not the profuse jungle foliage that she had grown accustomed to either.

They entered the barn area of the stables. Dr. Scroggins called out to make someone aware he was there. Across the yard, a man stepped out of the back door of his house. He was barefoot and was slipping his arms through his suspenders.

"Who is that?" Bill called back, rubbing his eyes with his hands. He squinted a bit and proclaimed, "Well, I'll be a treed coon! Give me just a minute. I'll be right there." He ducked back into his house for his shoes and returned quickly with a tankard.

"Here's some hot coffee for you two." He looked them over, and although he was dying to ask questions, he quickly realized that they needed transportation home.

"I have your buggy stored in the shed, Ezra. I can loan you a horse to pull it home if you'd like."

"That'd be just fine, Bill," Dr. Scroggins replied. "We've been away for too long, and I've got to get home as soon as possible."

Bill got busy hooking up the carriage, and Emily provided a bit of assistance. Dr. Scroggins tossed their luggage inside and climbed in with Em right behind him. Bill led them out of the barn, holding his horse's bridle.

"Welcome home, Ezra. You too, Miss Emily," he said, slapping the steed's hindquarters.

"Giddyap!" Bill shouted. The carriage lurched forward. Em and Dr. Scroggins were on their way home.

Bill's horse, Cotton, had travelled this road many times, and he did a good job pulling the buggy that day. Emily looked out on the farms and fields they passed while her dad concentrated on steering the horse and buggy. They were enjoying the ride immensely. The pastures and wildflowers were giving off a sweet fragrance after the rain.

Although Emily was excited to be almost home, she became anxious as she began thinking about how her mother must have felt after her disappearance. Emily felt guilty, even dismayed that her mom had to go through such a prolonged period of uncertainty.

Em forced a smile and looked over at her father. He read her face and said,

"It's going to be fine, Em."

It was still early morning when they approached their horse farm. Dr. Scroggins led the buggy around to the gate, where Cletus was standing holding it open. He smiled broadly at them as they passed through.

Ezra brought the carriage to a stop and jumped out. He could see Mary in the shed row working with the tack. He ran toward her and called out, "Mary! Mary!"

Mary turned her head and saw her husband coming toward her and gasped, "Ezra!"

She dropped the leather bridle and ran out to her husband. Ezra scooped her up by the waist and twirled her round and round. He set her down, gazing into her eyes and steeling himself for the distress he had anticipated seeing. It was not there. His heart was overcome with joy, and they embraced and kissed. They stopped for a moment. Mary brushed Ezra's hair from his eyes and asked, "Where's Emily?"

Emily had waited by the buggy. She wanted to give her parents a special, private reunion moment together.

When her mom looked her way, Emily could not stay back a moment longer.

"Mother!" she exclaimed. Em ran the short distance to her mom and they embraced. They laughed and cried tears of joy.

Cletus and Bessie had come to witness the reunion. Caramel began to whinny, kicking the stall with his hoof. Maybell stepped out the back door wiping a pan with her apron and yelled, "What's all the ruckus?"

She saw the family embracing, all three together.

Maybell shouted, "Lord be praised!"

Mary said, "I got the the letter you wrote, by God's grace, but it was hard to keep faith you'd be safe."

Emily smiled again at her mother and ran over to Caramel, who was still carrying on, bobbing his head and calling out for Em with short snorts. Em stopped directly in front of him and called his name, "Caramel!"

Caramel's ears turned forward. He calmed down and lowered his head. Emily hugged his neck and brushed his nose with her hand.

Em softly said to him, "Now, I know how Pedro and Chaca feel. I am so grateful for you."

"What happened, Ezra? How exactly did Emily end up on the ship? Where did you stay while you were gone? Did you find a cure for the sickness?" Satisfied that her family was safe, Mary began to ask one of the hundreds of questions she had been waiting so long to ask.

Dr. Scroggins said, "It was quite a time for all of us. Let's go inside and I'll tell you all about it."

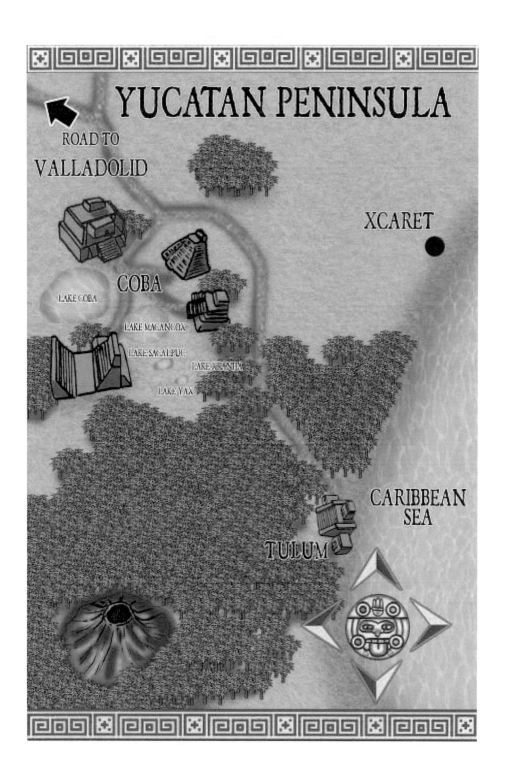

YUCATAN PENINSULA

ROAD TO VALLADOLID

XCARET

COBA

LAKE COBA

LAKE MACANCOX

LAKE SACALPUC

LAKE XKANHA

LAKE YAX

CARIBBEAN SEA

TULUM

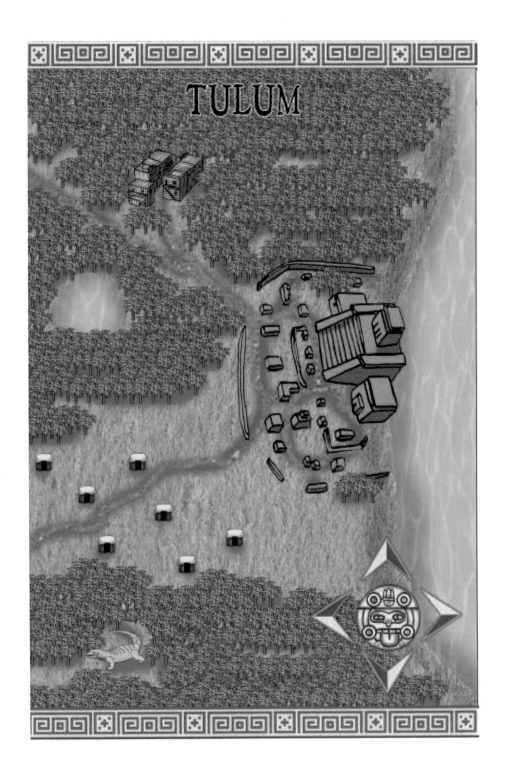

TULUM

About the Author

Since childhood, the author has been an avid naturalist and woodsman—observing, studying, and celebrating all of the amazing things Mother Nature has to offer. His real name may be unfamiliar, but thousands know Ken Panse as the Reptile Wrangler. Ken has been working with animals for over 20 years. Taking his show to schools, parties, and corporate events across the Southeast, his goal is to entertain and educate others about the exciting world of exotic animals.

In the young adult novel, *Into the Jungle*, Ken takes readers of all ages on an adventure that is replete with both wildlife and human nature. He shows the beauty and the savagery of the great outdoors, along with the remarkable ways people can learn to adapt to their surroundings and overcome adversity—for the good of both man and animal. This epic adventure explains more than any marketing material could about the author's passion and offers others the chance to escape and to explore unfamiliar terrain. In the jungle, true character will prevail.

In addition to writing a sequel, Ken is working on an animal adventure park called Rainforest Discovery, with tentative plans to open in 2015. He lives in the Atlanta area.